o
eanne—
always follow
your Heart
Anne D

HEART OF STONE

A Novel be Anne Denton

Daughter of AL + MARY NETZ

SUNSTONE PRESS
SANTA FE
NEWMEXICO

Printed in the United States of America

10 9 8 7 6 5 4 3 2 1

Library of Congress Cataloging in Publication Data:
Denton, Anne, 1958-
Heart of stone / Anne Denton.
p. cm.
ISBN 0-86534-224-5: $12.95
1. Diamond industry and trade—Mexico—Fiction. 2. Women pilots—Mexico—Fiction. 3. Cartels—Mexico—Fiction. I. Title.
PS3554.E5878H4 1994
813'.54+dc20 94-17835
CIP

Published by SUNSTONE PRESS
Post Office Box 2321
Santa Fe, NM 87504-2321 / USA
(505) 988-4418 / *orders only* (800) 243-5644
FAX (505) 988-1025

WINGS

"Be like the bird
That, pausing in her flight
A while on boughs too slight,
Feels them give way
Beneath her yet sings,
Knowing that she hath wings."

–Victor Hugo

For
Mom and Dad
Who gave me wings.

For
Grant and Lisa
Who gave me flight.

PROLOGUE
163 BC, CARIAN REGION, SOUTHWESTERN ANATOLIA

The early morning sun kissed the top of the rugged peak jutting out of the mighty Salbakos mountain range.

This was their first glimpse of the landmark. They had traveled all night and the persistent cloud cover had shielded the gentle moon light making travel on the uneven dusty road even more difficult. Now, reveling in the sight of the soft pink morning glow radiating from the distant mountain, the tired women quickened their pace, knowing the journey would soon end.

They had been traveling for three days. Barely stopping for food or rest, the young, heavily veiled princess felt a sense of urgency. Traffic along the road that paralleled the Maeander river, along which they had traveled since leaving their city of Aydin to the northwest, had been heavy. It was customary to see noblewomen with servants traveling together and no one approached them. The princess knew she must have been missed by now but much time would have been wasted in trying to puzzle out why she had left and in what direction. She tensed whenever she saw mounted soldiers but they all passed without giving them a second look. She knew this journey would probably cost her ancient maid servant, Kaati, her life and possibly even her own. Her life, however, would be worthless if she was to accept the fate planned by her father, the Emperor Trajan, who insisted she marry the disgusting Ziolios.

"Please, Kaati, I must rest." She sighed as she lowered her slight, draped body beside the crystal, tinkling spring. For a moment she longed for a soothing soak in the marble baths of the palace as she surveyed her dust encrusted, sandaled feet. For the first time in her privileged young life she was experiencing the pain of blisters.

Kaati moved to massage the tiny foot and tried to convince the girl to turn back. "Your father must be crazy with worry, Princess. Many people will lose their lives over this." She thought of the palace guards and felt guilty for the sleeping potion she had slipped into the drinks they gratefully accepted from her. It had been easy to slide past them in the night. "This journey will be fruitless. No one will question the wishes of your father."

Princess Lydia reached into a leafy branch and pulled down a fig which she bit into hungrily. "Ziolios is a beast," she said with a shudder. "I will be nothing but a brood mare used to fill his palace with screaming brats. I will kill myself before accepting a life sentence with that one." She looked longingly into the lined face before her. "Besides, I can only love Jason. He is the greatest warrior of our time. Together we will make strong, beautiful children who will strengthen the empire and bring us much joy."

Leaning back against the bank and closing her eyes she could picture him as he was the first day they met. The annual tournaments were drawing to a close and the most accomplished warrior had been given the honor of addressing her as she sat in her place at the arena beside her father. One knee was resting on the smooth granite floor and his head was bowed as he took her hand and addressed her reverently. "Princess," he said. She remembered the black curls on his head and how out of place they seemed with the torn and dirty tunic, the blood of his opponents still fresh in its folds. "Jason," she said. "You may rise."

As he tilted his head up to meet her gaze, she saw a pair of striking emerald green eyes over ruddy cheeks and a strong, firm chin with a slight cleft. The look in his face did not match the deference in his voice and she had the feeling that he was amused about something as the corners of his mouth twitched in a hidden smile. She fought for composure as her heart thundered and she tried to breathe evenly to calm herself. For once she was grateful for the veil over her face, but he had caught the passing glint in her eye and rejoiced inwardly at the love he felt for this warm and gentle woman.

Days later with the assistance of a frightened Kaati, their first meeting had taken place. They knew the terrible risk involved but the grip of young love held them firmly. They would sit for hours in the darkness of their secret place and whisper plans for the future. Although a fierce and loyal warrior, he envisioned a peace in their land and felt with her by his side, anything was possible. Anything, it seemed, except preventing her father from forging ahead with his plans to mate her with Ziolios. Her father knew the importance of joining the great kingdom of Ziolios with his own and was not to be swayed from his plans, regardless of her tearful pleading. Women had no rights and were mere possessions to be sold or traded as needed to advance the position of the men who ruled them.

Unconsciously, she reached under the white silk of her wrap and touched the gold medallion that hung from a heavy chain between her small, firm breasts. It was his parting gift before leaving to join the regiment that was marching north. "I will not fail you, Jason," she whispered.

Kaati could see fire in the black slanted eyes of her mistress. Although covered by the heavy veil, she intimately knew every curve of the legendary face, from the high cheekbones to the small, pointed chin, full lips over small white teeth and the delicate nose. She had been in charge of her since she was in swaddling clothes and loved the young girl as if she herself had borne her. "Come," she said resignedly, rising with a creak from old bones. "If we are to reach Aphrodisias today, we must hurry."

The road soon widened and activity picked up. Now they could make out the glistening marble columns of the famous temple. As they neared the edge of the city, the pungent aroma of thousands of flowering plants swept over them and they breathed deeply of the heavy, humid air. Passing through the gates, they turned toward the Basilica and, stopping a priest who was hurrying past, asked direction to the chambers of the high priest. He pointed up the steps of the towering temple to their right and scurried on.

The interior of the temple, after the crowds, clanging of stonemason's hammers and excited shouting of the vendors, seemed like a true haven. The dim interior was illuminated with flickering candles and a priest droned in front of an altar. The princess shivered slightly in the coolness. Slowly, they approached the stone lions that guarded the entrance to the main sanctuary and Kaati spoke haltingly to the guard.

"My mistress wishes to have an audience with the High Priest. She is princess Lydia of Aydin, and she wishes to seek council from the goddess Aphrodite."

The guard peered at them suspiciously. The Princess slowly reached up, gently grasped the edge of her veil and with great dignity, pulled the veil aside. Her glossy blue-black hairline could just be seen above the arched brows and the dark, slanted eyes. Two shining strips of the finest gold curved to a point between her eyebrows and met in a glowing ruby.

The guard gasped and stood aside. "You may enter, Princess, but the servant must stay here."

She looked longingly at faithful Kaati and wondered if she could continue without her. "Stay here, Kaati," she said. "I must do this myself." A large tear dropped from the old servant's eyes and she watched the dark spot spread as it disappeared into the porous marble steps. Lydia replaced her veil and stepped quickly into the holy sanctuary of Aphrodisias.

The high priest was at his esteemed position on the elevated altar. His round figure sat erect on an ornately carved marble throne and his beady eyes narrowed as she approached.

"Your Excellence, "she began while pulling aside her veil to identify herself. "I have come to seek the guidance of Aphrodite."

The priest was motionless as if carved out of the same marble as the throne. She tried to discern the emotion behind the folds of fat that covered his face but he revealed nothing.

The high pitch of his voice startled her. "The heart of Aphrodite is entombed in the magic vessel which transported it to Earth. Only one possessing pure, unselfish love for another will be able to remove it from this vessel. Many before you have attempted. All have failed. Are you aware of the power of Aphrodite's gift?"

Her eyes were lowered in respect as she nodded slowly.

"So you know," he continued, "that the one who is successful in removing the sacred stone will possess the power of Aphrodite. That power decides the fate of the fertility of the soil, the summer monsoons, the continuation of our race. If you remove the stone, you will mate with the source of your love and your offspring will rise up to rule this land. We will know peace and harmony for eternity. If you do not succeed, you will be put to death. No one who has seen the vessel returns to share its secrets. Do you accept this fate?"

"Yes, your excellency, I do," she replied, her eyes shining.

He reached into a marble container beside the throne and removed a blown glass amphora with a jeweled lid. The glass seemed to glow from within and the smooth exterior shone with iridescent opaline colors which shimmered in the flickering candle light as he held it out to her.

Slowly she reached and took it in her hands. She was surprised at its weight as she slowly sat on the step. It felt warm, as if the heart of another human beat within its breast. With trembling hands, the princess reached for the jeweled lid. She expected resistance and when there was none, her eyes widened in surprise. The priest looked on in shock as a small ray of light escaped from within. It lit her face as she peered into its depths and she reached her hand into the light to remove a large, glittering, heart shaped diamond. The disbelieving priest stood abruptly, towering above her as she gazed at the magnificent stone and felt the pulse of the great goddess in her hand.

Suddenly there was a deep rumble and the floor beneath them shuddered slightly. Then, as if a great animal deep within the earth rolled over and prepared to rise, the marble beneath them heaved with a roar and the priest fell against her as a giant crevice appeared and the polished columns swayed sickeningly like partners in a morbid dance.

Grasping the stone firmly, she fought to her feet and made her way across the thundering floor.

"The gods are angry!" screamed the priest. It added to her terror as she fell. The world pitched and rolled beneath her. She pulled herself to her knees and started to ease toward the door. There was a great cracking sound and, looking up, she watched in horror as one of the giant columns fell in slow motion toward her. She gripped the diamond tightly and breathed a desperate prayer to Aphrodite to unite her with her true love for eternity. The last thing on her lips before the tons of marble crushed down was his name, Jason.

VILLAGE OF GEYRE, SOUTHWESTERN TURKEY
JUNE, PRESENT DAY

Emil Popinopolis paused in the doorway to allow the group of tourists to gather around him. It was nearing the end of the one hour tour and he could tell they were getting restless. But the best was yet to come.

He cleared his throat and they stopped shuffling and looked at him expectantly. "Ladies and gentlemen," he began and paused for effect. "As you know, the University of New York received an archaeology grant in 1961 for the excavation of the ancient city of Aphrodisias on which we stand. During the past hour you have been allowed a glimpse of a few of the artifacts excavated from this site. The first archaeologists who came here were very enthusiastic as they uncovered a seemingly endless supply of magnificent marble statues, sarcophagi, columns and other priceless art forms from the Byzantine era. This excavation has continued for the past twenty-three years, yet it is estimated they have uncovered a mere one fifth of the treasures buried here."

He paused again, watching them closely. They had heard all this before. There were only so many artifacts you could view in one day without experiencing overload. They whispered among themselves and looked at their watches. He smiled. "Over the several hundred year history of this City of Aphrodite, the goddess of love, many made pilgrimages to this sacred place. Its fame extended not only throughout Greece and Turkey, but to the mighty city of Rome as well. One of these people was a beautiful princess. Her name was Lydia."

A few eyes turned toward him. Everyone liked a legend about a princess. "It seemed that Lydia was chosen by Aphrodite to mate with Jason, her true love. Her father, however, had different ideas. So she ran away from home to seek the council of Aphrodite, who could facilitate the joining of the two lovers through the possession of a sacred diamond, the Heart of Aphrodite."

The shuffling and whispering stopped. Was it his imagination, or were they leaning forward a little, to better hear his words? "But alas, the other gods were not in alliance on that day. Just as Princess Lydia grasped the stone in her hand she was killed during an earthquake. The high priest who witnessed this lived to record the story. It is written that a great famine descended on the land after that. The crops wouldn't grow, the rains refused to fall from the heavens, the cattle died of mysterious blights. Aphrodite mourned the loss of Lydia and perpetrated these plagues upon the people. Within a few years one of the greatest civilizations of that time had collapsed."

A hand went up toward the back of the group. "Yes, you in the red shirt. You have a question?"

"I do." The tourist stepped forward. "What kind of poppy cock is this? You expect us to believe some trumped up story about a princess and a diamond destroying the entire civilization?"

He had been expecting a question like this. It was a cue for what he had to say next. "Yes, sir. It was a mystery. Until about two years ago. A university student working alone in the temple area came across a startling discovery. Under a massive column around which she had been digging, her shovel struck something hard. Thinking it to be another of the artifacts and not wishing to incur damage, she got to her hands and knees and gently brushed the sandy soil aside. What she unveiled has changed our knowledge of this era forever. What that student uncovered, ladies and gentlemen, was the Heart of Aphrodite." He swept his hand toward the doorway and with great flair switched on a single light. A collective gasp went up from the group as their eyes fell on the stone. On a pedestal in the middle of the room resting on a simple piece of red velvet was the fabled diamond. A single light shone from above, the rest of the room in shadow. Tiny beams of light from the facets pierced the surrounding gloom and painted rainbows on the walls. The perfect clarity of the gem made it seem as if the source of light came from within.

The crowd pressed against the rail, pushing and shoving one another for a closer glimpse. "How do they know this is the Heart of Aphrodite?" someone called above the clamor.

"One member of the archaeology team was familiar with the history of that part of Asia Minor and he recognized the stone from Assyrian accounts of the legend. There can be no doubt of its authenticity. People such as yourselves travel from all over the world to see it."

He allowed them a few more minutes and then ushered them out the door. "That is the end of our tour for today, ladies and gentlemen. Thank you for your kind attention."

After the last member of the tour grudgingly left the room, he carefully locked the door and armed the alarm system before turning off the light.

The next morning when Emil returned to work, he went directly to the diamond room, as it was known, to disarm the alarm and check the stone.

It was gone.

Frantically, he phoned the police and shouted for assistance. The local authorities were anguished at the loss of their famous artifact and turned the country upside down. But it was gone without a trace. The search expanded and a staggering reward of five billion lirasi, equal to almost one million US dollars was offered for information leading to its return. There was nothing but dead ends. The search was fruitless. It seemed somone had pulled off a perfect crime.

CHAPTER 1
ONE MONTH LATER

The boy's father was a local legend on Tobago. Although details were beginning to fade, many of the older residents on the island remembered the story well. His father, a child of seven at the time, had been walking along the beach on a day much like this one. A vicious tropical storm had just torn through and his father had been walking the waterline searching for driftwood for the cooking fires. He had found a particularly large piece of wood and was digging in the sand to free one of the limbs when he unearthed a small, dull coin. It was heavy and appeared to be very old. He could not read the writing on it. He picked up a stick, and with small-boy enthusiasm started digging. In a short time, he had fourteen of the coins in his hands which was all he could carry. He ran up the sandy hill towards the little house shouting, "Mama, Mama, I have found some pennies on the beach." His father and brothers quickly appeared, hearing the excitement in the child's voice.

"These are not pennies, my son. This is Pirate's Gold," the father exclaimed.

The coins were soon melted and fashioned into a heavy gold bracelet the boy's grandmother still wore with pride.

Now the boy walked that same beach. The storm that had thrashed the tiny island most of the night had passed. A high swell had developed and the ground under his feet trembled like a giant kettle drum as the angry surf thundered into shore and boomed before receding, it's watery fingers grasping the sand. The wind had freshened and it keened mournfully in the rocky cliffs behind him. It caught the spray off the crests of the waves and he shuddered as the cool water dried on his skin, leaving behind a grainy film of salt. It stung his eyes, whipped his hair and he could taste it in his mouth. The tall, wiry grass of the dunes was flattened and, for once, the screaming gulls were silent. The small, puffy clouds chasing the front skidded across the cool morning sun, sending black shadows racing across the glistening sand.

He was thinking, as he often did on these walks, about his father's fame. Stopping to pick up a small round stone, he tossed it into the crashing waves. He had often fantasized about finding pirate treasure on the beach and returning home triumphantly to present it to his mother. He puffed out his small chest and walked a little straighter with the thought.

Ahead, a tangle of seaweed and driftwood had washed onto the beach. These tangles often trapped bottles or other items thrown or dropped from ships. He could see some dark blue cloth toward the end of the bundle. Curiosity drew him closer until, suddenly, a feeling of fear and dread gripped him so tightly that he found himself unable to vent the scream that seemed to be caught in his throat. He turned around and started to run. His heart was pounding and he thought he would die of the terrible pain in his chest before he could reach his mother's arms. There she was, on the porch, shaking a rug. A little farther; a little farther and he would be safe. She looked toward him and her face went white.

"What is it, Joseph?"

The boy was trying to speak, but he could not seem to force the words around his choking sobs. Finally, he pointed toward the bundle on the beach and collapsed into the protection of his mother's arms.

II

Normally, the black, moonless nights were the best. Jennifer Duncan sat in the cockpit of the twin engine Cessna and squinted at the glowing instruments. The inky night was otherworldly and you could feel it penetrate your skin, she thought. This was darkest part of her journey, paralleling the restricted airspace that was White Sands Missile Range. She had passed the scattered lights of Socorro, New Mexico, a few miles back and the next city, Las Cruces, was not for another hundred at least. The problem tonight was that she was bored. This was the fourth time this week she had done the Albuquerque to El Paso mail run and she was tired of it. Dragging around the country in the middle of the night, loading and unloading endless boxes of letters and packages and spending hours on end in her own company was getting old.

There was a momentary thrum thrum from the props and she reached up to make a small adjustment, bringing them back into synch. Pretty uneventful, she thought. Adjusting the seat, she leaned back and put her stocking feet on top of the glare shield. As she passed through a small rain shower, she watched the raindrops in the momentary flashes of the wing strobes. Each flash revealed what looked like a school of tiny silver fish swimming off her wing tip.

"Not even any turbulence tonight to liven things up a bit," she said to herself.

Reaching across to the other seat, she groped for her backpack. A small flashlight hung from a shoelace around her neck. As she felt for it in the dark, she thought of the dream. Every time another pilot teased her about this small flashlight, she told the story.

She had awakened in a dark airplane on a night exactly like this one. The autopilot was flying the plane but there were no lights, inside or out. A feeling of panic descended on her as she frantically searched for the light switches. The airplane was unfamiliar to her and she was not able to locate them. She didn't know how long she had been asleep or how far she had traveled. She could not tell how much fuel remained in the tanks or even if she was right side up or upside down. She remembered that her purse, with a flashlight, was in the back of the plane. She stood up and, feeling her way along the side of the plane, started making her way toward the back. That's when she woke up. She was standing in her dark bedroom holding the wall, drenched in sweat. The flashlight had been part of her night flying equipment ever since.

She used it now to search through the ever-present backpack for a snack. The backpack was another of her standard personal equipment items. Her job often took her across the wastelands of northern Mexico in single engine airplanes and it was filled with survival gear. She often joked with Brent, her husband, that if she ever went down there it would be years before they found her bleached bones. Now the only thing she felt she needed to survive was her bag of cheese curls. She was still fighting that pesky five pounds she had put on with her pregnancy six years ago but the cheese curl habit was a hard one to lick. Besides, these were diet cheese curls.

She finally found them near the bottom under the space blanket and beside the fire sticks. She dug them out along with her current book, something motivational about getting off your butt and doing something. The cheese curls went farther if she nibbled very slowly, taking tiny bites, and she did that now as she opened her book.

She propped the book on her knees and it fell open to a section on fear. She pondered the concept of fear while trying not to make too many crumbs. Brent hated it when she got crumbs all over the cockpit.

Fear was not necessarily a bad thing, she thought. It could be very motivational. As she nibbled she remembered several times in her life when she'd done something simply because she feared it. That was often the only way to get past a perturbation that stood in your way. Once you faced the dreaded thing, it never turned out to be as bad as you thought.

After the lessons she'd learned during her childhood on a small cattle ranch in northern New Mexico, she decided there were very few things left she feared.

One of her earliest memories was of a giant clay bank gelding her father had acquired in a trade when she was a toddler. He was a magnificent animal, seventeen hands high, a glossy chestnut coat the color of the deep red clay under his huge hooves and a flaxen mane and tail. His name was Jake. He had four white socks and a white blaze that shot up his nose to end between dark brown, intelligent eyes. Every hand on the place wanted him, but one by one he tossed them off into the thick dust of the corral. Adding insult to injury, he would bare his teeth, lay back his ears and charge the startled cowboys who high tailed it over the fence.

It was late summer and her mother was busy canning the harvest from their small garden plot. Jennifer was bored with watching her mother standing over the stove, stirring vegetables. Steam dampened her hair and caused small tendrils to stick to her face. The woman irritably brushed them away with the back of her hand and impatiently told Jennifer to go play as the child tugged at her skirt.

Unnoticed, she banged out the back screen door and toddled toward the barn to look at the chickens. Passing the corral, she heard a snort and noticed the big horse eyeing her.

"Pretty horsie," she said as she climbed through the rails of the fence and, holding her pudgy hand out, approached the animal. The horse stood with his front legs splayed, ears strained forward and nostrils flared to inspect this small human who approached him unafraid.

Her fingers stroked the velvety muzzle and he nuzzled her gently. She toddled to the nearest fence and slowly pulled herself up the rungs to have a better look at him. Reaching out to scratch his back, she could just picture herself as a cowgirl sitting astride this horse. Daddy would be so proud!

She leaned out as far as she dared and grasped the long wiry hair of his mane. Then she closed her eyes, held her breath and jumped. He quivered slightly as he felt her weight, but didn't move. She hooked an elbow over his broad withers and with much struggling, managed to claw her way onto his back until she was sitting astride, her short legs sticking almost straight out as she reached down to stroke the arched neck.

Her father came out of the barn from his evening milking and almost dropped the bucket when he saw her. Running to the fence, he spoke quietly so as not to spook the horse. "Jennifer, sweetie, get off the horse. Just swing your leg over and slide off, honey."

She reached down and hugged the muscular neck. "Nice horsy."

"I know, honey, but you have to get off the horse, now. Listen, Mommy's calling."

As her mother came out of the house, she stopped in terror as she saw the scene before her. "Oh my God," she said, putting her hand over her mouth.

As Jennifer's father approached, the horse bared his teeth and flattened his ears threateningly until he dared go no further.

They finally convinced her to get off the horse when her tummy started growling.

As she made her way across the corral toward her father's outstretched arms, the horse followed her like a dog, bumping her gently with his big nose.

Scooping up his tiny daughter, Roy Nolan removed his hat and scratched his head. "Well, don't that just beat all!"

The horse and child were inseparable after that. Initially, fearful for her safety, they had forbidden her to go near him. After days of crying and tantrums, they finally relented. Every chance she got, she opened the gate and let him loose. He followed her around as she explored the confines of her limited world.

He became a nuisance after a while, smearing the glass door of their dining room with his slobber and begging for bites of her peanut butter sandwiches at lunch time. Her favorite was strawberry soda pop, which she always shared with her big furry friend. When the bottle was half gone, she would hold it out to him. Grasping the bottle neck in his teeth, he'd tilt his head up, guzzling greedily until there was none left. She would laugh at the sticky pink foam around his mouth that ended up all over her as she scratched the favorite spot under his chin.

When she was six, she was fully indoctrinated as a tomboy. Running wild over the ranch with her brothers, having milk fights while milking the cows and practicing her lassoing on a stump, she soon felt cheated that she was not allowed on the fall roundup with the boys.

Her father found it hard to say no to her and so her education began.

One evening he took her out to a field behind the house and pulled a teardrop shaped leather case out of his saddle bag. From it he produced an ancient Colt 38-40 "peacemaker" pistol. He told her about how her great grandfather had used it in the Indian wars and how it had been passed down through the generations. If she was going to spend any time at all on the range, she had to know how to shoot.

Patiently, he showed her how to line up the sights on her target and squeeze, not pull the trigger. The first time it went off, the kick from the gun knocked her down. Rubbing her wrist, she got up, dusted herself off, and shook her head to try to clear the ringing in her ears. After that, he took her out every day for months until he figured she was safe and proficient.

Her first trail ride was on Jake's broad back, following her dad's bay quarter horse mare. As they moved into the mountains, he showed her how she could determine elevation from the vegetation. At six thousand feet, there was mostly juniper, piñon, mesquite and the fragrant sage. Around seven, the beautiful ponderosa pines started. He showed her how to identify these magnificent trees by their rough brown bark that smelled like vanilla and the long needles that grew in clumps. At eight thousand, the spruce and fir were intermingled with the other conifers, and at nine there were white barked aspen trees mixed in. He explained that aspen trees were nature's scab on a forest. They were the first to spring up after a forest fire, and would provide habitat for the animals and control erosion until the slower growing conifers sprouted. At approximately ten thousand feet was the timberline. Right at this mysterious line, the trees were stunted and knarled from their rough existence and beyond the timberline was barren tundra.

She fondly remembered that autumn as he patiently knelt and showed her how to survive in the woods, describing the different edible plants. In the spring the wild strawberries burst forth, small as the end of her little finger; sweet, tangy and delicious. Early summer through mid-July she could count on dandelion greens and rose hips. By mid-August, the juicy raspberries popped out of their prickly bushes, and her mouth watered as she gathered them for griddle cakes. Early fall, the piñon cones opened, releasing their small brown nuts and there was a two week period of time during which the edible mushrooms pushed out of the loamy soil. Her favorite were the giant white "puffballs" that her father sliced thickly and fried in butter over the campfire. He taught her that any plant with shiny leaves, milky sap, or a bitter tasted was poisonous.

She learned how to identify the tracks of the animals. The funny tracks of the jackrabbit, two small round ones close together followed by the two elongated tracks of his hind feet. Her father asked, "which way was he going?" She guessed wrong. According to her dad, the silly bunny was going backward. He patiently explained to her that it only looked that way because his hind legs passed his front feet when he was running. He showed her how to find his lair and set a snare for the rabbit or the big gray tassel-eared squirrels that lived in the trees above them.

The hoofed animals were more of a challenge. Deer and elk tracks looked a lot alike, two teardrops side by side in the soft dirt. She learned that the elk were much bigger than the deer and their hooves became more splayed with age. The tracks of the baby elk looked like the small crescent of a colt's hoof. Their hooves had not yet pulled apart enough to define the line between them in the dirt.

Raccoons left tracks that looked like baby hand prints in the soft mud beside the streams and these differed from beavers which had webbed feet. He taught her that beavers were the contractors of the forest and she was grateful for the plentiful ponds formed by their "lodges," which became home to the delicious trout, the browns, rainbow and cutthroat of the high country streams.

She learned that wolves and coyotes generally hunted in packs, but mountain lion, lynx and fox were solitary hunters. Black bear were common in the mountains, but they wouldn't bother you as long as they didn't feel their cubs were threatened.

Fire starting was an art in itself and cooking over the campfire was even more of a challenge. By the end of that first five week roundup, she felt like she knew all she needed to know to survive in the wilderness. The next year her father let her go with her brothers and she surprised them with her knowledge and ability to handle the animals. After that, the small dark-haired girl on the big clay bank gelding was a common sight among the weathered hands during the roundups.

Her father had owned a string of old airplanes for several years, using them as winter projects after dragging the derelicts home on a trailer and storing them in the barn. She longed to learn to fly and he promised her that as soon as she could reach the rudder pedals, he would teach her. On her ninth birthday, with the aide of a fat pillow behind her so she could reach the pedals, she had her first lesson. She was a natural. Her father declared that she must have been born with a saddle between her legs and a yoke in her hand as he proudly watched his small daughter maneuver the J-5 Cub expertly. She had a lot of opportunity to hone her skills on a variety of airplanes over the next several years. The Cub was followed by a Taylorcraft, a Luscombe, a Piper Pacer, and finally, a Cessna 180. The planes were invaluable on the ranch for spotting bands of cattle in remote areas, running to Taos, the closest town, for supplies, or locating herds of deer or elk in the fall before hunting season began. By the time she was seventeen, the legal age to apply for her Private Pilot Certificate, she had almost three thousand hours.

When it came time to go away to college, her father cashed in his CDs and proudly presented her with the money he had carefully put away over the past eighteen years. They both knew that ten thousand dollars wasn't going to cover her four year degree. Together, they shopped every small airport in the state until they found a nineteen sixty-four Cessna 172. Her dad spent a couple of weeks fixing it up, and after loading her gear in the back, she said good-bye to the folks with tears in her eyes and flew to Albuquerque to start her new life at the University of New Mexico.

After class and on weekends, she gave flying lessons in the small plane and managed to live pretty comfortably while she finished her degree. After graduation, she'd landed a job as a pilot with a small charter company in Albuquerque called Duncan Aero. That's where she met her husband, Brent. His dad had formed the company with the hope that his son would come back from college and take over. Brent had different ideas. He'd just gotten his degree in electrical engineering with a specialty in optics and he was ready to use his brain for research and development.

Their romance was swift and they were married within the year. She sold her little airplane and tried to give the money back to her father but he insisted they use it for a down payment on a house.

The first several years of their marriage were blissful as they each enjoyed the company of their best friend, each other. They spent all their weekends at the lake or in the high country. The second year, they broke down and bought a set of matching dirt bikes which they rode over the jeep roads of southern Colorado, exploring the national forests and scouting out fishing holes.

All seemed perfect in their world until he came home from work one evening to a white faced Jennifer who was just hanging up the phone. She wasn't sure how to tell him, so she was blunt. "Your father just dropped dead from a heart attack." Tears brimmed in her eyes and splashed on to her pale cheeks. She had been very fond of the quiet gentle man who was her father-in-law.

After that Brent brought his best friend, Dave Lark, into the business. They re-named it L/D Aerospace, the L and D standing for Lark and Duncan. Gone were the leisurely weekends and movies after work. They found that the business required twenty-five hours a day from each of them. Brent kept his engineering job and did what he could to squeeze both into his life. They kept promising themselves that it would get better. They would eventually get caught up and they could hire more help. Unfortunately, the bigger the business got, the more time it took.

Their daughter had been born the year after Brent lost his dad, and she became a permanent fixture at the offices and hangars of L/D Aerospace as her parents struggled to make the company go.

"Twin Cessna Five Lima Delta, contact Albuquerque Center one three five point eight five. Good night."

The voice from the radio made her jump from her reminiscence and she realized she'd been daydreaming. As she reached to key the mike, the cheese curls dumped on her seat and to the floor under her feet. "One three five point eight five, five lima delta, good night," she replied while looking at the mess with disgust. Tuning the radio to the new frequency, she checked in with the next controller. "Albuquerque Center Twin Cessna five lima delta one one thousand."

"Twin Cessna five lima delta radar contact."

She engaged the auto pilot and leaned over to pick up the cheese curls. "Thank goodness it isn't the Lear," she thought. November nine one lima delta was a Lear 35, the pride of their fleet, and the source of their near bankruptcy as well as many sleepless nights. They had decided early on that the piston airplanes were fine but they were making them nickels and dimes. What they really needed to break into the big time was a jet. This one seemed perfect when it came up at the customs auction. After mortgaging their land, house and anything else they could find, they had just been able to swing the purchase of the magnificent bird. The problem was that since it had never been used commercially, the previous owners had never bothered to have a fire-blocked interior installed. The Federal Aviation Administration required that if it was to be used for hire, it must have this interior.

"How much can a few seats and a headliner cost?" The answer was about one hundred fifty thousand dollars, which was about that amount more than they had. Fortunately, her folks were able to help out. The result was one of the most pristine aircraft of its type in the American Southwest. She had been delighted at the beautiful buttery soft, gray kid-glove leather seats, the plush carpet and the sparkling paint. The airplane would have to work long and hard to pay off the debt but she and Brent were determined to make it go.

"Cessna five lima delta, turn to heading one eight five proceed direct El Paso when able."

The crackle of the radio brought her back. "Five Lima Delta," she responded. It was time to get back to work.

Chief Inspector Samuel Cosgrove had just returned from his annual vacation in Bermuda. It was the first time he had felt reasonably relaxed since a year ago when he had returned from his last vacation to Bermuda. He did not mind his peeling nose and ears. The diving this year had been fantastic. It was going to be hard to go back to work tomorrow and face the ever-present workload at his office in US Customs.

The phone rang and he tried to ignore it but his wife picked it up in the kitchen. He heard her voice briefly and then her head appeared around the door of his den.

"It's the office, dear. I told them you were still on vacation until tomorrow but they said it was very important that they talk to you."

"Okay, thanks hon," he said with a sigh as he picked up the receiver. It was Montoya.

"Chief, I'm afraid there's some bad news..."

Cosgrove could feel the tension crackling over the line and the old familiar pain started in the pit of his stomach.

"What is it?" he asked.

"It's Charlie, sir. They found his body this morning washed up on a beach on Tobago. The sharks had been at him, sir, and..."

"A boating accident?" Cosgrove interrupted.

"No sir, he was dead before he hit the water. There was a bullet hole between his eyes."

The clouds had cleared but the winds were picking up when she returned to Albuquerque. A phenomenon called "canyon winds" by the locals had kicked up the gusts to over fifty knots. It is caused by a high pressure system building over the plains on the far side of the mountain range east of the city. There is a narrow gash in the range known as Tijeras (Scissors) Canyon, which acts as a giant funnel as the high pressure east of the mountains strives to equalize with the lower pressure to the west. The mountains act as a dam for the high pressure air and, as it is squeezed through the narrow pass on its journey westward, velocity increases. This phenomenon is common in Albuquerque. The main runway at the International Airport, runway eight, is perfectly aligned for canyon winds.

Jennifer was not thinking about this engineering foresight as she lined up on final for runway eight, she was just grateful that the wind was right down the runway. Fatigue was beginning to drag her down and fighting the turbulence from the gusty winds was already enough. The dark shoulders of the mountains loomed up before her above the glittering city lights. She could make out the sheen of white clouds draped over the rugged peaks, a ghostly cloak for the eerie giant monitoring her moves as she flared and the tires squeaked onto the smooth asphalt.

As she turned off onto the parallel taxi way and received clearance to parking, she tuned her second radio to the company frequency.

"Hey Tony, wake up!" she called to the night dispatcher.

"Hi Jen, I saw you come in. I'll be out in a minute to chock and help tie her down. The wind is really screaming tonight!"

He ran out of the office as she pulled up and, grabbing a chain, tied the right wing to the ground cable as she jumped out of the door and clicked the rudder lock into place. Her hair whipped into her eyes and mouth and she had to lean against the wind to make her way into the office. He was right behind her.

He could see how tired she was and offered to finish up her paperwork. "Thanks Sport," she said gratefully. "I'll sure be glad when we get another pilot on line. I don't know how much longer I can keep up this pace!"

She tuned her radio in her car to a jazzy station and stretched often to try to keep from falling asleep on the drive home through the deserted streets.

The porch light was on and as she walked into the side entrance of the house, she heard Brent call down to her.

"There's some double fudge nutty crunch in the freezer."

"You sure know how to treat your women right," she called back with a smile. Pulling the carton out of the freezer, she grabbed a spoon and dug in while she stood at the counter and read the latest flying magazine. After a five minute binge, when her stomach finally stopped growling at her and she was beginning to feel a little guilty, she returned what was left of the carton with a sigh and headed down the hall to her daughter's room.

The cozy alcove was softly lit by a night light and she walked to the side of the bed to look at the child. The dark fringe of her lashes lay against her rosy cheeks and her porcelain skin was luminous in the soft light. She reached down to hug her, breathing deeply of the fresh scent of her hair and she felt the familiar rush of maternal love. The child whimpered softly and turned to her side, grabbing in her sleep for the well-worn bunny next to her. After quietly leaving the room, Jen turned off the lights and started up the stairs. The little girl wanted a sister or brother so bad, but the way things were going she didn't see how she would ever have enough time in this lifetime to give this one kid the attention she needed, much less start another.

The shoes were off before her foot hit the first step. As she climbed the stairs she unbuttoned her shirt and slacks, pulling them off at the landing. Hopping on one foot, then the other, the socks came next, one by one and, reaching her closet, she had only to pull her underwear down to her ankles and with practiced precision, flip them into the hamper with her toes. She was not surprised that he was still awake. Even though he worked a full time job, as well as running the company, he always waited up until he knew she was safely home.

Climbing under the fluffy down comforter she shuffled over to his side of the bed, spooned against his warm body and nuzzled the back of his soft hair.

"I love you," she whispered quietly. "Love you, too," he returned. She was already asleep.

CHAPTER 2

From somewhere she could hear Brent's voice calling her. "Jen.... Jen, wake up."

Slowly she opened her eyes and blinked at the bright light. It took her a moment to remember where she was.

"Jen, we've got a trip. Annette's on the phone and she needs to talk about your fuel load."

She sat up. "What? What's going on?"

"We've got a Lear trip. Come on, you've got to get going. The guy's in a hurry."

Brent moved to the edge of the bed and sat down. He was in his middle thirties but the stress of the business had matured him. There was a lot of gray in the sandy brown hair now, but he was still slim and athletic.

"Look, I know you're tired, but there's nobody else who can do it."

"I can't have legal rest," she said, looking at the clock. "It seems like I just laid down!"

"Believe it or not, you've been asleep for nine hours."

"Can't Dave do it?"

"We're having some problems with the prop seal on the 421. We can't afford to have it out of commission another minute. He's put it at the top of his priority list because the parts are supposed to come in this morning. It will take him the rest of the day to finish the repairs. Besides, you know Dave can't speak Spanish."

"Dave gets along with everybody."

"I know, but smiling and passing out lifesavers is not exactly the most efficient means of communication in a foreign country."

She groaned and flopped back against the pillow, her hand to her face. "How about a co-pilot? Do we have anybody who's out of crew rest?"

"Annette says she's already called Mark and he's on his way."

"Okay, okay, tell her to tell Mark to call for weather, file a flight plan, and...where are we going, anyway?"

"San Jose Del Cabo."

"Okay, put forty-five hundred pounds of fuel on board and tell them I'll be there in thirty minutes. What about the Peep?"

At that moment, a six year old child with silky flaxen hair and enormous blue eyes peeked into the room.

"Mommy! You're home!" She ran into the room and jumped in the bed bouncing up and down enthusiastically.

"Only for a few more minutes, kiddo. Sorry, but I've got to go to work again."

The little girl's lower lip started to quiver.

"Oh hell, I'll ask Dave if he minds if she tags along with him while he works today," Brent said. He didn't think he was up to the whining that was about to start.

"Yeah!" Peeper cried and, spying the cat, took off in pursuit.

She had been given her nickname when she was a baby. People had looked at her enormous eyes and exclaimed, "Jeepers, creepers, where'd you get those peepers?"

"Sometimes I think she likes Dave better than me," Jen grumbled as she rolled out of bed and stumbled toward the shower.

"I think most kids like Dave better than most adults," Brent said as he headed for the kitchen to get her some coffee. "He's more fun."

Anyone seeing Dave and Brent together would wonder what they had in common and how they could be partners. Brent was tall and slim with clear blue eyes and an aristocratic carriage. His angled jaw was always clean shaven and his clothes impeccable. Dave was short and stocky with thick, bowed legs. All the lines on his face seemed to go up in his perpetual grin. With his dancing eyes, rosy cheeks, cut-offs and flip flops, he reminded one of a youthful, subtropical Santa. He bought wintergreen lifesavers by the case at Quantity Club and always seemed to have one in his mouth. They were generously shared with small children and dogs.

Dave had an annoying habit of talking constantly about airplanes. He walked, talked, breathed, ate and slept airplanes and often used airplane or flying analogies to make a point. Although most adults not interested in airplanes quickly became bored with the conversation, children flocked to him. He seemed to have unlimited patience with them and would often spend hours in the hangar on a simple task like installing a rivet or tightening a bolt because he wanted to allow them to help. He would put the wrench in their hand, show them how to adjust it and cheer them on as they accomplished each task. Although an accomplished pilot, Dave was just as happy working on airplanes as flying them. People tended to underestimate him because of his appearance and sunny personality. Behind the merry eyes, however, was a brain of near genius ability. He had a bachelor's degree in aeronautical engineering with a master's in electrical engineering. His troubleshooting abilities were legendary and he could always be counted on to deliver when it involved anything mechanical.

A bachelor, he treated his planes like members of his family and constantly worried about their well-being. He could not stand to have anything wrong mechanically and had been known to engage the auto pilot in flight and, flopping upside down with his feet sticking straight up in the air and his head under the panel, troubleshoot a radio problem.

Because of his eccentricities, Brent and Jen tried to steer him toward the maintenance end of the business. It wasn't difficult, since with a fleet of nine airplanes something was always requiring repair or an inspection. Dave didn't seem to mind. He went about his work smiling and uncomplaining and he accomplished an unbelievable amount for one guy.

Dave's constant companion was a small, short-legged dog named Sandy. She was a cross between a Pekinese and a Lhasa Apso and seemed to have gotten the worst qualities of both breeds. Brent often said she was the ugliest dog he had ever seen. She was long and slung low to the ground. Her front legs had big knobby knees and her toes pointed outward. She had a tremendous underbite and the teeth jutting up from her jowls could be frightening unless you looked at her face. Her big dark eyes would instantly endear you to her and you would quickly overlook the shortcomings of her little body.

Sandy loved to fly almost as much as Dave and often went with him on his road trips. His favorite plane was a single engine Cessna 182. He had an oxygen bottle he often took with him for those times when going higher meant a better tailwind and thought nothing of flying the little plane around at sixteen or seventeen thousand feet. Once he had donned his oxygen for these high altitude forays he would faithfully put a mask over Sandy's stubby nose. She would then paw it off and he'd wait until she passed out from oxygen starvation and place it on again. After landing, he would crumble a baby aspirin and mix it into her food for her headache. She didn't seem to mind. She, like the kids, adored Dave.

Thirty minutes later Jennifer wheeled her Bronco II into the L/D Aerospace's offices parking lot. She noticed a plain looking car with government plates.

As she came through the door, Annette looked up from the dispatch desk. As usual, she had a phone in each ear and was carrying on both conversations simultaneously. Raising four kids had been good training for her job.

In a corner of the reception area sat a man in a crumpled blue suit. He was staring straight ahead and didn't seem to notice he had a cup of coffee in his hands. His brown hair fell over his forehead and there were dark smudges under his eyes. It looked like it had been a while since his last shave. She could tell the suit was expensive and the shoes had a shine that would rival those of a Marine cadet in boot camp but he looked more like a homeless person.

On her way through the office to the hangar she looked at Annette, raised her eyes and tilted her chin in the direction of the man. Annette shrugged and went back to scribbling on the pad in front of her.

Once in the hangar, she was pleased to see Mark finishing up the pre-flight. He looked fresh and well rested. She couldn't understand how a young bachelor like him, with his unusual hours and many interests, found the time to launder, let alone iron his uniform shirts.

He looked up. "Hi Jen, we're about ready to go. I'll ask Roger to tow her outside. Weather looks good. Typical summer day. Scattered thunderstorms, turbulence and gusty wind in Cabo. Other than that, nothing in particular."

"What are the winds aloft?"

He broke into a grin. "Seventy knots on the tail."

"All right!" she said. "What's with smiley?" she asked, indicating the reception area.

"That's Inspector Sparks, US Customs."

She couldn't resist. "Does his name describe his electric personality?"

Mark smiled. "I get the impression he's having a bad day."

"Why are they using us? Doesn't customs have a Citation?"

"Yea, but it's down for maintenance."

"Okay, if you'll finish up here, I guess I'd better go introduce myself to Mr. Sparky. Oh, and one more thing." She turned at the door. "Make sure we've got extra barf bags. This guy looks a little green to me. If he barfs in my airplane, his day is going to get worse."

Inspector Royce Sparks was having a bad day. He'd had another fight with his wife, Donna, about work. His already heavy workload had increased with the boss on vacation and two inspectors assigned to the smuggling case in Mexico. Then the jangling phone woke him at two o'clock this morning and the first thing to penetrate his fuzzy mind as Cosgrove filled him in on the recent chain of events was that his good friend, Charlie Adams, had been found murdered on the beach of some obscure island in the Caribbean. Now, in spite of his protest, Cosgrove had put him in charge of the investigation which involved flying to Mexico and dealing with the bureaucracy that made the US system look like a well-oiled machine. He had argued that he was having personal problems and really needed to stay around the home front for a few days. Besides, he was personally involved, since it involved the death of a friend.

Cosgrove was not sympathetic. "There isn't anybody in the office who wasn't Charlie's friend, Royce. Besides, you're the best investigator I've got on the force and your Spanish is impeccable."

Three months earlier, the El Paso office had received a tip from an informant in southern Baja about a smuggling operation of enormous proportions. Two of their inspectors had immediately been assigned to Cabo San Lucas to investigate. Shortly thereafter, they had discovered that the merchandise was coming up from Venezuela and the Albuquerque office had been asked to provide backup personnel to help with the investigation in South America.

Like most government agencies, their office seemed to be chronically short of staff. The President's War Against Drugs sounded great in theory but the new programs had spread the already overworked staff thinner. Charlie's newly acquired partner was a rookie who had barely arrived at the Albuquerque office before being assigned to him as an assistant and mailed off to South America to investigate the elusive smuggling ring. Cosgrove hadn't been real happy about doing that to a new inspector, but staffing problems being what they were, he didn't feel that he had a lot of choice. Now Cosgrove was anxious to send in reinforcements and continue the investigation while the trail was warm and the informers still talking. Besides, he was nervous about the thought of a rookie inspector in charge of the case, even if only for a day or too. It was just too damn important, and they had already spent an unbelievable amount of time and the taxpayers' money to get to this point.

Royce thought about Donna, who had not spoken to him as he left the house this morning. The fear that his marriage was finally going down the tubes for good almost overshadowed the fact that he was deathly afraid of flying, especially in small airplanes.

A feminine voice broke through his thoughts and he looked up. Before him stood a tall slender woman in her mid-thirties. Her glossy black hair was short and brushed back from her face and he noticed that her cocky smile was made up of a set of large, incredibly white teeth and an impressive dimple in her right cheek. Long, thick lashes curled over dark eyes and there were bright spots of pink on the crests of her high cheekbones as if she had recently stayed too long in the harsh, New Mexico sun. She was wearing a crisp white short-sleeved shirt and on each shoulder was a navy blue epaulet with four silver stripes. Navy pleated slacks covered her long legs and completed the uniform.

She held out her hand. "Inspector Sparks? Hi. I'm Jennifer Duncan. I'll be your pilot today."

A hundred thoughts went through his mind and none of them were good. He had to suppress a groan. Just what he needed today, of all days. A cocky female pilot!

The Learjet crouched on the hot pavement, sleek and low slung like a feline about to pounce on its prey. The morning sun glinted off the bullet-shaped fuel tanks at the ends of the wings, designed to hold extra sustenance for the ravenous turbofans on either side of the fuselage. Each engine could develop thirty-five hundred pounds of thrust. Even at gross weight, the airplane could climb out of Albuquerque at five thousand feet per minute.

The graceful bird was painted in what is known as a "waterline" pattern. The belly up to the wings was a soft dove gray. A black stripe separated the gray from the clean white of the top half of the plane. Racy black pinstripes completed the theme.

They were loaded and off within twenty minutes. Leveling off at thirty-seven thousand feet, she marveled at how much faster they covered the same ground she had flown over last night as they skirted the restricted area over White Sands, whipped over Douglas, Arizona, and headed south, on a direct course to San Jose Del Cabo.

An hour and twenty minutes into the flight, she turned around and looked at her passenger. His knuckles were white on the armrest and his eyes were closed tightly. It looked like he was holding his breath. An untouched brief of his assignment lay in his lap.

"Inspector Sparks, are you okay?" she asked.

His eyes popped open. "Yes," he said. "I'm okay."

"Would you like a drink? That might help you relax. There's a ton of booze in that cabinet in front of you. Help yourself."

"I'm on duty," he replied. "Isn't there something you can do about this turbulence?"

"There's only one guy I know of can do anything about turbulence." She broke into a grin. "Him," she said pointing up.

Hell, it was worth a try. Flying might even persuade him to take up religion.

He chanced a look out the window. A vast expanse of water was bordered by a thin strip of land on the distant horizon. Mainland Mexico. Through the window on the opposite side of the plane he could see the rugged coast of Baja. He leaned over for a better look.

"How much longer?" He was feeling queasy.

"We're about to start our descent. About another twenty minutes. Be a bumpy approach. The wind's blowing pretty good down there."

He didn't reply. His eyes were closed and he was gripping the armrest again.

"This guy's a real mental case," she said into her headset mike.

Mark smiled. "At least he hasn't barfed yet."

The landing was bumpy as promised. The wind was gusting up to forty knots and as he glanced out the window, Royce thought it looked as if they were flying sideways along the ground toward the runway. He didn't realize that this was called "crabbing," and was necessary for landing in a crosswind. Just as he thought they were going to land sideways, the airplane smoothly straightened out and the left wing dipped. He felt his stomach slam to the other side of the plane. Just then, a gust hit them and they momentarily rose up a few feet before finally settling on the runway.

As they started their shutdown procedures, Jen said, "Why don't you let Mr. Sparky out so he can get some fresh air?"

"Too late," Mark said as he turned around and noticed the open door. Inspector Sparks was hurling his guts out into a trash can while the Mexican refuelers looked on.

CHAPTER 3

Jennifer cleared Customs and Immigration, paid the fees and returned to the airplane to supervise the fueling. She climbed into the cockpit and dug out her charts so she could plan her trip home. Suddenly, without warning, a black leather-gloved hand clamped over her nose and mouth and she was unable to breathe, or scream. She struggled and clawed at the hand but her movements were restricted by the small space.

"Stop struggling and I will relax my grip so you can breath," a man's voice with a British accent hissed beside her right ear. She stopped struggling and tried to relax but the blood was roaring in her ears and she felt an icy panic constricting her throat.

"I have a knife at your throat," the voice continued. "I am going to remove my hand from in front of your mouth. If you scream, I will not hesitate to kill you. Do you understand?"

Slowly, she nodded. The hand came away and she sensed, rather than felt, the sharp blade a hair's breadth from her neck.

"Now I am going to talk and you are going to listen," the voice said. "I am a desperate man. I need to get to South America in a hurry and you are going to take me. Can you fly this plane by yourself?"

She hesitated, then said, "No."

"You are lying."

"This plane is not certified for single pilot operations."

"I do not care about your bloody certifications! I wish only to know, can you fly the plane without crashing in the ocean?"

"I could, but it would not be a smart thing to do."

"Why?"

"Because if anything abnormal happened, I could not handle it by myself. The plane is too complex. There would be too many things for one person to do."

"Then we will just have to make sure that nothing abnormal happens," he replied. "Here is what you are to do. You go in and file your flight plan to Albuquerque. You order the maximum amount of fuel. You say nothing about this to anyone. Then you return to the plane and we depart. Do you understand?"

"What if I refuse?"

"Then your co-pilot is dead."

"Okay, I understand. Can I move now?"

"Yes. Hurry. There is no time to lose."

II

Jennifer went into the office. She hoped no one noticed the trembling in her hands. She did not want to have to answer any questions. She thought about trying to pass a message to someone but she had no idea what he had done with Mark and was afraid for him. The man behind the desk sat before an ancient Underwood typewriter and, with two fingers, typed out her flight plan to Albuquerque.

"Color of plane?" he asked, bored.

"Azul," she answered.

He looked out the window at the white, gray and black jet sitting on the ramp. It didn't look blue to him but if the Señora said it was blue, he would write that it was blue.

He finished and gave her a carbon copy.

"Hasta la vista, Señora."

"Hasta la vista. Gracias." She turned and left.

Taxiing out she was distracted by the stranger in the right seat and the change in procedure. She was busy as she ran the checklists herself, double and triple checking everything. She couldn't afford to make an error. It could mean her life. High performance jets were not known for their forgiving characteristics. Many pilots had paid the ultimate price for that lesson.

There were no other aircraft taxiing and she was immediately cleared for departure. It was a struggle on the takeoff roll to monitor all the engine instruments, the airspeed, the usual cross-check through eighty knots, while dividing her attention with the equally important task of keeping the airplane aligned on the runway through the rapid acceleration. At rotation speed she grabbed the yoke firmly with both hands and pulled. Once clear of the ground and climbing rapidly, she raised the gear, engaged the auto pilot and ran her after-take-off checklist.

"Lear Lima Delta, contact Mazatlan Center on one two nine decimal five," the heavily accented voice of the controller came over the radio.

She reached to change the frequency so she could check in with the controller but he laid a restraining hand on her arm. "Don't talk to them."

"I have to. I'm on an instrument flight plan. I've got to be in contact with someone at all times. If I don't check in with them, they'll wonder what happened."

"Let them wonder. There will be no future radio contact with anyone."

She had a sick feeling in the pit of her stomach. "You're calling the shots."

"How far out are we?"

She looked at her distance measuring equipment. "About twenty-five miles."

"Turn right in a southeasterly direction toward the mainland coast. When we are about fifty miles off the coast, turn so that we are paralleling the mainland but we are not to fly over land as long as we are paralleling the coast of Mexico."

"What have you done with Mark?" she asked.

"He is unharmed."

"Where are we going?"

"We'll fly the coast all the way down to Central America. Once we reach Panama's airspace we'll turn east, cut across the Isthmus of Panama and turn southeast again to fly over Caracas into the interior of Venezuela."

She looked at her ground speed and mentally computed fuel burn. "How far into Venezuela will we have to fly?"

"About two hundred miles."

"We may have to stop for fuel."

"That's not an option."

"You're talking about over two thousand miles with this circuitous route you've mapped out for us. If we keep the tailwind we've got now we may be okay, but I expect it to diminish as we get into the lower latitudes."

"Just do what you need to do to keep this aircraft in the air as long as possible. As I said, stopping for fuel is not an option."

"Then I'd better take a look at my range charts. We're limited to forty-one thousand feet until we burn off a little. After that, we'll go to forty-five thousand. That will give us the best fuel economy as well as the most favorable winds, hopefully."

He didn't answer. His back was turned to her and he was staring out the window. Quietly, she reached to her transponder, the instrument interrogated by the ground radar, and entered the emergency code that means hijacking.

II

Brent's Saturday chore was the books. He had been working in his study all morning and was getting depressed. He had run the numbers three times but it was useless. They were going to be in the red this month. He leaned back in his chair and rubbed his face. Life used to be so simple. Where had they gone wrong? They only wanted to make an honest living. Every time they started to get a little bit ahead, however, one of the airplanes came due for an engine or a prop. The monthly payment on the Lear alone was half what he made in a year at his engineering job. He couldn't understand how his Dad had done it all those years.

As he leaned forward to resume his task, the phone rang.

"Yeah," he said sharply, aggravated at the interruption.

"Is this Mr. Duncan?" the voice asked.

Sounded like another sales pitch. "Look, whatever you're trying to sell, I'm not interested," he said, and started to hang up.

"Wait, sir. This is Albuquerque Flight Service. I'm calling regarding Lear november nine one lima delta. This phone number was listed on the flight plan.

Brent sat up. "Yes, what is it?"

They departed San Jose Del Cabo at seventeen forty-five Zulu today and no one has heard anything since. Has the aircraft returned?"

Brent closed his eyes and mentally calculated the time. Since this was summer, Zulu, or Greenwich Mean Time, was six hours later than New Mexico time. He looked at his watch. "Oh my God," he said as he slumped in his chair.

"I take that as a negative, sir?"

"That's right." Brent felt sick to his stomach. "We have not heard from them."

"Then we have to presume they've gone down. It might be a good idea to come down to our office Mr. Duncan. It's not easy to organize a search on the other side of the border."

"I'll be there as soon as I can," he replied and hung up.

Dave was on the floor of the hangar on his hands and knees with Peeper, still looking for a washer that he had dropped twenty minutes ago. She was at the "Why?" stage and he was patiently answering.

"Dave." He looked up. It was Brent and he looked strange. "Dave, can I talk to you for a minute?" With a look at Peeper he added, "In the other room?"

"Sure," Dave said, getting up. "Hey Peeper." "Will you keep looking for that washer?"

She looked at him with big eyes and nodded.

"And, if you find it, would you hold it real tight so it doesn't sneak away again until I get back? Your daddy and I are going to go look at a new tire we got today."

Closing the door behind him, Dave turned to his friend. "It's Jen, isn't it?"

Brent's composure cracked. "She didn't want to go, Dave, and I made her. Now she's gone," he said as he covered his face with his hand and a sob escaped his throat.

"Wait a minute," Dave said. "Give me the details."

"They left San Jose Del Cabo at about eleven forty-five this morning but never showed up in Douglas. Flight Service has waited a reasonable amount of time and they can't figure out what happened to them. The flight plan was opened by San Jose Tower but they know nothing after that. Flight Service is convinced they've gone down."

"So, that doesn't mean she's dead," he exclaimed.

"Dave, Flight Service has heard nothing. It's like they just dropped out of the air."

"Has anyone looked at the radar track?"

"You know the phone lines in Mexico. They've been unable to reach anybody at San Jose or Mazatlan Center."

"I also know Jen, and I know that she wouldn't go out without a scrap. The only thing she couldn't survive in that airplane is a structural failure and, since I know the mechanic personally, I know that's not possible. They haven't found a smoking hole, have they?"

"No," Brent replied.

"Then there's hope. We're wasting time. Call your mother and see if she can watch the Peep. I'm going to bolt the prop back on that animal out there and we'll go have a look for ourselves."

"Thanks, Dave."

He was already out the door.

II

It was one of those crystalline summer days that occur so often in New Mexico. Visibility was well over a hundred miles and the sky was a deep indigo blue that is only found in high altitude, dry climates. There were a few puffy cumulus clouds on the horizon, their stark white a brilliant contrast to the summer sky. At twenty-five thousand feet above sea level, the features of the earth were stunted, huge mountains reduced to rock piles, deep canyons mere gashes in the planet's tender skin.

Dave had offered to fly, but Brent took the controls hoping it would help him stop thinking about the morbid possibilities he faced. He thought about how he had begun to take Jennifer for granted and kicked himself mentally for all the lost opportunities. How stupid he had been! He wanted another chance. To turn back the clock and do it over. Next time he would pay more attention to what was happening to his family, change a few priorities. Suddenly the business seemed unimportant compared to the idea that he might never see her again.

The Gila wilderness spread beneath them, an emerald in the expanse of the rock and rubble of southern New Mexico. As he looked out the window of the twin engine Cessna, he was not seeing the magnificent panorama unfolding before him. He was trying to capture the image of his pretty wife. In his mind's eye he could see the red-gold highlights in her dark hair, the single dimple in her right cheek. He smiled to himself as he thought of it. The dimple was definitely one of her most arresting features and friends often commented on it. She loved to tell the story of her cat fight with Tammy Sutter in the third grade. They were arguing over the ownership of a pencil. When Jennifer appeared to be getting the best of her in the disagreement, Tammy picked up the pencil and stabbed her in the cheek. She had never received stitches for the odd wound and it had scarred into the striking dimple that everybody found so appealing.

Brent's eyes casually scanned the instruments, always alert for a problem. Dave appeared to be lost in his own thoughts. It was one of the few times Brent had seen him still for more than a few minutes. He turned back to gaze out the window. He figured they had crossed the Arizona border as he looked out and saw the colorful slashes of the copper mines. They would have to stop in Tucson for fuel. Another delay. He wanted to scream and shout and pull his hair and tell the world that it wasn't fair to lose your soul mate. He had always assumed they would grow old together although they often joked about safety.

"Keep the greasy side down!" he would call playfully as she picked up her flight bag and rushed out the door.

"Don't worry!" she'd call back. "I don't want to be the first one at the scene of the crash!"

How could they have joked about such things? He supposed it was some weird kind of defense mechanism that helped them deal with the hazards of this profession.

The worst part of all was the guilt. He felt personally responsible for sending her on this trip. He could still picture her as she lay this morning, the right side of her face jammed into the soft down pillow, mouth open slightly as she sighed in her peaceful sleep. Then the way she bumped around the house until she got her first cup of coffee. Oh, how she loved her coffee! Always threatening to give it up because the caffeine wasn't good for her. Now it didn't matter. All those little things that were just memories. He wondered, once the people who remembered you were gone, if you ceased to exist. After all, that's all that was left of any life...memories.

He forced himself out of these thoughts to glance at the chart in his lap and cross check it with his instruments. Dave was rooting around in his flight bag for a roll of lifesavers.

"Another twenty minutes and we'll be in Tucson. You want to file the flight plan while I arrange for fuel?"

"Sure," Dave replied as he found the candy and started peeling the paper. "Anything you want. You okay?"

Brent turned tired eyes to his friend. "If she's dead, my life's over Dave."

"Hey, what kind of talk is that! Jen's okay. She probably had to park it somewhere and is trying to call us as we speak."

Brent reduced the power slightly to slow for the descent. He knew there would be turbulence over the mountains. "I hope you're right, Dave. God, how I hope you're right!"

II

The Commandante's office was hot, humid, and smelled of sweaty bodies and stale smoke. He leaned back in his chair, produced a wooden match and, with a flick of his wrist, lighted the cigarette hanging out of his mouth. He inhaled deeply, held his breath for a moment and exhaled the smoke in a rush. It curled around his head and he blinked his eyes.

"I've already told you four times, Señor. The Señora filed her flight plan to Albuquerque. She departed San Jose Del Cabo, she signed off with San Jose tower, and that is all I know. You must understand this is very messy for us. We do not like to lose airplanes in our airspace."

"That's my wife, you bastard!" Brent started out of his seat and Dave grabbed him.

"Our apologies, Commandante," he said. "You must understand that Señor Duncan is not himself since Señora Duncan disappeared."

"Of course," the Commandante replied through narrowed eyes. "Now, if you will excuse me, I am a very busy man." He turned to some forms on his desk. Brent and Dave took the hint and left.

Outside the office, Brent clenched his fists and gritted his teeth. "Now I know why I don't like to come to Mexico," he said. "My nerves can't take the frustration."

"He's only one guy," Dave replied. "There have to be at least twenty people around here who saw Jennifer and might know something. We're not going to leave until we talk to every one of them."

II

It was a beautiful afternoon. The sun was putting on a brilliant show as it hung low on the dusty horizon and the wind was starting to let up. The airport guard popped open a can of beer, lit a cigarette and absently scratched his crotch. The dog whined softly and he reached down to rub his ears. He decided he needed to relieve himself and ambled toward the shed where the wooden crates were stacked. The dog trotted ahead and, sniffing around the base of one of the crates, started barking. The guard was suddenly alert. He set down the can of beer, picked up his assault rifle and slowly approached the stack of crates. There was a muffled sound coming from one of them. He approached cautiously and, holding the gun on the crate, slowly removed the lid and peered inside. Looking back at him with wide eyes was a young man in a pilot's uniform and an older man in a rumpled blue suit. They were both bound and gagged. The Commandante is not going to like this, he thought as he reached to untie them.

CHAPTER 4

Dave and Brent tackled the task of interviewing every person on the airport. There were customs and immigration, the man behind the weather desk, the guys on the ramp who handled fueling and parking of aircraft, the air traffic controllers in the tower and the guards. Brent had never been able to get used to the sight of young kids who were still wet behind the ears running around an airport with assault rifles. He looked at them warily as they moved from one group of people to the next, trying to break the language barrier and get some answers.

Between them, they knew a little Spanish. It had always been enough to get by when there was absolutely nobody else who could do a trip and they had to fly into Mexico. Most of the Mexicans knew a little English. Cabo San Lucas was becoming more popular with the tourists and they were flying into San Jose in increasing numbers to escape the cold from up north during the winter months.

How do you ask someone in pidgin Spanish what they know about the fate of a Learjet? How do you say, "Did you see the airplane crash into the ocean?" in Spanish?

Brent was chafing at the reception they'd received in the Commandante's office. The man was arrogant! He wished Dave hadn't kept him from punching the guy in the nose but he knew it would only have landed him in jail. That wouldn't have helped Jennifer.

They decided to start with the tower. Those guys would definitely be able to talk to them. The men were polite but unable to answer many of their questions. Yes, they had cleared the airplane for takeoff. No, there were no apparent problems. The aircraft climbed normally and turned northbound. No, there was no distress call, no mayday.

"Who was speaking on the radio?" Brent asked the man.

"The Señora."

Brent looked at Dave. "Mark must have been flying if Jennifer was working the radio."

"Doesn't make any difference. Mark is an excellent pilot. I'm sure he could easily have handled any abnormalities."

Brent turned back to the controller. "How did she sound?"

He shrugged. "Like a Gringa."

"You handed them off to Mazatlan Center?"

"Yes, Señor. I asked them to report twenty-five knots north. After the report, I handed them off to Mazatlan Center."

"Did you see them after that?"

"No, Señor. They were out of sight when I handed them off."

"Thank you." Brent held out his hand. "You have been most helpful."

"Señor."

They paused at the door as the man called out to them. "Good luck."

II

He had been brief in his demands. His accomplice was holding Mark. If he did not check in with this partner every forty-eight hours to let him know that she was co-operating, the partner was under strict orders to waste him.

She watched him out of the corner of her eye. He had been quiet since his short speech, and he was sitting in the co-pilot's seat watching the Pacific slip under them at five hundred miles per hour. He was good looking, this hijacker of hers. His ruddy blonde hair was short and curly and he had a firm, square jaw. There was the faint shadow of blonde stubble on his face. His gray eyes were hooded and she wondered what haunted him. There was a large elongated bruise on his arm and he seemed to favor it. When paying for the fuel, he had produced a large roll of hundred dollar bills. The guys at the fuel pumps had taken one look at the wad in his hands and their eyebrows had shot up. So had hers. There had been no sign of the knife and he didn't look that threatening. Now that the initial panic had passed and she had her hands on the yoke, she felt a little more in control. She sighed quietly and thought about her options. She was afraid to press him further about his intentions, but until she got more information, it would be difficult to plan an escape.

Brent must be frantic, she thought. I've got to get word to him somehow.

She wondered if anyone would notice that she had listed the color of the airplane as blue on the flight plan. It had been a long shot. She knew there would be an investigation after her disappearance. Her only hope was that they would notice the inconsistency. Brent would surely know that she'd never call the airplane blue. She hated blue. She'd picked the colors for the Lear. It was her baby. She only hoped they didn't think the aircraft had gone down in the Sea of Cortez. That would just delay their search for her and her captor while they tried to find the wreckage. He hadn't seemed to notice the emergency transponder code. She could see the transmit light flashing on the instrument as it should but she did not have a lot of faith in Mexican radar. It seemed it was down more often than it was working. Oh, well, her fate was in their hands now. She had to trust them. Her job was to keep Mark and herself alive and keep from bending the airplane in the process.

"It's against the law to deviate from your flight plan while in Mexican airspace," she ventured.

"It is also against the law to kidnap and hijack," he replied and turned back to the window.

"They've got radar. They can see us."

"For all they know we are a fish-spotter."

"Fish-spotters don't go four hundred and eighty knots at forty-five thousand feet above sea level," she replied.

"Do you have a comment for everything?" he asked sarcastically.

"It would be helpful if I knew where we were going. Flying a heading is fine for a while but eventually you'll have to clue me in if you want to get there."

"Does your Global Positioning System work?" he asked, indicating an instrument on the crowded panel. GPS, as it was known in the industry, was the newest state of the art technology in satellite navigation and Jennifer was very proud of it.

"To within fifty feet of wherever you tell it you want to go."

"Good," he said. "Here are the coordinates." He handed her a crumpled piece of paper.

"That's pretty far south."

"I know."

"Which airport is it?"

"None that you've ever heard of. It's unpublished."

She looked at him incredulously. "This doesn't have anything to do with drug running, does it?"

"Us or the airport?"

"Either one!" She was starting to get angry. "Listen. This is not amusing! Those people have big guns. They shoot first and ask questions later. They are mean. They are nasty. And I don't think I want to be part of your little scheme, whatever it is!"

He turned back towards her and she was thinking that he didn't meet her expectations of a hijacker. Somehow, she had always pictured hijackers as wild-eyed radicals from some camel riding country that waved machine guns around and screamed demands to their captives.

"Listen," he said resignedly. "If I tell you the purpose of my trip, the source of my desperation, will you try to cooperate and most of all try to keep your mouth shut?"

"It depends. I'm listening."

He turned back toward the window and she could not see his face. He began to talk.

"They have my little girl. She is going to be five on her next birthday. If I don't get them what they want within five days, they are going to start mailing me her fingers, one a day." He was silent. His jaw was set and Jen had never seen such a look of fear, pain and desperation on a human face.

She was horrified. She thought about Peeper's tiny dimpled hands and cringed. How could anyone do that to a child? She shuddered and reached to rub the goose bumps off her arms.

"Look," she said. "I'm a parent myself. My little girl probably thinks I'm dead right now. I've got to at least call them and let them know where I am and that I'm okay."

"I'm afraid that's not possible," he replied. We don't have much time. I need your services. When I'm done with you, you're free to go."

"If you wanted my services, why didn't you just hire me? It doesn't look like you are exactly hurting for money!"

"You would not have gone willingly to our destination."

"So you're going to hold a gun on me and make me go there against my will?"

"I don't have a gun," he said flatly.

She was amazed. "You don't have a gun?"

"I had a gun but I lost it."

"You lost your gun?" she said. "I don't believe this. This is too much. He lost his gun."

"It's a long story," he replied.

"How do you expect to go against a bunch of bad guys without a gun?"

"I'll think of something."

She was quiet for a few moments.

"You're not really going to let your friend hurt Mark, are you? He's just a kid!"

"His safety depends on your cooperation."

She wasn't sure she bought the story about the little girl.

Dave and Brent weren't getting very far. Dave popped open his fourth roll of lifesavers and tossed one in his mouth. "We definitely need to find someone who speaks Spanish and English," he sighed. Frowning, he quickly moved the candy back and forth from one side of his mouth to the other. "I think those guys at the fuel pumps know something but we just can't seem to get around this communication barrier."

"Señor Duncan." A man approached. "Come." He started toward the Commandante's office.

Mark was sitting in front of the Commandante's desk in a worn gray chair. A somewhat tired and dusty man in his mid-forties was sitting beside him.

"Mark!" Brent was ecstatic. If Mark was here, Jennifer couldn't be far!

Mark stood up and held out his hand. "Good to see you, Brent. This is US Customs Inspector Sparks." He gestured to the man standing next to him, holding out his hand.

"Mr. Duncan," Sparks said. "We have to talk."

CHAPTER 5

Juan Carlos Jose Emilio Fuentes de Lopez was the ultimate middleman. He had come a long way from his peasant roots to become dictator of one of the largest drug cartels in South America. However, the thing that had made him rich was the insatiable greed of the wealthy Americanos for diamonds, not drugs. Junkies had no money. Sure, they could knock off a convenience store or mug some guy in Central Park to get enough for the next fix or two, but Juan Carlos had been shrewd enough in the early days to figure out that the real money lay with the gentry. Their pockets were deep, their resources seemingly endless. They had it all it seemed, but they were always greedy for more.

His father had been a worker on a coffee plantation. When Juan Carlos was six years old, his father had developed an addiction to cocaine. He had helplessly watched his father's steady decline as he sank deeper into the clutches of the drug. He would snort a couple of lines first thing in the morning to get him going. Initially, he would be euphoric, rushing around speaking rapidly, making grandiose plans for the future. After the burst of frantic energy wore off he would fall into his bed and often sleep for two days.

The meager furnishings in the small home disappeared as he desperately sought to raise cash to feed the habit.

One morning his startled mother had answered the door to a frightened friend who stood on the stoop, hat in hands and, with downcast eyes informed her of her husband's arrest for the theft of some jewelry from the big house.

Juan Carlos never saw his father again. His second night in jail he bled to death from a hemorrhage in his nasal passages.

His mother seemed very old after that. Her kind face was pinched and dried up and the lines became deeper. There was never enough food and, although she took in laundry to help support Juan Carlos and his baby brother, the little house sunk into a lower state of repair. There was no longer laughter and Juan Carlos developed a cold hate for the father who had deserted them by dying.

That spring, the baby developed dysentery and, within a few days the diarrhea had left him severely dehydrated. His cries were weak and his fingers thin as they gently picked at the tattered blanket while his mother whispered desperately to Juan Carlos to fetch the neighbor.

He had pulled the startled woman down the dirt track to the tiny house. As she passed through the door ahead of him, she gasped and screamed in horror.

Turning, she tried to push him back. But it was too late. He had seen the grisly scene. His mother was lying on the floor in a spreading puddle of dark blood, her throat slashed. Clutched in the birdlike fingers of her right hand was a bloody kitchen knife. In her other arm, pressed against her sagging breast, was the body of his infant brother.

Life was cruel to a peasant boy with no family and no friends. He promised himself that he would never again allow love into his heart because it meant vulnerability. He was determined to survive and he haunted the streets of his village, quietly stealing when he could, relying on a diet of small rodents and bugs when necessary.

By the time he was twenty-three, he had used his cunning and determination to overthrow a famous drug king pin and quickly became the feared dictator of the largest drug cartel in Venezuela. He was both respected and feared by his employees as well as his enemies.

He felt he had finally arrived. He was using the source of his father's death as a weapon against society. As his arrogance and power increased, so did his vanity. With dark Latin good looks, he spent hours on his grooming, standing in front of a mirror while barking orders at subordinates. His clothes were expensive and impeccable. His blue-black hair was meticulously trimmed weekly and women found the sensuous pouting lips irresistible.

But life had one more nasty card to deal. One morning he woke to a strange, numb feeling on the right side of his face. Looking in the mirror, he saw with horror that the right side of his face sagged grotesquely with the paralysis of Bell's Palsy. The doctors assured him that most patients fully recovered from this mysterious ailment, with no lingering effects. But this was not to be the case for Juan Carlos. The paralysis persisted and he grew a long drooping mustache to hide the constant dribble of saliva that escaped the helpless corner of his mouth. His speech sounded like that of a drunk but those who knew him, knew he was always coldly sober. Juan Carlos did not engage in vices that made him vulnerable—drugs, booze or women.

In nineteen eighty-seven, he had sent his first shipment of cocaine to a contact in South Africa. In return, he received a handful of diamonds. It had taken five weeks to smuggle them from Venezuela through Baja, California into the Port of Los Angeles. The wait had been worth it. The return was twenty times what he would have made on the shipment of cocaine, had he sent it directly to the United States. He took great pride in the fact that he had never been caught and was convinced that his system was perfect.

Juan Carlos picked up the bottle of red wine with the South African label. He turned it over in his hands and ran his finger over the small embossed mark that told him what it contained. This one was special. He was tempted to uncork the bottle so he could actually hold the stone in his hands, feel its weight and admire its brilliance. Above all else, though, Juan Carlos was a business man. He knew that the undisturbed bottle was a necessary vessel to transport the precious cargo to the States. He smiled as he thought of the famous Hope Diamond, now displayed at the Smithsonian in Washington, DC. The one he held in his hand, safely entombed in the green glass and red wine, would make the Hope diamond look like a child's toy. It was priceless. Almost. In the world of Juan Carlos anything could be bought for enough money and power.

The little girl was frightened. She was cold as she huddled in the corner of the small dark room in the damp ship and the pitching movement gave her a stomach ache. She missed her parents and nanny and all the things that were normal in her life. She whimpered softly, afraid to cry, because the man might hit her again. Her dress was torn and dirty. For once in her young life she wished for a bath. She closed her eyes and dreamed about Nanny serving a delicious tea in the nursery and, afterwards, taking her dolly for a walk in the pram through the park. The man said her father was going to come and get her in a few days, but he wouldn't come if she wasn't good. She crossed her fingers. "Please Daddy," she said softly. "Please come. I promise I will be good."

Inspector Royce Sparks held out his hands. "I'm sorry," he said. "This is really embarrassing and I don't know where to start."

"Just start when you got out of the plane." Brent was impatient.

"Well, I wasn't feeling too well," he began. "After getting out of the plane and throwing up in the nearest trash can, I was still feeling ill, so I went into the john."

They all looked at him expectantly. The short man in the corner was making sucking noises around the lifesaver he had just popped into his mouth. Sparks' head was throbbing and his eyes were scratchy from lack of sleep. It was becoming more difficult to concentrate.

"Anyway," he continued, "I was sitting on the john with my elbows on my knees and my head in my hands when suddenly the stall door is kicked open by someone on the outside. The door cracked me in the head and knocked me off the can. My pants were down around my ankles. I kept trying to get up but my pants kept getting tangled in my legs and I would fall down again. All the time this guy is trying to push his way through the door."

He looked around the office. He had their attention now. The short guy in the corner had even stopped sucking the lifesaver. It was the first time he had seen him still.

"I finally managed to get up on my feet and I saw an opportunity, so I threw myself against the door, crushing his arm in the opening and causing a gun to fly out of his hand."

"So you got the gun," Brent said. He was leaning forward in his seat.

"Not exactly." Royce looked down. "It landed in the toilet."

They were silent for a moment as this sunk in.

"But you had your gun." Brent was looking at him expectantly.

"You have to realize this all happened very fast." They looked disgusted. "I was in the crapper, for god's sake!" he added defensively.

"Go on." The Commandante leaned back in his seat and drew leisurely on a cigarette.

"He had the advantage of surprise and I had my pants around my ankles. I was also still stunned from the whack on the head. Anyway, he was able to overpower me, tie me up and throw me into that crate. The kid was already there." He nodded to Mark.

The Commandante leaned forward across his desk and spoke around the cigarette. "Why do you think this man would want to tie you up, kidnap the Señora and hijack the airplane, Señor Inspector?"

"It's possible it has something to do with our customs investigation in South America. If that's the case, however, I don't understand why they took her and left me behind. Maybe it was a mistake."

"You've never seen this hijacker before?"

"I don't know who he is," Royce replied, "but I got a good look at him. I'll call in the info to my office right away and have them fax me dossiers on anyone who meets the description and might have a reason to be in this part of the world."

II

Brent went with Mark on the thirty minute taxi ride into Cabo San Lucas. There had been recent heavy rains in southern Baja and the normally parched desert had bloomed. There was a patina of green everywhere as the seeds that had lain dormant for months germinated and burst forth overnight. He watched the red rocky bluffs give way to the deep sapphire of the sparkling Sea of Cortez.

The town of Cabo San Lucas, once a sleepy fishing village, had experienced a bloom of it's own. Once word got out about the giant marlin and mahi mahi, whale migrations off Todos Santos and spectacular diving in the crystal water, the tourist industry had boomed. Condominiums and resorts had shot up and American hotels started moving in. Brent hardly recognized this bustling village from the last time he had been here almost ten years ago.

The taxi pulled up to the Hotel Plaza de Las Glorias and Brent got out to stand before Mark. "Sorry about the way things turned out, buddy."

"Just make sure you get Jennifer back in one piece." Mark looked down as tears formed. "I feel like I let her down."

"Nonsense!" Brent put his arm around the thin shoulders. "There was absolutely nothing you could do! Jen wouldn't want you to be talking like that!"

Mark looked up gratefully. "I'll do what I can to keep things going at home."

"Do you have your ticket?"

"Right here. I'm booked on the first flight out in the morning."

There was an uncomfortable silence. Finally, Brent pulled the young man to him and gave him a hug. "Give the Peeper a kiss for me, will you?"

"Sure. Anything," Mark replied. "Listen, you'd better get back." He didn't want to prolong this good-bye any more than he had to. "You guys have a lot to do before tomorrow morning. I wish I spoke Spanish. At least that way I might be able to help you out a little."

"You'll be more help to us back home. Someone needs to fly all those airplanes while Jen's gone."

"I've got a buddy who's between flying jobs right now. Do you want me to call him up and see if he can help out for a few days?"

"No, it would be too difficult to get him checked out while we're gone. Hopefully we'll have Jen back and be home within a day or two. Thanks for the offer."

Brent watched out of the back of the taxi window while Mark's solitary figure got smaller and smaller. Finally, they turned a corner and he was gone.

CHAPTER 6

They skirted the Pacific Coast of Mexico for over two hours before passing into Central American airspace. As directed, she turned due east over the Panamanian coast, crossing the Panama Canal and leaving the Pacific behind for the translucent waters of the Caribbean. Ahead on the horizon, a shrouded peak had been growing steadily. High pressure had been building over the Pacific and they were fortunate to have clear skies. Below them, the ocean sparkled in the late afternoon sun. She looked again at her chart and then at the GPS.

"Pico Cristobal Colon," she said, pointing. He looked at the massive peak looming on the horizon. "Over nineteen thousand feet," she added. "Looks like we're still about three hundred knots from the fix you gave me." The fuel gauges were getting dangerously low. She only had about an hour's worth left at cruise power. She figured she could just make it to the fix he had given her, but one hundred miles past Caracas was a point of no return. They were committed. There would probably be only one chance on the landing. A go-around at take-off power would gobble up the low reserve she would have. "Can you tell me anything about this field we're landing at? Elevation, length," she paused, then turned to him suddenly. "It is paved, isn't it?"

"Yes," he replied. "It's paved. I don't know the elevation or length. It's in the mountains. The paved part of the strip is probably something over a kilometer."

She didn't know if she liked this.

The city of Caracas appeared off the left wing and she looked at the International Airport longingly as it slipped beneath them. They passed over fields of bananas, coffee and cocoa beans before crossing the rich Orinoco River Basin. They could see large herds of cattle grazing on vast plains.

One hundred miles out, she started her descent. The terrain rose rapidly as they started over the rugged wilderness of the Guiana Highlands. The neat, cultivated fields had abruptly given way to a tangled rain forest.

When she estimated that they were about one thousand feet from the ground, she leveled off and slowed as much as she dared. He had his nose pressed against the glass, watching intently.

"There!" The eagerness in his voice made her jump.

She followed the point of his finger with her eyes and saw the tiny gash of dark pavement going up the side of the hill.

"We can't land this airplane there!" she cried. "That isn't a runway, that's a scratch in the side of the mountain!"

"Relax," he said. "I've been into this field before in an airplane just like this."

"You have?" She was incredulous as she banked the plane for another pass. As they crossed a second time, she noticed a small metal building at the top end of the strip. In her mind she was rapidly calculating landing distance. It looked like the elevation was about forty-five hundred feet. The grade was unbelievable. My goodness, she thought, I bet it's off the charts! She couldn't tell which direction the wind was blowing but there was no question in her mind that she would land up hill. The steep grade would decrease the landing distance significantly. Just then, the red master caution light on the glare shield started blinking and she heard the alarm. Looking at the annunciator panel, she saw what she expected to see, the low fuel warning light. She had exactly eight hundred pounds of fuel left. At take off power, that was about ten minutes worth. They were committed to this runway, like it or not.

"Hand me that gray book," she said, all business. He picked up the heavy manual and handed it to her as she checked the reading on the outside air temperature gauge. She turned again to keep the field in sight and engaged the auto pilot before turning to the performance section of the book. She scanned the chart for five thousand feet elevation, no wind, two percent grade (that was the maximum they gave) and a temperature of eighty-six degrees. She groaned. According to the table, at their weight, they would need forty-eight hundred feet to land. She thought of the little girl. She thought of the Peep. She thought of Brent. She thought about poor Mark. She thought about all the things she shouldn't be thinking about. Time to stop thinking and start flying. The important thing at that moment was getting on the ground in one piece.

"Hold on Kimosabe," she said, disengaging the auto pilot and turning to line up on a five mile final. "We're going in."

She noted the five degree crab to the right and hoped that it was a head wind, which was what her instincts told her. Extending the flaps fully, she lowered the gear and slowed to the least possible speed as the wheels missed the treetops by a few feet and she dropped the airplane into the clearway at the end of the runway. The landing was firmer than usual, but she wasn't shooting for perfection. She just wanted to get the wheels on the ground so she would have braking. At the moment of touchdown, she jumped on the brakes and yanked the whining engines into full reverse. The building at the end of the runway was approaching at an alarming rate and, the closer it got, the harder she stood on the brake pedals until the disks between the tires were smoking and she feared the pedals would snap off under her feet. Five hundred feet from the building, the anti-skid on the left side failed. The brakes immediately seized and the tires locked. They slowly started to rotate to the left as the burning rubber on the locked tires grabbed at the pavement. The tortured engines screamed for mercy until finally, in a spay of gravel, they skidded to a halt, sideways, in front of the building. In the end, the steep upward grade, about seven percent by her estimate, saved them. The right wing rested only six feet from the front of the building.

Jen let out her breath with a rush and didn't realize she had been holding it. Drenched with sweat, her ears were still ringing from the whining engines. Her right hand was clamped so tightly on the throttle knobs that her fingers were frozen. Reaching her left hand across the yoke, she pried them loose. Her passenger was pale and she could see the bones of his jaw standing out as he clenched his teeth.

She was angry. "You've never been into this field in an airplane just like this, or any jet for that matter, have you?"

He turned to face her. "I told you, I am a desperate man."

"Don't ever lie to me again," she said coldly and pushed the door open to a rush of searing tropical air and the sharp smell of hot rubber. Jumping to the ground she looked at the flattened tires with a sinking heart. "There goes our ticket home."

"Looks like I am no longer in need of your services," he said.

"Look, Mister," she shot back. "You forced me down to this god-forsaken hole and you are not about to waltz off into the sunset and leave me here for ant bait. Wherever it is that you're going, I'm going."

"Do you speak Spanish?" he asked.

"Fluently," she replied.

"Okay," he said. "You can tag along as long as you don't slow me down. I don't have much time."

Dave mumbled something about needing something out of the airplane and disappeared into its dark interior. Brent was gratefully tagging along with Inspector Sparks, who appeared to be fluent in Spanish. They were slowly making their way through interviews with every person on the airport who may have seen Jennifer or her hijacker.

The men at the fuel pump knew the Señora well. "She always brings us the flaky bread," they said rapidly in Spanish. Brent was puzzled when Sparks interpreted this. "I think they mean croissants," he told Brent, noting the puzzled look on his face. "The Mexicans love them and they are almost impossible to get down here." Yes, the men had seen the Señora get into the airplane. Yes, they had seen the fair-haired gringo. No, they did not hear where they were going. Didn't she live in Albuquerque, Nuevo Mexico?

They moved on to the guards who claimed they had not seen or heard anything unusual. Finally, they landed at the weather desk. The same questions were asked the man behind the typewriter. He was thoughtful. "The Señora, she seemed different today," Sparks interpreted.

"Why do you say that?" he asked.

"Because," the man went on. "She said her airplane was blue." He shrugged.

Brent and Sparks looked at each other. "Why would she possibly say the airplane was blue?" Sparks asked.

"I don't have the slightest idea," Brent replied, thoughtful. "But, knowing Jen, I'm sure it's important. She loves that airplane. She would never call it anything other than what it is without a good reason."

"Gracias, Senior," Sparks said and, turning to Brent. "I need to call the office. I'll be over at that pay phone. Let me know if you decide to leave."

"Okay," Brent said. "I need to find Dave."

Brent went back into the simple terminal building. His friend was nowhere in sight. He knew better than to try asking someone if they had seen him. He barely knew how to ask where the bathroom was.

Walking back out into the heat of the ramp, he shielded his eyes from the harsh sun and squinted at the horizon. He could imagine the outline of a Learjet disappearing over the low hills to the northeast and fading from sight. Where was she? What was she thinking? A cold cloak of loneliness settled on him and he shivered in spite of the heat. If he had to spend every cent he owned and kill himself trying, he was not going to rest until she was safe. The thought bolstered him slightly and he shook himself. In his gut, he knew it was going to take every bit of ingenuity and dedication he owned to get through this ordeal.

CHAPTER 7

Sparks filled Cosgrove in on the latest developments. He had given him a description of his assailant which matched the description of the hijacker. "I'm afraid we don't have much to go on, Chief. We don't even know which direction they turned after taking off from Cabo. Have you been in touch with the FBI since our initial report?"

"Yes," Cosgrove replied. "They've called in the Hijacking and Terrorist Tactical Response International Cooperative Team from Houston."

"Boy, that's quite a mouth full. I've never heard of them."

"They call them the HAT-TRIC team. The FBI put together an assortment of individuals from several different government agencies to deal with international incidents like this. Their specialty, as their name implies, is hijacking and terrorist activity. They've got guys from the FBI, CIA, International Intelligence, and just about any alphabet soup government agency you can think of. They've been talking to the Mexican military who has the best surveillance radar coverage in the country, at least in the coastal areas. They reported picking up an emergency transponder signal traveling at high altitude and high speed about fifty miles off the coast heading south. The target turned inland just as it reached Panama, turned eastward until crossing Caracas, Venezuela, then turned southeast toward the highlands. That's when they lost it. The FBI is working with the Mexican and South American governments. They've let them know this is a hijacking and they've agreed to leave it to our authorities. Anyway, it's out of our hands. The FBI deals with these things all the time. I'm sure they've got it under control."

"I just feel bad about the girl," Sparks said.

"She'll be okay, I'm sure," Cosgrove replied. "Getting back to our case," he continued. "Have you talked to our contacts in Cabo San Lucas yet?"

"I haven't had a chance," Sparks apologized. "Things haven't been going real smooth so far."

"You've got to get down to Caracas as soon as possible, meet up with Melendez, and take over where Charlie left off. We're too close to let this one go."

"I'll be on the next Mexicana flight through Mexico City."

"When does that leave?"

"Tomorrow at ten."

"Not soon enough. Charter an airplane and leave now. I'll wire you some cash as soon as I get off the phone and it'll be waiting for you at the Cabo San Lucas Branch of the Banco de Mexico. While you're in town, make contact with the guys from El Paso at the secure number I gave you. See if there are any new developments before you leave."

"All right Chief," Sparks sighed, and hung up the phone.

II

In the airplane, Dave smiled and slowly removed the headsets of his small portable FM radio. Walking to the pay phone, he looked left, then right before stepping into the booth. Picking up the receiver, he unscrewed the mouthpiece and removed a small silver disc about the size of a dime from inside, slipping it into his pocket.

II

Sparks approached Brent. "I need to charter your airplane."

"It's not for rent," Brent replied coolly. "Try somebody else." He was displeased that Sparks refused to reveal classified information about the Customs investigation.

"Look," Sparks was apologetic. "I know you're distressed about your wife, but think about it. If you take me to my destination that gives you one more piece to your puzzle. I need to go to Caracas to meet with another inspector who has been working on this case for the past three months, if that tells you anything, and while I'm with you, my Spanish might come in handy. Besides, I'm desperate. You guys are the only charter aircraft on the field."

Brent looked at Dave as he approached. "He wants to charter the 421 to Caracas. What do you think?"

"I think that's a long way in a twin Cessna. We'll probably have to stop twice for gas, but we can do that."

"Okay," Brent said. "How soon do you want to leave?"

"As soon as I get back from Cabo. I've got to go into town to pick up some cash. It will probably be dark by the time I get back. Is that a problem?"

"Not a problem," Brent said.

"By the way," Sparks added. "Do you have a fax phone in your plane?"

"Sure do," he replied, reaching into his pocket for a card with the number.

II

The gleaming white Finestera Hotel in Cabo San Lucas clutched the hill overlooking the harbor. Nestled among the rocks, its grip looked tenuous as the balconies hung precariously over the steeply sloping terrain. The battered Volkswagon bus pulled up the steep driveway and slowly came to a halt to the sound of squeaking brakes. Sparks paid the taxi driver and jumped out.

The directions given him by the other Custom's agents were easy to follow and he was soon at their door. His knock was answered by Wally Connors, an old friend from the Academy. He never could remember Wally's real name. He'd gotten the nickname Wally from the impressive red drooping mustache that made him look like a walrus. His blue eyes crinkled in a smile and Sparks knew it was there even though the mustache covered his mouth in a bushy mass. It was hard not to stare at the thing.

They walked out onto the balcony and sat at the table flanked by two chairs facing out over the cliff and the harbor beyond. Russ Talbot, the other agent from El Paso, set a pitcher of iced tea on the table between them.

"How was your flight?" Wally asked his friend with a sheepish grin. He knew well Spark's aversion to airplanes.

"As bad as I expected. What's worse, I've got to leave shortly for South America."

Wally whistled through his teeth. "That's a long trip. Glad I don't have to go!" He was watching his friend closely and was appalled at his condition. Spark's normally impeccable appearance was frazzled and it looked like he'd slept in that suit. His face was drawn and he was pale as if just getting over a serious illness. "How's Donna?"

Royce took a long pull from his glass of tea. "How's the investigation?"

Ah, so that was it! Wally took the hint to change the subject. "It's been slow. By the way, my condolences on the loss of Charlie. He was a good guy."

"It was a shock. Any idea who did it?"

"Your team in Venezuela has fingered a drug lord in South America. His name is Juan Carlos Lopez. He trades cocaine to a contact in South Africa for diamonds which he smuggles to a fence in Cabo. From there they travel up the coast to the Port of Los Angeles. We don't know who actually pulled the trigger, but I'm sure Lopez is responsible."

"How are they smuggling the diamonds?"

"That remains the big question. Our contact was able to give us information about the people involved but we have yet to figure out the means. We received one tip that ended up a dead end. Unfortunately, we wasted a lot of time chasing around before we figured that out. They told us the diamonds were being placed in the claws of lobsters being imported to the United States from Cabo. You've seen those lobsters in the tanks at the grocery stores? You know how they have the big rubber bands around their claws?"

"Sure, I've seen them. That would be a great way to smuggle diamonds. Who would want to take off those rubber bands!"

"Exactly. That was our theory. But then we went down and talked to the lobster fishermen. After seeing the lobsters, we figured out it wasn't possible."

"Why?"

"Those lobsters you see in the grocery stores are Maine lobsters. They have giant claws. The ones they catch in the Sea of Cortez are called spiny lobsters. They have no large claw, only little pinchers on the ends of their legs. There is no way you could get a diamond in one of those pinchers. Even if you did, it wouldn't stay there. They don't band them."

"So now you need another angle?"

"Yes."

"Have you been in touch with Melendez?"

"Melendez is the one who gave us the information on Lopez. They were able to figure that one out just before Charlie was killed."

Sparks looked at his watch and stood up, holding out his hand. "Thanks for the tea, Wally. I've got to run. It's going to take us all night to get to South America as it is."

Wally's freckled face once again lit in a smile. "It was good to see you, Royce. Take care of yourself. You look tired. We'll keep the investigation going on this end. Let us know if you find anything new."

The sights and sounds of the rain forest overpowered her senses. The air was heavy with humidity and the scent of rotting vegetation. A roar of sounds pulsed from the dark forest as thousands of insects, birds and animals went about daily routines. The screech of howler monkeys rose above the deafening din.

"It smells like something crawled in here and died." Jennifer was holding her nose as she pulled open the large front doors of the metal building. The rusty hinges resisted loudly as she lifted her flashlight and cautiously peered inside.

"Looks like something did die," he said, pointing to the unrecognizable remains of an animal that was swarming with ants. "See anything in there?"

"A couple of rusty fuel cans, a spider web with the second biggest spider I've ever seen and a lot of rust and mold. Doesn't look like there's anything in here we can use. When do we have to leave?"

"No time to go anywhere tonight," he said, noting the fading light.

"I'm going to go to try to get some sleep. I'll be in the airplane. You can have the shed or the tarmac, your choice."

He had no opportunity to argue. She had already disappeared outside.

"What's that?" Sparks asked, indicating the small oblong package on top of the dash. They had leveled off over the Sea of Cortez and turned south over the dark water. The fading light of dusk was rapidly disappearing and the tiny sliver of moon was not going to provide much illumination. The earlier wind had calmed and there was no turbulence as the droning props pulled the little twin engine Cessna through the air.

"That's my burrito," Dave replied, reaching to unwrap the bundle. "I got a deal on these at Quantity Club last month and got six dozen to throw in the freezer. I put one on the dash of my car or airplane in the morning and by supper time it's cooked and ready to eat. Want a bite?" he asked, holding the thing over the back of the seat.

"No thanks," Sparks replied. He was starting to feel ill again.

He hadn't seen her since she had gone out to the airplane. She had left him the small torch but it was scarier to turn the thing on than to leave it off. He was trying to get comfortable on the hard floor of the shed. The smell of mold was overpowering and everything was damp. He jumped up and pounded his pants as he thought he felt something crawl up his leg. There was a scuffle and a loud squeaking as a rat overpowered a field mouse. In a few moments he could hear the crunching of bone.

Jennifer sat up as he started banging on the door of the plane.

"What is it?" she asked crossly.

"Let me in," he said contritely. "Please?"

"What's wrong?" she asked.

"There are some pretty big rats out here."

Jen opened the door. "Drop dead." She pulled the door closed and turned the lock.

The droning of the engines had finally put Sparks to sleep. He was snoring in the back seat and Dave and Brent were busy with the business of flying the airplane. The red light on the fax machine started blinking and, within a few minutes, it had spit out seven pages.

Dave picked up the top page read quietly through the headset mike.

"Classified information. Authorized personnel only."

He thought about that for a moment. "We're authorized personnel, aren't we? I mean, we're authorized to drive airplanes, vote, walk down the street, just about anything we want to do, right?"

"Sounds good to me," Brent replied, smiling.

Dave didn't waste any time. The next six pages were pictures and dossiers of the hijacker suspects. They all fit the same basic description for build, color of hair and eyes and all had alias names listed. Only one was known to have a British accent.

"Betcha this is him." Dave held the picture out for Brent's inspection. "Ex-international jewel thief. Went into retirement about five years ago just before the birth of his daughter." He paused, thinking. "Wonder if there's any connection? Convicted only once. Out on parole within a year. Considered non-violent, never maimed or murdered anybody. Want one?" he asked, holding out the roll of lifesavers.

"No thanks," Brent replied. "Go on."

"Last known location was Baja California del Sur, Mexico." They looked at each other. "Thought to be in retirement. Not suspected of any recent jobs."

Sparks was starting to stir so Dave quickly placed the pages back in order. "Why don't you handle this," he said, handing them to Brent. "I'm going to listen to the radio for a while and see if I can catch a few."

"Inspector Sparks." Brent turned around and held the pages out to him as he sat up and rubbed his eyes. "These just came for you."

"Thanks," Sparks mumbled. He took the dossiers and quickly began to scan them. The picture seemed to jump off the page. "That's him," he murmured. He read the name. James Dover King. He looked up at the pilots. The tall thin one in the left seat had his pilot's headset on and seemed to be flying the plane. The short one was reclined with his feet up. He had the earphones of his portable radio plugged into his ears and his eyes were closed.

"Can you hand me the air phone, please?" he shouted to Brent as he tapped him on his shoulder.

"Sure," Brent said, handing it back. "We'll be landing in Guadalajara in about thirty minutes."

"Thanks!" Sparks yelled above the noise of the props. "Chief," he said in a low voice as Cosgrove came on the line. "I recognize him. It's the one with the British accent."

Dave smiled.

CHAPTER 8

The bar stood on a cobbled thoroughfare on the east side of the once prosperous market district. Over the years of its colorful past it had been a home to a family of twelve, a vegetable stand, a whorehouse and, for the last three years, a bar. The plain exterior was decorated by a collection of winos and junkies. There was a thick layer of mossy mold covering the walls both inside and out and the smell almost managed to overpower that of cigarette and cigar smoke, unclean bodies and an overflowing toilet. A young man in a white shirt and cotton pants was making out noisily with a woman in one of the booths. An old pool table slouched in one corner. There was a game with stakes taking place between a large bald gorilla and a wizened man whose mouth curved in over toothless gums. The ancient derelict seemed to be winning and the bald gorilla would occasionally make roaring or grunting sounds as an assortment of beer guzzling spectators egged them on.

Annaliza Louise Melendez sat in a sagging booth in another corner and waited for her contact. He was late. She hated it when people were late. A man at the bar was making ridiculous eyes at her and she stared him down coldly. He finally turned away. She sipped slowly at her margarita. She always liked to have her full faculties at her disposal and never ran the risk of getting drunk.

She thought about the events of the past three months. Although a career in US Customs was not her first choice she could not complain about the excitement so far. She tried not to think about her partner, Charlie Adams. He had treated her well and she considered him a friend, if not a confidant. She had struggled to keep their relationship strictly professional and he had not pressed her, although they were mutually attracted. He had played college football and managed to maintain his physique through workouts. She admired that. She herself had always placed high value on physical fitness.

Growing up with three older brothers and a father who was a career Marine was good practice for her. She got tired of always losing in the constant tussles with her brothers and enrolled in a karate class when she was eleven. Her father encouraged her. She earned her black belt the summer after she graduated from high school. Her brothers weren't winning anymore. They had received a good pounding from her hands and feet a few times and begun to steer clear of their beautiful, but ruthless sister.

After finishing her degree in criminology at the University of Texas, she signed up for four years in the Marines. Nothing matched their hand to hand combat training and she wanted to be the best. She had her heart set on the FBI, but they turned her down. Probably couldn't stand the thought of working with a strong female, she thought.

Her striking looks had attracted a lot of would-be suitors but she wasn't interested. Maybe after I'm well established in my career, she thought.

She looked over at the gorilla at the pool table. Although his chest and shoulders were enormous, he had no ass and his dirty jeans kept slipping down to reveal the suggestion of a crack between his buns. She watched, fascinated, as he continually hiked them up. He was leaning over the table now and she jumped as she heard one ball crack against another. There was some loud cursing in excited Spanish and she figured out that the game must be over as the fight broke out.

She put down her glass and moved to leave. The door was on the other side of the room and she deftly sidestepped as a body crashed to the floor in front of her. The guy rose, grabbed a chair and charged back into the fight. The noise was deafening now as the sound of splintering wood, breaking glass and Venezuelan curses were added to the loud Spanish music coming over the speakers. Ducking, she avoided a flying glass. A guy stumbled into her and, unable to resist, she tossed a punch. It wasn't much fun beating up on drunks so she eased through the obstacle course toward the door.

"Damn," she said looking at her watch. "Am I going to have to wait all day for this turkey?"

Sparks opened his eyes and sat bolt upright in bed. Looking at his travel alarm on the dusty beside table, he groaned. He had only eight minutes to shower, shave, dress and get to the establishment four blocks away where he was supposed to meet Inspector Melendez for a briefing. There was no way he was going to make it. His head was throbbing and the insides of his eyelids felt like they had sandpaper glued to them. He felt dizzy as he stood up, and recognized the after effects of air sickness.

He looked at his bloodshot eyes in the cracked mirror as he shaved. "She's going to think I have a hangover and I feel like I do!"

Pulling on his clothes, he tied his shoes and ran out the door.

Dave and Brent were sweating as they stood on the airport ramp in the suffocating heat and watched the airplane being fueled. Dave was holding the small silver disk in his hand.

"What is that?" Brent asked. "It looks like a camera battery."

"It's an FM receiver," he replied, slipping it back into the pocket of his cutoffs. "I saw it advertised in the back of Popular Science last month. You know I can't resist gadgets and it was only thirty-nine ninety-five, so I ordered it. I had to have one. It came in the mail a few days ago. I've been playing with it, trying to figure out what frequency it receives on."

"And did you figure it out?" Brent asked. He wondered where this was going.

"Sure did." Dave smiled, and popped a lifesaver into his mouth. "One oh two point seven."

"What does all this have to do with us, Dave? We need to figure out Jennifer's whereabouts instead of playing with electronic gadgets!"

"It was in the mouthpiece of the pay phone in Cabo. I was able to hear Sparks' entire conversation."

Brent's eyes widened. "Don't tell me."

"Yep," Dave was pleased with himself. "It was also in the mouthpiece of the phone in the airplane. I've got all the hot news from Albuquerque, El Paso, Cabo San Lucas and Caracas right here," he said, smiling and tapping a finger against his head.

"Dave, you're brilliant!"

As Sparks stepped out of the small hotel onto the cobblestones, he was hit by a blast of hot tropical air. Two blocks later, he was already drenched with sweat. As he was pulling his handkerchief out of his pocket to mop the rivulets running down his neck, he had to jump up against a building to avoid being run over by a screaming police car. Turning a final corner he saw a collection of flashing lights, cops and bodies flying out of the doors and windows of the bar he was headed for. He was concerned that Inspector Melendez might have been hurt and picked up his pace with concern. Then he saw her.

She was standing in front of the bar with an expensive looking navy leather clutch under her arm looking on benignly at the turbulent scene. She might have been standing in air conditioned comfort. There was not a drop of perspiration to be found on her. Her crisp navy suit was well pressed and she wore a beautifully draped white silk blouse. Smooth dark hair hung to her shoulders, gently turning in toward her perfect cheekbones and arched eyebrows. As she turned towards him, he could see recognition in her black eyes. They turned up gently at the corners. Her full lips lifted into a smile and parted over perfect teeth as she took a few steps forward and held out her hand.

"Inspector Sparks." Her speech was cultured. "Welcome to Venezuela."

II

He was pounding on the airplane door again. "Go away," she yelled and turned over.

"I'm leaving in five minutes. If you want to come with me, you bloody well better get your act in gear," he called.

She jumped up, grabbed her backpack and headed for the door. Her stomach was mumbling and she couldn't remember the last time she had eaten. Opening the door, she saw the rosy streaks of early sun in the sky.

"Take a good look at the sky," he said. "Be the last time you see it for a while."

"I'll be right back," she said, disappearing behind the shed. When she returned, she saw that he was chewing on beef jerky which he offered to her.

"No thanks," she said, digging into her backpack. "I've got some slim bars." Digging a couple out of her pack, she finished them quickly. Her canteen was about three fourths full and she took a long pull on it before capping and returning it to her pack.

The night before she had taken stock of supplies in the airplane. They kept a tool kit in all of the planes and she used a screwdriver to remove the whiskey compass from between the windscreens.

It was the only piece of navigational equipment that would be any use to her without electricity and gyros. It was small, with a clear domed lid. Inside was the compass suspended in a special solution. The instrument had gotten the name whiskey compass when early aviators had problems with leaking fluid. The specific gravity of the solution was critical to the smooth operation of the instrument. If the solution was too thick it would drag on the top of the clear dome. Too thin and it rested on the bottom. Some innovative alcoholic figured out that whiskey had the same approximate specific gravity of the magic solution in the compass. So when it started to leak there was a cheap plentiful source of replacement fluid.

She had placed the compass as well as the aeronautical maps of the area into her pack. To this she added a small pillow and a blanket kept on hand for passengers. She also brought several warm sodas from the liquor cabinet and had hesitated before heaving in a bottle of Tequila. What the hell, she thought, it may come in handy. Looking around the cabin and cockpit of the plane she did a final quick inventory, not willing to leave anything that might be useful. "I hope I see you again," she said to the plane.

"Okay, I'm ready," she said, slipping the heavy pack onto her back.

He pulled on his satchel and looked up at the sun before heading under the dark tree canopy. She followed closely.

Jen was surprised to see that he was following a trail. Once inside the forest, it was cooler. An eerie, filtered light escaped through the dense growth and softly illuminated the ground. The screeching, cawing, scratching sounds of creatures around them were unnerving and she shuddered involuntarily. She didn't know if it was fear or the drying sweat on her back. Swarms of large mosquitoes descended on them and they both swatted furiously as they pushed through the dense vegetation. Occasionally there was the woof woof of the wings of a large bird as it swooped overhead.

He cursed as he ran into a giant spider web between two trees and she shuddered as the sticky remains brushed her bare arms. The ground was uneven and they frequently tripped on exposed roots. The unrelenting heat and humidity sapped her energy and her legs were leaden with growing fatigue. But she was determined not to be a burden so he would have no excuse to leave her behind.

After about six miles, they came to a fork in the trail. He slouched out of his satchel and sat down on the slimy surface of an overgrown log. With a sigh, she pulled off her pack and settled down beside him. He pulled out a map and squinted at it in the dim light.

"Where are we going?" she asked, looking over his shoulder.

"Here," he pointed to a spot along a river marked Crystal Falls. "Our landing strip was about twenty-eight miles to the southwest of Crystal Falls. We should make it there by tomorrow afternoon if nothing happens."

She looked at him closely. His face was red and swollen from insect bites. She wondered if she looked as bad.

"What you're looking for is at Crystal Falls?"

"No, but Crystal Falls lies along a tributary of the Orinoco River. We're going to a place called Villa de Lopez that lies along the Orinoco River. I'm hoping to steal a boat from a small tribe of Indians that live at the base of Crystal Falls. With the canoe it will be easy to float down the Orinoco and right to the Villa de Lopez. It will be much quicker to travel by water than over land."

"These Indians, how do they survive in this environment?"

"Their culture is ancient. They've been living here for thousands of years and are well adapted."

"Do they farm, fish, hunt?"

"A little bit of all of those things. Their primary source of food comes from the forest itself. They hunt with darts dipped in curare and shot through a blow gun. Their aim is amazing most of the time. It takes several darts to kill even a small animal like a monkey. They'll shoot a dart into him and chase him through the forest until they can get another dart off. Sometimes it will take as many as seven or eight darts to kill a twenty pound howler monkey."

"You mean those guys we see flitting around eighty or a hundred feet up in the tops of the trees? I'm impressed."

"It's really impressive to see them climb up there to get the monkey after he's dead. I've seen men in their sixties scurry up trees like it was nothing."

"Don't the monkeys just fall out of the trees when they die?"

"You've seen the density of the canopy. It's rare for the monkey to fall to the ground."

"What kind of farming do they do?"

"They don't really farm, exactly. They gather roots and fruit from the forest. The roots they grind into a flour which they use to make a large pancake. It's a funny sight to see those pancakes thrown on top of the roof of the hut to dry. They take it very seriously. It's an important part of their diet."

"Pancakes, fish and monkey meat. That's quite a menu."

"The Yekuana are not known for fishing abilities although they manage an occasional catch."

"Then why do they have boats?"

"You've seen how difficult it is to travel on foot through the rain forest. They use the rivers like we use highways. They travel to other villages to visit and trade."

"I won't feel right stealing from them."

"Then you are welcome to bloody walk," he said as he stood stiffly and lifted his satchel. Maybe there would be an alternate plan. As she got up to follow him, she pulled the compass out of the side pocket of the back pack. They were heading northeast, as he said. She was wary but in this, at least, he seemed to be telling the truth.

CHAPTER 9

Agent Henry O'Brien settled into the uncomfortable seat of the Blackhawk. The sleek black chopper was cruising at twelve thousand feet above the southern Caribbean at one hundred and forty knots, heading east. Although fast as choppers go, the Blackhawk still wasn't getting him there as quickly as he would have liked. He had been flying from the right seat for the past thirty-five minutes and his back was kinky from the strain of trying to peer over the glare shield out the front of the windscreen. He silently cursed the engineers who always seemed to design everything for tall people. As he gazed absently at the instrument panel in front of him, he thought about the case. As team leader of the HAT-TRIC team in Houston, he had been notified yesterday when information came in regarding the hijacking of the US registered aircraft out of San Jose Del Cabo. The Mexican military had been surprisingly open and supportive in sharing the tapes of the radar track showing a target moving off the coast of Mexico across the Panama Canal and into Venezuela.

They had spent half the night chasing around the coconut coast of Mexico gathering information before arriving in San Jose Costa Rica at dawn. HAT-TRIC had bases all over the world. Several years of intense diplomatic negotiations had allowed the United States to forge agreements with foreign governments. As a result, tactical aircraft were stationed at critical locations on virtually every continent. The Blackhawk had been sitting safely tucked away in a hangar in Costa Rica awaiting a mission such as this.

The size of the team varied with their assignment. This one was fairly small, eight members in addition to O'Brien, who was in charge. They believed they were after only one suspect. O'Brien, however, felt that a minimum of eight men was necessary for twenty-four hour reconnaissance. Once they picked up a scent, they worked constantly until the perpetrator was brought to justice. The members were all volunteers, most coming from other branches of security or law enforcement in the United States. They ranged in age from twenty-seven to sixty-six. All had a fierce patriotic spirit and were loyal to death for this cause.

Henry O'Brien had been involved with HAT-TRIC since its inception in nineteen eighty-two. The veteran of many missions, he was gruff and pessimistic, but his men admired him. They knew he could be counted on to be fair and never asked of them anything he wasn't willing to do himself.

The whole thing is coming off too easily, he thought pessimistically. The Venezuelan government is going to give us grief. I can feel it in my bones.

"Chief," the voice of the pilot brought him back to the present. "That's Colon, Panama straight ahead. Do you want to skirt around their airspace to the north or talk to Colon approach?"

He pulled himself up to squint out at the city coming into view, scattered over hills and spilling down to the edge of the water. A large Cuban cigar was jammed in his mouth and the end bobbed up and down as he chomped on it. Although nobody had ever seen him light one of the things, he always seemed to have one protruding from his pouting lips. The members of the team used the cigars as a barometer to his moods. He would suck and chomp until only a small stump remained which he would then toss into the trash can with a grunt before inserting another. The quicker the cigar disappeared, the more stressed out he was. From the look of things, this one would be gone before they cleared the Isthmus of Panama.

"Give em a call," he said. "The trail is already getting cold. You take it for a while, Bob. I'm gonna try to catch a few winks."

The pilot took control as O'Brien eased back against the seat, closing his large blue eyes and wriggling slightly to get more comfortable.

The pilot looked at him for a moment. He was always amazed that such a gruff character lived under that baby face. With long dark curly lashes over baby blues, round rosy cheeks and full lips, he looked like he belonged in a nursery rhyme instead of leading a tough group of individuals against a bunch of terrorists. The cigar could almost pass as a pacifier as it drooped from his mouth, hanging limply as he began to snore quietly.

Dave and Brent were sharing a couple of icy club sodas in the airport cafe as Dave filled Brent in on the information he'd gathered from his eavesdropping. Condensation ran off the side of the cool glass and formed a ring at the base. He idly moved the glass in circles, widening the ring as he talked.

"Evidently, they're after this guy called Juan something something else unpronounceable Lopez who's the head of a major drug cartel here in Venezuela. He's been smuggling diamonds into the US under their noses for several years."

"Wait a minute," Brent interrupted. "What does the leader of a drug ring have to do with diamonds?"

"I was just getting to that," Dave continued. "He smuggles cocaine into South Africa in return for diamonds and then ships the diamonds up to the United

States for a big profit. US Customs is normally geared toward the drug smugglers so it took them a while to figure this one out."

"Why do they care?" Brent asked. "Diamonds are not illegal."

"They're losing millions of dollars a year in import tariffs since the rocks are not coming in through legitimate channels."

"So how does this guy that nabbed Jennifer fit into the picture?"

"Since the Brit's a known jewel thief, they think that this Lopez guy might have something the Brit wants. It's a long shot, but the only theory they have right now. There's no other apparent motive. He's wanted in Venezuela for a big job he pulled off a couple of years ago so he couldn't just jump an airline and whiz down here to rip the guy off or whatever he plans to do."

"God, I can't believe she's in his hands." Brent put his hand over his face.

"I know this is tough for you, buddy, but you're going to have to keep it together or you won't be able to do her any good. The dossier on this guy says he's conspicuously non-violent. Besides, you know how resourceful Jen is. If I know her, you'll be feeling sorry for the Brit before it's all over."

Brent smiled gratefully at his friend. "So what do you suggest we do now?"

Dave stood up, popped a lifesaver in his mouth and tossed a couple of bills on the table. "I suggest we try to find somebody in this god forsaken place that speaks English, find out where this Lopez character hangs out, jump in the airplane and go take a look see."

II

She heard the rushing water before she saw it. He stopped beside the stream and, pulling his satchel off his back, sank to the ground and dug the map out, carefully unfolding it to check their progress.

She stretched back, letting the pack fall from her shoulders and swung it around in front. Unzipping the main compartment, she searched for her canteen.

There was a faint, familiar sound and she recognized it as the quick staccato beat of hooves on hard earth. Surprised, she looked up just in time to see a giant boar burst from the underbrush. She barely had time to shout a warning. Startled, he stood up, dropped the map and threw up his left arm just as the porker slammed into him, knocking him into the brush and ripping open his forearm with a razor sharp tusk. He knew he was dead. The red rimmed beady eyes glinted with anger and he could smell the animal's putrid breath as the snapping teeth closed in. Then he heard the gun. The pig collapsed on top of him, the hooves still pawing. Red-tinged bubbles appeared over its slobbering jaw as the mouth gaped open. The weight was crushing and he gasped for breath. Looking over the shaggy ears of his attacker, he could see Jennifer standing in the small clearing by the stream. The ancient Colt Peacemaker was clutched in her hand. A thin wisp of smoke still lingered around the blue black barrel.

She moved to pull the boar off his chest.

"My God," he exclaimed, looking at the carnage. "Is this blood mine?"

"No, I think some of it belongs to your little friend there. This was probably his personal watering hole. We were trespassing."

"Next time I'll remember to ask permission," he said sarcastically.

She ignored the remark as she picked up her pack and rummaged for the sewing kit she kept on hand for buttons that always seemed to be popping off her shirts. "Why don't you get in the stream and wash off so we can figure out where all your blood is coming from."

He stood slowly, but felt dizzy. Recognizing the blackness closing in, he dropped back down on the wet ground and passed out.

"What next?" she sighed and, picking up her canteen, dunked it into the stream to wash out his wounds. Most were merely bruises and abrasions but the gash on his forearm needed attention. It looked like an artery had been cut as the bright blood was seeping out of the wound at an alarming rate. Holding pressure over the gash with one hand, she grabbed her bottle of tequila with the other and uncorked it with her teeth. She hated to waste good tequila on the rascal but he was, after all, a human and even had a mother. She had a soft spot for mothers.

After cleaning the wound with the amber liquid, she settled down to stitch the ragged edges together. She was glad he was out. Twenty minutes later, she rocked back on her heels to admire her stitchery. It wouldn't win a prize in a quilt contest at the county fair but the blood flow had stopped and she was satisfied. It was obvious that he was in pretty bad shape. She decided their progress for the day was over. Searching him quickly she turned up a knife and ran her fingers lightly across the blade as she looked at the boar. If I can get a fire going, she thought, we can have pork chops for supper!

II

They had finally found a quiet place to talk and, settling down across from her, he took in her appealing features. Although her fighting skills were legendary in the force, looking at her now, with the long painted fingernails and perfect makeup, it was hard to picture her as a killing machine.

"Charlie lost his life to this bastard and I will not rest until he's behind bars."

"Do you know what happened to Charlie?" Their appetizer of fried bananas had arrived and he was eyeing it suspiciously.

"We had just cracked the South African connection," she said, slicing the fruit with a sharp knife. "We suspected a steamship with South African registration as the link between South Africa and South America. Charlie stowed away on board after we noticed our main suspect leaving the ship late at night. That's the last time I saw Charlie alive. It was a foolish thing to do. But you know how Charlie was...impulsive."

He took a bite of the sticky fruit and found it tasty. "By the main suspect, you mean Juan Carlos?"

"Yes. There wasn't any other reason for him to be aboard a South African steamship so we figured this ship was our connection. Actually, I don't think Charlie intended to go anywhere, just to snoop around a little but for some reason, they tossed off the lines and set sail ahead of schedule." She stopped momentarily as their main course of hervido arrived. He sniffed at the fragrant soup before digging in hungrily.

"What's that interesting flavor?" he asked.

"Yucca roots," she replied matter-of-factly. "Anyway, the good news is, I've gotten a position as a maid at Villa de Lopez. You've arrived just in time. I'll bug the place and you can set up a reconnaissance station outside to listen in. We've got to catch him red-handed or we don't have a case."

"What can I use for a cover?"

She thought for a moment. "There's a small church in the village just outside the walls of Villa de Lopez. It's in the process of restoration. It should be easy enough to park a worker's van next to it. You can set up the equipment in there."

"Infiltrating this guy's home sounds dangerous. Are you sure you're up to it?"

She looked at him like he was an idiot. "Do you want dessert?"

"Wrong question. Sorry. Sure, I'd love some. Everything I've eaten the last two days, I've thrown up."

She called to the waiter in rapid Spanish and ordered passion fruit ice cream for both of them. "I need to go back to my place and get myself roughed up a bit to look like a maid. See what you can come up with that resembles a construction worker's van. I'll meet you back here at seven this evening so we can work out the rest of the details.

He finished his ice cream and leaned back in his chair, enjoying the feeling of saity as she rose to leave. "I'll see what I can find. See you at seven." As he watched her shapely body walking across the room he wondered how she was going to pull off a cover as a maid.

Outside the restaurant, Sparks hailed the first taxi and handed him an address before leaning back against the cracked naugahyde and taking in his first real view of the city. The driving was as bad as any he had seen in Mexico City as the cabby sawed the accelerator, honked the horn continuously and dodged pedestrians. Soon they turned on to Avenida Bolivar, the main avenue through town. Traffic was heavy and the fumes from automobiles, buses and scooters was choking. Sparks was grateful when they finally pulled up in front of the post office main branch. Paying the driver and adding a healthy tip, he stepped lightly to the sidewalk and quickly made his way inside It was crowded and twenty minutes later he was finally at the counter. He gave the clerk his name and a will call number and she disappeared into a back room, returning in a few moments with a small parcel wrapped in brown paper and tied with string. He signed for it, slipped it into his pocket and made for the door.

Back in his hotel room, Sparks anxiously pulled the small package from his pocket, cut the string and carefully unwrapped it. In a bed of white tissue was a giant heart-shaped diamond. Holding it up to the light, he turned it left and right to admire the brilliance. Smiling, he returned it to its wrappings and looked around the room for a hiding place. On his hands and knees, he discovered a loose floor board. Pulling it up carefully, he placed the package underneath and replaced the board, tapping it lightly until it lined up with the others.

It was dusk before he started to come around. For a moment, he forgot where he was. His head was pounding and there was a painful throbbing in his left forearm. Then with a start, it all came back. He could swear he smelled pork cooking. Opening his eyes slowly, it took a moment to focus. He wondered if he was dreaming. What was left of the carcass was hanging from a heavy leather thong in a nearby tree. There was no sign of the head, skin or entrails. She was tending a small smoky fire over which a spit laden with meat hung. Her metal canteen was perched between two rocks at one side of the fire slowly boiling water. Occasionally, a log would pop and a few sparks would fly up. She seemed unconcerned. The front of her white shirt was covered with dried blood and he noticed that her eyes were almost swollen shut from the insect bites. As he watched, she got up, walked to the stream bed and, scooping up some soft mud, packed it against the skin of her face. She noticed him.

"Among the living, I see. Hungry?" She pulled a chunk of meat off the skewer and held it out to him. He reached for it gratefully and pulled hungrily at the soft flesh until it came off the bone.

"Do you have a name?" she asked.

"Why do you ask?"

"I usually don't provide emergency medical services to folks I don't know. I definitely don't share a meal with them."

"James," he replied.

"Do they call you Jim for short?"

"No. My name is James. Those of us from the UK do not have that bloody annoying habit of shortening everything like you Americans do."

"Excuse me."

He felt guilty. "Sorry," he offered. Then, to change the subject, "Did you dress and skin our friend, as you called him?"

She looked around. "See anybody else?"

"It seems I can't keep my foot out of my mouth. Let me try again. Where did you learn such amazing skills and where did that leather thong come from?" he asked, pointing to the hanging carcass.

"The leather thong is my jump rope. It's the only way I know to stay in shape when I'm on the road. As for the rest, I grew up on a ranch in Northern New Mexico." She pulled a piece of meat off the spit, settled against a log with her feet to the fire and started her story. "My dad used to say I was born with a saddle between my legs and a yoke in my hand. We had five thousand acres of rough rangeland, and leased another seventy-five hundred from the forest service to run the cows on. It was all my brothers, Dad and I could do to round up the lot of them every fall before first snow. We would often be in the high country alone for weeks. My dad gave me the Colt revolver when I was five and taught me to shoot. He wanted me to be able to defend myself against varmints like you." She looked at him coolly before continuing. "The horses and cows were always getting tangled up in barbed wire or some other mischief. That's where I learned my veterinary skills." She indicated his arm. Looking down, he was surprised to see the neat row of stitches. It was dark now and the firelight was flickering on her face as she reminisced.

"My dad owned an old J-5 Cub that he kept parked in the barn. We used it often to scout out remote bands of cattle or to locate herds of elk or deer in hunting season. It was also useful for running into Taos or Questa for supplies. We lived a good hundred miles from the nearest outpost. Out of necessity, I learned to fly when I was nine. I soloed when I was tall enough to reach the rudder pedals, about eleven. When I reached the legal flying age of seventeen, I got my private license. The Cub was followed by an additional assortment of various airplanes through the years, a Luscombe, a Taylorcraft. The last thing my dad laid his hands on before I left home was a Cessna 180. He was real proud of that one. He was always finding derelict airplanes with flat tires laying around small airports and he would buy them, fix 'em up and fly them for a while before he sold them for a profit and went looking for the next one. We brought most of them home in pieces on his big old flat bed. I got my instructor's certificate and put myself through college teaching others to fly. My first real job was with my husband's father's charter company, Duncan Aero. That's where I met Brent, my husband. Anyway, his father passed away shortly after we were married leaving the whole mess to us. He was an only child. He brought in his best friend Dave as a partner, and they renamed it L/D Aerospace. Anything else you want to know?"

"You saved my life."

"I reckon I did." She was staring at the fire.

"Thank you." He didn't know what else to say.

"Oh, I almost forgot. I borrowed this." She handed the knife to him, handle first.

He stared at it for a moment before taking it slowly, re-sheathing it and returning it to his belt.

"Have another pork chop," she said. "This meat won't last long in the heat."

"What did you do with the entrails?" he asked, curious.

"I dumped everything we didn't want to eat in the stream. That carcass is going to be next. After we're full, it all goes overboard. I don't want to attract any other hungry critters. This place is spooky enough as it is."

She dug through her pack until she found the silver space blanket which she spread on the ground in front of the fire, before placing her blanket and pillow on top.

"That's a good idea," he said. "Keep your bedroll dry that way."

"That's not why I'm doing it," she replied. "I once did a raft trip down the Colorado River through the Grand Canyon. The guide made us lay our sleeping bags on a sheet of plastic. Seems snakes don't take to slithering across plastic. Hate to wake up with one as a bed mate."

CHAPTER 10

The heat of the day still lingered with the setting sun but it was cool and dark in the control tower radar room at the Simon Bolivar International Airport in Maiquetia. The center supervisor was dressed in a crisp white cotton shirt, black pleated pants and a striped tie. English is the international language of aviation and all controllers are required to speak it at least nominally. But Joseph Quintana had a four year degree from Berkeley and his English was impeccable.

As they reviewed the previous day's radar tapes a green glow illuminated their faces in the dark room, giving all a ghoulish cast. Agent O'Brien's cigar was disappearing rapidly as he watched the screen's blinking blip pass over Caracas, heading southeast approximately two hundred and twenty miles before circling and disappearing abruptly over the vast uninhabited area of the Guiana Highlands.

"Any idea what's there?" he asked the supervisor as he pointed to the place on his screen with the end of his cigar and the green dot slowly faded.

"From the coordinates, we've identified an abandoned airfield used in the past by the drug trade. There has been no known activity at that field since a major bust about two years ago. It is usually closely monitored by our authorities. You can imagine our surprise when an aircraft squawking the emergency transponder code landed there!"

"Our suspect allegedly hijacked a Lear 35. Does that jibe with the numbers you observed?"

"They were cruising at flight level four five zero with a ground speed of four hundred eighty knots before starting their descent. With the winds aloft at that time, I'd say it's possible that our target is a Lear. There is just one question in my mind." He took off his glasses, pulled a clean folded handkerchief from his pocket and polished them absently. "I've flown over that strip in a light aircraft. Although I've never actually landed there, I would be very surprised if someone could successfully land a high performance jet on that strip. The air field was built for the old DC 3s they were using for their low altitude drug smuggling operations. It was never designed to accommodate a jet."

O'Brien was thoughtful. "Run that tape again, please."

Quintana pushed the appropriate buttons and the tape whirred, then clicked as it began to run again. The blinking green light reappeared on the screen and they watched it make its way over northern Venezuela to the now-familiar landing point.

"Looks like they circled a couple of times before deciding to land," O'Brien observed. He pulled the cigar stub from his mouth, squinted at the end and tossed it with deadly accuracy into the trash can across the room. Pulling a fresh one from his pocket, he began to remove the cellophane. "Peterson."

"Yes, sir." A man wearing combat fatigues and a billed cap stepped forward.

"Didn't you fly Lears in the Air Force?"

"Yes sir."

"What do you think about their chances of surviving a landing there?"

Peterson walked to a wall map and found the approximate position of the tiny airfield. "Well, sir, I've been thinking about that myself. We know they left Cabo with full fuel. Since it doesn't appear they stopped to refuel, they would have been getting pretty low by the time they reached this point. With only the two of them on board and no baggage to speak of, they would be pretty light. Can you give me an estimate of the temperature at this place around the time they landed?" he asked Quintana.

"I would guess around thirty degrees centigrade. The field elevation would be around fifteen hundred meters."

Peterson pulled a calculator out of his pocket and quickly converted to degrees Fahrenheit and elevation to feet. He whistled through his teeth. "Wow," he said as he shook his head. "That's eighty-six degrees at around five thousand feet elevation. Even if they were light, they'd still need close to five thousand feet to land unless they had one hell of a head wind or a significant slope to the runway."

Quintana raised his hands, palm up in front of him. The air field is uncharted and I have never landed there, but based on what I have observed from the air I would be surprised if it was over one to one and a half kilometers in length. It's very difficult to judge such things."

"Then I would say it's highly unlikely they successfully landed there without major damage to the aircraft or themselves," Peterson said with finality.

"Son of a bitch!" O'Brien slumped down in a swivel chair, leaned back and propped his heels on the desk. The cigar was already half gone. "This one really has me stumped. We just don't have a motive here! This guy grabs a US registered aircraft with a girl on board, takes only half the crew, flies to some god-forsaken abandoned runway in the middle of a rain forest which they can't possibly land on without crashing and we haven't received any kind of demand or ransom request. Furthermore, the suspect is a known jewel thief who has been in retirement in Mexico for five years. Why does he suddenly leap up and hijack an airplane to the middle of nowhere?"

Quintana was thoughtful as he gazed at the blip on the screen. "I have a theory," he said.

O'Brien rocked forward in the chair and looked up hopefully. "I'm glad somebody does, because I'm tapped out here!"

"This is a long shot," Quintana continued. "But there is a notorious criminal who lives about forty miles to the southwest of this landing strip. He's the kingpin of one of the largest drug cartels in Venezuela. There have been whispers for several years that he is involved in smuggling diamonds from South Africa. This may be just a rumor." He shrugged his shoulders.

"Actually, that theory has come up. Wonder if it has anything to do with that Custom's investigation. Sounds like their sort of thing." O'Brien stood up and looked at his watch. "No time to go anywhere tonight, it's getting too dark. I say we rest up, get the chopper refueled and buzz up there at first light tomorrow morning and check out the landing strip. For all we know, they're still in the airplane, injured or dead. Can you show me where this druggie hides out?"

"His name is Juan Carlos Lopez," he replied, pointing to the map. "Villa de Lopez sits on the Orinoco river to the south of this little fishing village. You can't miss it."

"Thanks," O'Brien said, reaching up to slap him on the back. "You've been a tremendous help."

The little girl looked dully at the plate of unappetizing food growing cold in front of her. Her stomach still hurt and she was too frightened to eat. Her guard was in an adjoining room. He hiked up the dirty cotton jeans and tucked in his sweat stained T-shirt before picking up the mike.

"Baby bear callin papa bear, you copy?"

There was some crackling before the blurred reply. "Yeah, what is it?"

"It's the kid. She ain't eatin' or drinkin'. She don't look too good. What do you want me to do?"

There was a short pause. "It's only been two days. She ain't gonna die from not eatin' in two days. Give it to her and if she don't eat, she don't eat. We don't care what shape she's in when we throw her to the sharks!" There was a short burst of laughter before the static moved in. The man shrugged and replaced the mike.

After a long afternoon of pounding the pavement, Brent and Dave finally hit pay dirt. It came from an unusual source. They had asked everyone from street venders to waiters about Juan Lopez. When they got a reaction, it was usually a frightened look. It was difficult, at best, since everyone they approached spoke nothing but Spanish. Tired and dirty, they sank down on the curb and watched the late afternoon melee pass on the street in front of them. They had never seen such a disorganized mob of buses, cars, trucks, bicycles and venders. Neither knew what to say. They were at a dead end.

"Hey Meester," the sharp voice of a child made them look up. "You want buy cheekles?"

He was holding out a worn cardboard tray with small colorful packages of gum. The little urchin was not more than seven or eight and his cocky grin showed two or three gaps where he had lost some teeth. He wore a short-sleeved shirt that was sizes too big, the sleeves hanging almost to his wrists. The pants were too short and skinny brown ankles showed beneath the hems. They were hiked up around the slim waste with the oversized shirt stuffed in and a piece of cotton cord holding it all together. His short black hair was spiked on the crown of his head.

Brent pulled some change from his pocket. "Here kid, now beat it. We're kind of busy."

The child pocketed the change. "You need a guide? I be good guide!" He smiled and stood up straight as he jammed his thumb into his chest.

Brent and Dave looked at each other. They couldn't believe he was speaking English.

When's the last time you had a good meal?" Dave asked, offering him a lifesaver.

The kid eagerly took the candy and shoved it in his mouth. "I always hungry," he said. "You got food?"

"No, but we'll buy you supper," Dave said as he stood up and put his arm around the thin shoulders. We just might need your services."

They walked into the nearest cafe and watched as the boy hungrily downed everything placed in front of him. "Where you want go?" he asked around mouthfuls.

Dave leaned across the table. "We want to go visit a guy called Juan Lopez."

The boy's black eyes grew large and he stopped chewing abruptly. "Juan Carlos, he bad man!" He got up to leave.

"Hold on a minute, now," Dave said gently as he pushed him back in his seat. "We just want to talk to him. There's something in it for you if you tell us how to find him."

Frightened, he looked from Dave to Brent and back to Dave who had pulled a roll of bills out of his pocket. The kid had never seen so much money. "How about twenty bucks?" Dave asked as he peeled off the top bill. The boy's round eyes stared but he didn't say anything. "How about fifty?" Dave pulled off another couple of bills.

"How about a hundred?" Brent interrupted and threw a hundred dollar bill on the table. "Come on, Dave, we don't have a lot of time."

"What do you think, kid? A hundred bucks, just like that. Ready to talk?"

The kid was ready. "Juan Carlos, he live on big river to south. River called," he screwed up his face and looked at the ceiling. "Onco or Arin or something. He have big villa. Name of town, lady name like Lorena or something."

"How far south?" Dave asked, still holding the bill.

The boy thought for a moment. "It take eight day on donkey."

"Thanks, kid." Dave held the money out to him. He snatched it and disappeared out the door. "Come on," he said. "We need to find a good map before everything closes for the night."

A soft darkness enveloped the quiet library at Villa de Lopez. The man sat in his favorite wing chair and idly perused the glowing tip of his cigarette. The bottle of wine sat on the table next to him. He hated to pass it into the hands of those amateurs. Perhaps he should accompany it, at least to Cabo San Lucas. This one was too big to lose or to have fall into the wrong hands. He smiled ruefully.

"Grog," he said, pressing the intercom button. There was an answering grunt. "I need to see you for a moment."

The door eased open and, although he couldn't see him, he felt the burly presence.

Grog had been his faithful companion since his days on the streets. He didn't know his real name. Everyone had always called him Grog. Short and burly, his long, hairy arms ended in enormous knuckles that almost touched the ground. He had large, bushy brows over black, glittering eyes and his entire body was covered in a thick matte of black, curly hair. He seldom spoke full sentences, conversing in a series of grunts. They made an unlikely pair, the tall, handsome Juan Carlos and the short, burly Neanderthal, but the team of brains and brawn had come a long way. After Juan Carlos woke up to the horror of Bell's palsy, which disfigured him for life, he was able to relate to the ugly man even more. Juan Carlos trusted him explicitly and Grog had never let him down. Several would-be assassins had succumbed to Grog's crushing bear hug or the quick neck snap or eye poke for which he was famous.

He shambled into the room. "Argh."

"Grog, how would you like to take a vacation?" he lisped.

"Argh."

I've decided to accompany our pretty friend here on her way to Cabo San Lucas." He paused to wipe some spittle from the side of his mouth. "Book us passage on the Pacifico Azul for the twenty-second of this month. We'll leave day after tomorrow for Caracas."

"Argh?" he grunted.

"No, that's all. Thank you, Grog."

He heard him shuffle out and the door clicked shut.

He watched blearily as she heaved herself to her feet, threw another soggy log on the smoking fire and settled back down on the damp earth, her back against the log. The almost-empty Tequila bottle sat between them. He tried to shove the cotton in his brain aside long enough to figure out how much was in the bottle when they started. At least the throbbing in his arm was beginning to let up a little.

"How far you reckon we have to go tomorrow?" She was looking at him through swollen slits. God, she looked awful.

"About twelve miles," he slurred. "Think you can make it?" His head rolled around on his shoulders as he looked back at her.

"You're the one I'm worried about. You look like hell and you're going to have one heck of a hangover tomorrow." She was quiet for a moment as she stared at the fire. "It would help if I knew what you were after."

The booze had loosened his normally-reserved British tongue. "A very large diamond."

"Is that the ransom for your kid?" she asked.

"Yes," he replied. "They kidnapped her and told me I had to produce the diamond or I wouldn't get her back."

"Who has this diamond?"

"A cunning and evil man named Juan Carlos Lopez. The diamond is very famous. Juan Carlos arranged to have it stolen from a museum in Turkey. It is the largest cut diamond known and has virtually no defects. It's about two thousand years old."

"I didn't think they had the technology to cut diamonds two thousand years ago."

"It's one of the great mysteries of man." His eyes were closed. "Like the great pyramids and the Aztec calendar."

"Can't you just offer to buy this diamond?"

He opened his bloodshot eyes and looked at her, trying to focus. "It is priceless. Besides, Juan Carlos would just as soon kill you as look at you.

"Does he have a phone?"

He wasn't sure he heard her right. "What?"

"Does he have a phone? I need to call my family to let them know I'm all right."

He didn't answer. She got up, re-corked the bottle and grabbing him by the ankles, pulled him out straight on the ground, facing the fire. Stretching, she made her way to the bed she had fashioned and lowered her aching body to the hard ground. She was missing Brent more and more. What must he be thinking? She thought about Peep. That was even more painful. She hoped her child was unaware of the predicament her mother was in. She was asleep before her head hit the pillow.

Brent and Dave pushed through the door of their small room and looked at the depressing surroundings. The smudged and sooty window barely let in any light from the setting sun and did little to block out the traffic noise from the busy street below. There were two twin beds with faded spreads and the linoleum between them was worn through so that a black path was visible. It looked like an army had marched through this room.

A single light bulb hung from a wire in the middle of the tiny space and it flickered as they set their bags on the sagging beds and began to unpack. Only the cold water tap seemed to work, but they wouldn't mind a cold shower after the sweltering day. There was a small jar of drinking water and two chipped glasses beside the stained porcelain sink.

After a shower and shave, they settled down to get some sleep. Within minutes, Dave was in his usual sleep state of snorting, snuffling and hacking that went along with his summer allergies. Decongestants didn't help.

Brent lay awake and stared at the ceiling, unable to contemplate sleep. He was wondering what he'd done in his life to bring him to this low point and knew without asking that he wasn't living his life the way he should.

A chronic worry wart was what Jennifer called him. He spent a lot of time worrying about things and sometimes found it difficult to make a decision.

Somehow, he had stopped living his life and his marriage and allowed fate to chart his course without taking control and directing events himself.

He'd been proud of himself when he graduated from college and, at the risk of hurting his father, stood up to him and refused to be dragged into a business in which he had no interest or talent. When his father died and it was dropped into his lap, however, he just took it on and tried his best to do it all.

What had happened to the bright young man who was so excited about pursuing his research and making the world a better place to live? Good, sweet, Jen. She had gone along with whatever course he mapped out and now she was the one paying for it. She was a victim of his indecision and inability to take control. He had been taking her for granted and it took a crisis to point that fact out to him.

Oh, Jen, he thought. Please hang in there so we can have another chance. The priorities are going to change when we get home. If we can only get you back!

CHAPTER 11

Although the sun hadn't made its full entrance yet, it promised to be another steamer. Dave and Brent were already sweating as they preflighted the airplane on the dark ramp. They loaded the few provisions they had purchased the day before and climbed in. The engines only turned over once or twice in the warm air before sputtering into action. Dave smiled to himself as he listened to the turbo-charged piston motors warm up and settle into a smooth hum. Turning on the radios, they listened to the field conditions before obtaining clearance to taxi.

The landing lights of an American 767 glowed off the end of the runway as it turned for a final approach. There was no other activity on the field. After the big Boeing had cleared the runway, they were given a clearance for takeoff and, taxiing out without delay, were soon airborne.

As they climbed through ten thousand feet southbound, the sun eased over the mountains to the east. Brent squinted at the map in the dim light and Dave maneuvered the plane as if she was an extension of himself.

After studying the map until eleven the night before, they had finally agreed that the river the boy was referring to must be the Orinoco. It flowed from the south. There was a small village called Lorna about one hundred and eighty miles south along the river. There had been some lively discussion about what constituted a burro day or how far a burro could travel in one day. They finally decided twenty to twenty-five miles at the outside. That distance times eight put them just over this little village of Lorna on the Orinoco River. It was their best guess from the sketchy information the boy gave.

They were content to sit in companionable silence as the graceful Cessna winged south across the grasslands and toward the Guianas highlands. They picked up the Orinoco River easily and turned slightly to follow its meandering course.

"Oh no," Brent was looking out the window at the right engine. There was oil flowing up and over the top of the nacelle. But the engine hadn't missed a beat.

Dave leaned forward to look around his friend. "Damn! It's that prop seal again! The new one they sent me must have had a defect!"

"Everything is covered in the warranty except parts and labor," Brent said as he elbowed his friend.

"It looks worse than it is." Dave ignored the jab. "It's just making a hell of a mess. Damn I wish they had better quality control on those parts!"

As they approached their target, Dave reduced the power and started a slow descent. "There," he said, pointing. "That must be it."

The early morning sun glinted off the windows of a small village surrounded by a green patchwork of lush fields. Small herds of cattle and sheep grazed below. As they passed over at about two thousand feet, they saw what looked like a fortress. On the side of a small rise, a rose-colored mansion spread into multiple stories. Gracefully carved woodwork faced the many balconies and there were wrought iron bars on the windows. The magnificent grounds were enclosed by a tall masonry wall. Inside the wall were flowering plants, citrus trees and fountains.

"That's gotta be it," Dave said, turning for another pass.

"Wow." Brent was almost speechless. "Do you think Jen's in there?"

"There's just one question I have about that theory."

Brent looked at his friend. "What's that?"

"No airport. Not even a road long and straight enough to land a single engine Cessna on, let alone a Lear." He turned again. At a hundred and fifty knots, the place passed under them quickly.

Brent was stumped. With no airport, they had obviously not come here to land. He pulled out his aeronautical chart. "The closest published field is about fifty miles to the north."

"I wonder where the closest unpublished field is?" Dave was thoughtful. "I wouldn't be surprised if there was a private strip around here somewhere. Why don't we just fly in ever widening circles with this mansion in the center and see what we come up with?"

The first circuit didn't turn up anything. As Dave widened out and started toward the thick jungle, Brent put his hand on his arm. "No use wasting our time going that way. I can't imagine an airport in that wilderness." They looked below at the thick canopy of trees.

As Dave started his turn, he peered out the window to his left. He had caught a flash out of the corner of his eye. He turned back.

"What are you doing?" Brent asked.

"The sun flashed on something there a second ago. It's got to be a metal building or something else reflective. There's nothing natural down in that forest that would catch the sun like that. It'll just take a minute to check it out."

Then they saw it. Dave wagged the wings of the small plane in excitement and dropped down to treetop level, passing over the small strip to make sure. The Learjet sitting sideways at the end of the pavement was unmistakable.

Dave made two more passes to gauge the elevation, distance and wind, then set the little plane down lightly at the far end of the strip, surprised at actually having to add power to taxi up the steep incline to the end. As they pulled up to the sleek jet, Brent jumped out and Dave shut down the engines.

"Jen, Jen!" Brent yelled as loud as he could. His voice was almost drowned by the din coming out of the forest surrounding them. They walked over to the Lear and looked at the flattened tires.

"Jen must have had a hell of a time getting this baby in here." Dave pointed to the black marks on the pavement. "Anti-skid must have failed her." They inspected the plane and pulled the rusty shed doors to inspect its interior. No sign of Jen or her captor.

Brent looked at the intimidating wall of trees. "Unless they flew another plane out of here, they would have to go through the jungle."

Dave had to agree. Here they were at another impasse. Without a map or compass, they wouldn't last two days in that wilderness. Besides, they weren't sure which way the pair had gone. It looked hopeless.

Henry O'Brien rallied his team early. After a large breakfast, he loaded them into the Blackhawk and headed south. In their briefing over breakfast, they decided to post two men on the only road that led from Villa de Lopez toward Caracas which was the only major town for hundreds of miles. Then the plan was to find the tiny landing strip they had identified the day before.

The helicopter pilot expertly hovered a few feet off the ground just to the north of the village of Lorna. The reconnaissance team jumped lightly to the ground and Peterson tossed them their survival gear. "See you guys later," he called as the chopper rose gracefully and moved southwest over the mountains.

The huge chopper rotor moved the sleek beast through the air over the forty miles effortlessly and they were in the area within fifteen minutes. O'Brien was peering out the side and when he saw it, he motioned to the pilot excitedly. As they approached, he blinked and rubbed his eyes. There was not one, but two aircraft parked at the end of the field. He could just make out two figures next to the planes and couldn't believe his luck. Could they nail them this easily? Excitedly, he growled to the pilot. "Let's get down there quickly before they have time to beat feet into the trees." Then, to the team in the back, "Get your weapons ready, boys, the suspects are at twelve o'clock and less than a mile!"

"Listen." Dave put his finger to his mouth and looked around.

"What is it?" Brent asked impatiently. He was frustrated and ready to do something.

"Sounds like a rotor," Dave said. He squinted and had a difficult time seeing anything as he looked directly into the sun that was low on the horizon. The whoof whoof of the rotor was unmistakable.

Suddenly, it loomed over the building and swooped over the top of the roof, missing the corrugated steel by a few feet and landed twenty feet from them. As they stood there, stunned, the door flew open and the heavily armed men in battle fatigues rushed upon them, knocking them to the ground and pulling their hands behinds their backs. The sharp gravel cut into their faces as a booted foot was pressed against the backs of their heads.

"Hey, what's going on here?" Dave yelled as the handcuffs clicked into place and he was frisked. Invisible hands behind him pulled him to his feet and he had to look down to meet the pale blue eyes of a round-faced elf chomping on a giant cigar. Brent was shoved into position beside him.

"So," he said, "I see you speak English."

"Of course I speak English, you son-of-a-bitch! I'm a United States citizen!"

O'Brien's eyes narrowed. Neither looked like the suspect. "What are United States citizens doing at a drug smuggler's airfield?"

"Is that what this is?" Brent looked around. "Both of these airplanes belong to me. My wife was hijacked in that Lear day before yesterday. I'm trying to track her down."

"Got any identification?" O'Brien was suspicious, but the story was too unbelievable not to be believable.

"In my back pocket," Brent said, turning. "My name is Brent Duncan. Jennifer Duncan is my wife. She's the one who was hijacked. The registrations are in the airplanes. Check them out."

"And who is this character?" O'Brien pointed at Dave with his cigar after checking out the New Mexico driver's license in the wallet.

"This is my partner, Dave Lark."

"Uncuff 'em," O'Brien ordered.

"And just who, may I ask, are you?" Brent said as the handcuffs fell free.

"Agent Henry O'Brien, head of HAT-TRIC, FBI."

"HAT-TRIC?"

"Stands for Hijacking and Terrorist Tactical Response International Cooperative. It seems we're both on the same mission. Any sign of your wife or the hijacker?"

"We've only been here a few minutes, but there's no sign of them."

"Maybe they'll be back for the plane."

"Not possible." Brent pointed to the flat tires. "This baby isn't going anywhere until she gets some new shoes."

"Damn." O'Brien looked toward the jungle. "Must have taken off cross country. I don't envy them the trip."

"Do you guys have any clues?" Brent asked.

"Maybe." O'Brien was non-committal. "You guys need to climb in your airplane and go home. I'll do my best to find your wife."

"We've got to go with you," Dave said.

"No chance." O'Brien was on his way back to the chopper. The turbines were starting to spool up. "Can't have civilians tagging along on an official investigation."

"But we're stranded here," Dave said. Brent looked at him knowing there was nothing wrong with the airplane except the pesky leak.

"Look." Dave pointed to the oil covered nacelle. "This engine is shot and blowed, as you can see. It's obvious we're not going anywhere any time soon. You can't leave us here like this." He spread his hands.

O'Brien didn't see that he had a choice. "Okay," he said grumpily, throwing the cigar stump into the weeds. "Hop in."

Dave smiled at Brent as he climbed into the helicopter. Brent couldn't believe the audacity of his friend, but he was grateful for it.

She slowly came awake at the sound of the droning overhead. Sitting up, she shook her head and strained to hear above the sound of chirping insects, cawing birds and screaming monkeys. The plane passed a few hundred feet above the canopy and seemed to be headed toward the landing strip they had left the day before. She wished the vegetation was open enough for her to wave her arms. At least it would have been something to do.

She walked stiffly to the inert figure next to the dying fire. Looking down, she felt like kicking him. Instead, she nudged him with her foot. "Hey, Kimosabe. Wake up."

He groaned and rolled over. "Hey, you! I need to find a phone and you're the only one around who can make that possible. Get the lead out!"

He opened his eyes slowly and looked up at her. His eyes were still scratchy and sore and everything was bleary. There was a pounding in his ears that sounded like the percussion section of the Boston Philharmonic and his head was about to explode. On top of that, the throbbing in his arm had returned. As he started to move, everything tilted sickeningly and he knew he was going to lose it. He bolted for the bushes.

As she watched him empty his guts she wondered if she was doomed to spend the rest of her life watching men throw up.

II

The two HAT-TRIC men huddled in the brush at the edge of the village. Although stakeouts were rarely exciting, this one was particularly miserable. It didn't take long for the tropical sun to turn their hiding place into an oven and the bugs were big enough to carry you away. They sipped on canteen water and slapped at mosquitoes as they watched the entrance. The only activity had been a painter's van that had pulled up next to the little church outside the villa walls. As it stopped, a woman in a maid's uniform jumped out and approached the gates, pressing the intercom button and speaking rapidly in Spanish. The gates swung open and she disappeared. They stretched and dug through their pack for a snack.

II

Annaliza was on her knees in the kitchen, scrubbing. Pausing to look at her hands, she decided it had been a waste of time to chew off her fingernails and dip her hands into kerosene to roughen and redden the smooth skin. They were already getting sore from the harsh detergent. She was in a hurry to finish the floor so she could start the dusting. That would be a good excuse to check out the rest of the house.

The head housekeeper returned for a breakfast tray and growled at her. "Aren't you finished here yet? There are many outside who would take your place in a minute, you lazy bitch." Without waiting for a reply, she grabbed the tray and pushed through the heavy door.

Annaliza paused long enough to throw a bird at the ample bottom retreating through the doorway.

II

Sparks sat quietly in the dim van interior and waited for something to happen. He would rather have been the one inside. The waiting was worse. So far the only thing he had heard was the quick orientation Annaliza received and the assignment of her duties. He wished they had two-way communication so he could talk to her. They had decided it was too risky. So here he sat.

This idle time gave him a chance to think about his marriage and his mind wandered back to Albuquerque. He wondered if he still loved his wife after he had come home, exhausted from a trip and found her in bed with another man. As he thought of it, all the feelings of rage, anguish and betrayal had returned. He felt the constriction in his throat and the pounding of his heart as he pictured the two of them nuzzling and giggling, unaware of his presence. At that point he understood how somebody could be capable of murder. He had felt like murdering them both. All the wonderful years of their marriage, the companionship, the laughter, the love, dropped from him in that instant. He felt empty and devoid of feeling and wondered if he could ever chance loving again.

Everything became clear. He wanted a divorce. He did not think he could bear to go on with the strained silences, the separate beds and the deceptions any longer. It was not possible to regain what they had.

The decision made, he felt better. Leaning back in his seat and propping up his feet, he desperately hoped Annaliza would be able to place the bug without being caught.

CHAPTER 12

She tore into her emergency rations for breakfast. He offered her some of his but it didn't look appetizing. Anyway, she preferred her trail mix concoction of mixed nuts, raisins and M&Ms. The chocolate hit the spot.

Their map was torn and spattered with blood so it was almost illegible. The wandering trail forked often and they were now depending on her compass to keep them going in the right direction. Her shoes rubbed from the sweaty cotton socks and her hair was matted and oily. If she could just wash her hair, she knew she would feel better.

The barrage from biting insects had not let up but they no longer had the energy to swat and scratch. Rest stops were more frequent than the day before, as he was weakened from pain and loss of blood. She was beginning to wonder if they would ever see civilization again as the forest seemed to stretch endlessly in front of them. Logic told her she had seen open grasslands not forty miles away as they flew overhead but each time she parted the huge leaves hanging across the trail, she just saw more of the same.

She was in the lead since she had the compass and was more able to navigate the maze of game trails. He was somewhat incoherent, stumbling along behind her, blindly following. There was no effort wasted talking.

Her mind was wandering as she ducked under a branch and reached to brush aside a hanging vine. Suddenly, she felt something drop on her and realized too late that the vine was a live snake that quickly wrapped its supple body around her arms and then her neck. The part she had brushed away was just the tail of the monstrous anaconda. She had no time to react or fight as the snake started to squeeze. She dug her nails into the scaly skin wrapped around her throat and fell to the ground as everything started going black.

It took him only a moment to realize what was happening. He pulled his knife and jumped on top of the writhing bundle. In desperation, he hacked away at anything that looked like snake. Her struggling was weak and he knew he didn't have much time. The snake's head hung away from the body. Its eyes glinted at him, the forked tongue flicking in pain and anger. He managed to bring his hysteria under control long enough to take a strong downward stroke and sever the head from the body.

It took a moment for the giant coils to relax and he started freeing her as he heard her choking and gasping for breath. She struggled to inhale air in rasping gasps.

His wound was bleeding again and he collapsed beside the trail tired and discouraged. The desire to lie down and give up was powerful. The only thing that was keeping him going was the thought of his little girl in the hands of those animals.

Her voice was hoarse as she spoke. "I guess we're even now."

He didn't have the strength to reply. He just lay on the cool damp earth waiting for his heartbeat to slow and his breathing to return to normal. She pushed the scaly body aside and sat with her head between her knees trying to get more oxygen to her brain. There was a roaring in her ears that sounded like water. She looked at him.

He had sat up and was staring down the trail. "Do you hear it?"

"A river?" she asked hopefully.

"A major river!" he replied, scrambling to his feet, the pain and fatigue disappearing.

Pushing through the trees, he made his way along the trail toward the roar. She smelled smoke and knew they were approaching a village. They slowed as they heard the excited shouts of children playing above the crashing water.

Crouching behind some bushes, they carefully pulled aside the branches. The mist rising from the thundering waterfall hung over a small village of thatched roof huts. The dirt paths leading through the settlement were swept clean. Small boys played in a clearing, batting a ball made from the hide of an animal in a game that looked like polo without horses. They were naked from the waist up, wearing only slight, colorful loin cloths. The boys laughed and bantered good naturedly as the leather ball was kicked back and forth between them on the soft dirt. Dugout canoes lined the bank of the broad, slowly moving river.

They heard someone calling. A woman emerged from one of the huts and rapped on a stick to get the boys' attention. Jennifer did not understand her language but she was fascinated with the woman's appearance. Her black hair was cropped short over her ears. Her teeth were very white and made a beautiful contrast against the smooth nut-colored skin. Around her neck were strings of beads in bright, primary colors. She was naked, like the boys, from the waist up, but a skirt-like garment hung over her upper legs, stopping just above her knees. The vivid red, yellow and blue were repeated in this garment and Jennifer thought how beautiful the woman was as she herded children into the hut for their meal. The village soon became still and quiet.

"This is our chance," he whispered. "We'll grab one of those canoes and be at the Villa de Lopez by dark."

"How can you steal from these people? Can't we buy what we need?"

"Money means nothing to them. What would they do with it out here?

Besides, it would raise suspicions. We could be here all day wasting precious time. I don't speak their language and you don't, either. Have a better suggestion?"

"Yeah," she replied, turning and making her way back down the trail. "Follow me."

The woman picked up the remains of her simple meal and left the hut to walk down to the river. As she neared the water's edge, she saw that one canoe was missing. There was a large mound in its place. As she got closer, she stopped abruptly and gasped, backing away. A large snake rested at the water's edge. She called to the men. Raising spears, they approached the snake carefully. It did not move. One man nudged it carefully but the giant reptile lay in the mud as if dead. They sighed with relief. The snake's head had been severed cleanly and they determined that the kill was fresh.

The men raised their spears and shouted with joy. A delicacy this size would feed the entire village. The story of the anaconda with no head that mysteriously appeared in place of a canoe would be told over cooking fires for a very long time.

O'Brien had a difficult decision to make. He had talked to the reconnaissance team on the ground by radio and they had reported no activity at the villa except the maid's arrival. His guts told him the villa was King's destination, since there was nothing else for miles. Why else would he risk his life to fly into that godforsaken place and beat his way through the jungle? He was irritated that he had two unwelcome passengers in tow. That made everything more complicated.

"I've made my decision," he said to the pilot. "Find a place to set this baby down. I'm going to unload the rest of the team, surround that place and set up a network that this King character is going to have to pass through to get to the villa. Then you go on and take these guys back to Caracas. You can come back in the morning and we'll be in radio contact. I have a feeling King is close, so hopefully we won't be out here too long before we pick him up."

Dave was sitting behind him leaning back with his arms folded. He seemed to be asleep. But above the whining turbine engine and the steady beat of the rotor, he had heard the entire exchange. Going back to Caracas would not do them any good, especially now that they were without transportation. He had to think quickly.

Opening his eyes slowly and stretching, he acted as if he was just waking up. Pulling a roll of lifesavers out of his pocket, he passed them around to the men sitting near him. He waited until he was sure he had their attention. Then he abruptly stopped chewing the candy and cocked his ear. "You guys hear that?" They looked around at one another, then back to Dave.

"Hear what?"

Dave was looking up. "There it was again, did you hear that?"

Now he had the pilot's attention. "I didn't hear anything," he said, looking at the engine gauges.

Brent had crawled forward to join the conversation. He thought he knew what Dave was up to. "You'd better listen to him," he said. "He's an aircraft mechanic."

He had their attention now.

Moving forward to where he could see the engine instruments, he pointed. "There it is again. I saw the oil pressure spike that time!"

The pilot nervously looked at the gauge. "I don't see anything wrong."

"It was just a spike." Dave studied the instruments. "Practiced auto rotation lately?"

O'Brien jumped in. "You don't think the engine's about to quit, do you?"

"You know how it is with turbines," Dave said matter-of-factly. "They don't give you much warning before they go. A couple little blips and then blam! If you want to set it down, I'd be happy to check it out for you."

O'Brien was reluctant but they were approaching the villa and he had planned to unload the guys in this area anyway. "Okay," he said, finally. "I guess we'd better take a look." He jammed his cigar back in his mouth. The team knew one of his foul moods when they saw one and they were quiet as the pilot carefully maneuvered the heavy chopper into position to land.

On the ground, Dave picked up a small canvas bag of tools that was his constant companion and climbed to the top of the chopper as the rotor slowly wound down. "This is going to take me a while," he called down, pulling out a wrench. You guys might as well make yourselves comfortable."

O'Brien called them together. "I want you fellas to fan out around the villa and watch for any activity. Take some gear with you. We're liable to be out here for a few days. I want everybody to check in by radio once every two hours. Unless you hear differently, we'll meet back here in two days to compare notes and re-provision." The team quickly dispersed, leaving him with the chopper, pilot and two civilians.

Brent climbed to the top of the fuselage to talk to his friend. "This is a scam, right?" he whispered.

"If it wasn't disabled before, it is now." He smiled as he held up a critical part. "I won't break it too bad. We might need it later. I just wanted to buy some time and give you a chance to poke around a bit. Going back to Caracas isn't going to do us any good at all!"

"Find anything?" O'Brien squinted up at them.

"It'll take me a while to trouble-shoot this problem," Dave replied. "I'll work as fast as I can." He winked at Brent, who slid off the side, landing on the ground with a thump.

"Where are you going?" O'Brien asked Brent, who was heading for the river.

"I haven't had a bath in two days," he tossed over his shoulder. "I'm going to wash some of this sweat off."

"Don't go too far." The cigar bobbed in front of the blue eyes. "As soon as that thing is air-worthy, you guys are on your way back to Caracas."

The man left another plate of unappetizing food. There were lumpy mashed potatoes and congealing gravy next to a stringy piece of meat. Getting up and edging around the disgusting food, she peeked through the crack in the door. He was leaned back in his chair with dirty boots propped on the desk and eyes closed. He seemed asleep.

Holding her breath so as not to make any noise, she crept past him to the door beyond and gulped fresh air as it rushed in with the opening of the door. Turning and quietly closing the door behind her, she ran across the short, open expanse and skidded to a halt in front of the rail. Grabbing the edge, she cautiously peered at crystal water twenty feet below. The height and the movement of the rolling boat made her stomach turn, but she was determined not to be sick.

Looking around, she saw that there was a shoreline not far away. Could she make it? She'd had swimming lessons and considered herself proficient in her stroke. On Sunday afternoons, her Dad often took her to the beach where they played in the gentle surf of the Sea of Cortez. But her confidence flagged as she saw how far it was to the shore.

"Hey Frog, where do you think you're going? Wanna go for a little swim?"

She whirled around as he grasped her right ankle and swung her over the rail, dangling her slight body upside down. She gasped and swallowed the scream in her throat as she looked down at the water below. He belted out a braying laugh that showed his broken yellow teeth and held his side with his other hand.

"Had enough Frog?" He wiped away tears of laughter as he hauled her back over the rail, bruising her thin limbs on the metal piping. Dropping her on the deck in a heap, he gave her a nudge with his boot. "Better get outta here afore I change me mind."

As she scrambled down the stairs to her bleak room and the untouched meal, she could hear his laugh echoing off the ship's metal superstructure.

She edged to an isolated corner and threw herself on the thin mat, drawing her knees up to her chest and hugging her legs. Sobbing softly, she prayed, "Please, God. Please bring my Daddy to me!"

Annaliza was slowly making her way through the house with a giant feather duster in her hand. After checking out the austere bedroom, she decided there was definitely no business conducted there. The simple pine bed and the single dresser looked like they had come from a garage sale. There was no desk or phone and the cool tile beneath her feet had no rugs or carpeting. The small, high windows were barred and there were no pictures on the wall. No woman's touch here, she thought. It took only five minutes to dust the spare furnishings and she moved on to inspect the rest of the villa. She felt like a rat in a maze as she made her way through the network of narrow hallways, peeking in doors and around corners.

Finally, she came to the library. There was a large desk with a sophisticated phone system on it. Picking up the receiver and unscrewing the mouthpiece, she placed the bug inside. She felt better now that it was installed and no longer in her pocket.

A computer sat on a credenza to the side and a large map of Venezuela was tacked to the wall. A huge fireplace loomed in one corner but it looked like it had not been used for years. Next to a massive oak bookcase set an aged brown leather wing chair. There was a small table beside it, holding an intercom, a brass lamp with a tiffany glass shade and a bottle of red wine.

She picked up the bottle and examined the South African label.

"What are you doing?" the sharp voice hissed at her and she almost dropped the bottle.

Staring at her feet, she tried to alter her Spanish to sound more like a peasant. "Cleaning, Señor."

"Clean someplace else, woman!" he spat. "Servants are not allowed in here!"

She slipped past him into the corridor. It was difficult to hide the horror she had felt when she caught a glimpse of his face. He slammed the door angrily behind her.

Sparks sat up in the van as he heard the exchange. He knew the bug was placed as he heard the man rustle around the room after her departure. He didn't have long to wait as he listened to Juan Carlos summon Grog. He turned on his tape recorder.

"Did you get the tickets?"

"Argh."

"What time do we depart on the twenty-second?"

"Four PM."

"I trust we have first class accommodations?"

"Yes."

"In what country is the Pacifico Azul registered?"

"Brazil."

"So our crew will be Portuguese. That will suffice." He walked to the window to gaze at the magnificent river valley view. "Once this deal is consummated, I will be the richest man in Venezuela. But all the money in the world can not buy back my childhood or my face."

Grog did not answer, but waited in the doorway.

"That is all, Grog." He blotted the side of his mouth with the white handkerchief and thought that with all his money, he was no happier now than when he had lived on the street.

Meanwhile, Sparks had turned off the recorder and thought about the conversation. So, they would be sailing on a ship called the Pacifico Azul at four PM on the twenty-second. Juan Carlos was obviously going on this trip to conduct an important business transaction. It had to be related to the smuggling ring. He figured the latest that Lopez could leave the villa to travel to Caracas in time to make his boat was the morning of the twenty-second. Maybe even the day before. Somehow, he had to figure out how to get Inspector Melendez out of there before then. He just hoped and prayed that she was not exposed as a spy in the mean time.

The muddy water moved slowly beneath them as the tiny canoe bobbed northward down the river. They weren't making more than three knots. He was reclined in the bow as she sat in the stern, using the paddle for a rudder. They had on the same clothes they'd been wearing for the past two days. She could pass as a local, he thought, looking at her tanned skin and dark hair. He, on the other hand, stuck out like a sore thumb with his blonde curly hair and fair complexion that was red from sun burn.

She reached for her back pack and rummaged around until she found her Swiss Army knife. Grabbing one of her pant's legs, she sawed at it with the knife. Soon, she had a ragged pair of shorts. Leaning back against the stern, she stretched and propped her bare legs on the edge of the canoe, soaking up the afternoon sun. "What's your little girl's name?"

"What?"

"Your little girl, what's her name?"

"Kristen."

"Where's her mom? She must be frantic."

"She was killed in an auto accident when Kristen was four." He looked away as the familiar pain appeared and he felt the stinging behind his eyes."

She watched him closely. Looked like the guy had some feelings after all, she thought. "Isn't that kind of tough being a single parent and trying to work?"

"I don't work anymore. I'm retired. Kristen is my whole life. I don't know what I'll do if something happens to her!" His eyes were brimming now and the tears were genuine as they spilled over the red rims of his eyes and down his swollen cheeks. She began to soften.

"What did you used to do?"

What the hell, he thought. He might as well tell her. "I was a jewel thief."

"Great," she said. "I'm taking a boat ride down the Orinoco River with a criminal!"

"It's not what you think!" He was defensive. "I'm not a violent person. I never even carried a gun on any of my jobs. I depended on cunning and deception. I only stole from the rich."

"Well, hell, Robin Hood. Excuse me if I don't play my violin for you. Stealing is still stealing."

"I know. That's why I quit. I didn't want to bring Kristen up that way and I was afraid for her because of some of the sleazy characters I was dealing with. That's why I moved to Cabo San Lucas. I figured it was remote enough that they wouldn't find me there. I was wrong." He studied his hands.

"So how did you get involved in this deal?"

"This chap, Lopez, stole a famous diamond from Turkey. He has a very extensive smuggling operation between South Africa and the US which passes through Venezuela and Baja, Mexico. His contact from the States has a fence in Cabo San Lucas. That's where the exchange of this diamond was going to take place. Then this contact got greedy and decided he would rather steal it from Lopez than buy it from him. Since none of his goons have the finesse to pull it off, he tracked me down, kidnapped my little girl and is holding her for the diamond."

"I had no idea," she said. "How far are we from this villa place?"

"About fifteen miles."

"At this rate, that's five hours." She was thoughtful. "Hand me that other paddle and get back here to take over the rudder for a minute."

Pulling her jump rope from her pack, she placed the paddle's flat end against the side of the canoe extending over the edge so that it rested about a foot into the water, the handle sticking up vertically, Then, using the rope, she tied the paddle firmly to the middle seat.

"Give me your shoelaces," she ordered, taking the blanket out of her pack and laying it next to the Swiss Army knife.

He didn't have any idea what she was doing, but he reached down and pulled the heavy laces out of his boots.

She folded the blanket in half as a triangle and started punching holes along one side with the knife. She used her own laces down the long side of the blanket to the handle of the paddle. She tied off the top and, grabbing the free corner of the triangle, adjusted the little sail until it caught a breath of wind and ballooned out. He felt the little boat leap forward and the water whooshed noisily under the bow as they picked up speed.

"There," she said. "That ought to give us an extra two or three knots. At this rate, we might make it by dark!"

This woman never ceased to amaze him. He smiled.

"Are you going to check in with your partner as soon as we get to the villa so he won't harm Mark?"

"I never had an accomplice. I just told you that so you would cooperate. I'm sorry I drug you in to this mess."

"I think I understand," she said as she pulled two warm sodas from her pack and used the knife opener to pop the top off one before handing it to him. After hers was opened, she held it up in a salute. As the two bottles clinked, she said, "I christen this boat, The Peeper. Cheese curl?"

CHAPTER 13

Brent sat on the edge of the soft bank and watched the muddy water move slowly past. He tossed a stick and watched it turn lazily and drift with the current toward the mighty delta below. Grasping his knees, he thought about his wife and tried to puzzle out his next move. He ached to feel her in his arms and silently cursed the man who took her away. He didn't know if she was dead or alive, injured, needing his help. He was impatient with the authorities for not moving faster but he knew there wasn't much more they could do than he was doing right now...waiting.

He heard a rustle behind him and looked up as a cow and her calf ambled to the water's edge for a drink. She stopped momentarily and gazed at him with liquid brown eyes. A part of one of her ears was missing and it gave her face an odd, unbalanced look. She seemed to sense that he was no threat and moved to the river where she silently drank great mouthfuls of the murky water. The calf huddled close to his mother's side. After quenching her thirst, the cow began clipping the lush grass at the river's edge with her sharp teeth.

He stood, stretched and took a long look up and down the river bank. He wondered if O'Brien knew his job. Slowly, he turned and made his way up the incline toward the grove of trees that sheltered the clearing where the helicopter rested. He was hungry and couldn't remember the last time he had eaten. He hoped O'Brien had some extra provisions. He wasn't up to a supper of wintergreen lifesavers.

The sun had just disappeared over the horizon when he came into the clearing. O'Brien was nowhere in sight and Dave was climbing down, wiping grease off his hands with a shop rag.

"See anything?" he asked, noting the dejected look on his friend's face.

"Afraid not," Brent replied. "I don't even know where to begin." He sat down and leaned against the chopper's tire. Dave eased down beside him.

"The way I see it, is we do like these guys are doing and wait. With the chopper stranded here, they aren't going anywhere and they can't get rid of us. We'll be privy to every piece of information. Besides, I have this feeling that Jen is close. I'd be willing to bet a week's pay that we'll be talking to her in the next twenty-four hours."

"As much as I'd like to believe you I'm not as optimistic." He leaned his head back and closed his eyes. "There are so many things that could have happened to them. Besides, they had forty miles of wilderness to travel through to get here. I can't believe they covered that distance in just two days."

"We'll see." Dave was worried about his friend. He wasn't looking too good.

A faint glow that turned out to be the village of Lorna appeared around a bend in the river. She moved to take down the makeshift sail. They had traveled the fifteen miles in less than three hours and she was anxious to have her feet on the ground again.

She stuffed the blanket and jump rope into her backpack, handed him his shoelaces and retied her own. As they approached the sleepy village, she worked the canoe toward the bank with the paddle. The bow eased into the soft mud of the bank and he jumped out to pull them ashore.

As she stepped out a snort startled her. She jumped and looked around warily, but it was only an old cow and her calf grazing beside the river. "Look at that poor thing," she said. "Half her ear is missing!" King wasn't interested.

Picking up her backpack, she followed him up the bank toward the villa's towering walls. He wasn't wasting any time. The few hours of rest had revived them both and before long they were standing at the base of the great wall.

Dropping his satchel to the ground, he pulled out a length of nylon rope and organized it into neat coils before attaching a collapsible grappling hook. Swinging the hook around his head like a lasso in a cowboy movie, he let it fly. There was a metallic clang as it landed on top of the wall. He pulled the rope to test it.

"Why didn't you tell me you had that rope before I bloodied my jump rope on that lousy boar?"

"You didn't ask," he replied, looking up the wall.

"Are you sure you're up to this?" she asked, indicating his arm.

"Have to depend on my left arm. It won't be easy." He reached as high as he could and grasping the rope with his left hand, started to pull himself up. Sweat broke out on his brow and his muscles bulged with the strain. His left arm was doing most of the work, pulling him up a few inches at a time until he could grab the rope with his right hand momentarily, long enough to reach up for another grip with his left.

When he was about halfway up the twenty foot wall, he heard a metallic clank beside him. Rotating on the rope, he looked to his right and couldn't believe what he saw. An aluminum expandable ladder was up against the wall and she was scrambling up it. "See you at the top," she said as she passed him.

Swinging sideways, he was able to grab the ladder with his foot and pull himself over. Reaching the top, he looked at her. "Where did you get the bloody ladder?" he asked.

"I borrowed it off the side of that painter's van," she replied, pointing to the dark vehicle. "They weren't using it!"

Pulling the ladder up behind them, they placed it on the other side of the wall. As they dropped to the ground, they heard the angry growl of guard dogs and looked down into the black faces of two large dobermans.

Sparks was startled when he heard the clang as someone lifted the ladder off the side of the van. He held his breath. To be exposed now would be disastrous for them both. When nobody appeared at the window, he breathed easier. Who could be stealing the ladder? He curiously looked out the back window. The ladder was disappearing over the wall as two dark figures pulled it over the top. A nylon rope dangled from the wall next to where the ladder had disappeared. He had an idea. Maybe there was a way to get inside and alert Melendez that he had all the information needed to crack the case. They could leave tonight and get to Caracas in time to purchase tickets on the Pacifico Azul. Once on board the ship, he felt confident that they could nail Lopez in the middle of his smuggling act.

He quietly got out of the van, grasped the end of the rope and started climbing the wall. He would have to make plans as he went along.

Down the road, behind their sheltering bush, the reconnaissance team watched the explosion of activity along the wall with fascination. Since nightfall, they had been using night vision goggles and binoculars to monitor the villa. The older man, Alan Netts, picked up his radio.

"Hey, Henry," he whispered. "We've got some action on the wall."

O'Brien's voice rasped back. "What's going on?"

"Two individuals went over the wall, using a ladder. One of them seems to be injured. Shortly after they disappeared, a third man followed them."

"Was the girl with him?" O'Brien asked.

"It's hard to tell at this distance, but I think one of the first two was a female. The others were definitely men."

"That's strange." O'Brien was puzzled. He hadn't reckoned on a third. "Must be an accomplice."

"Couldn't say." Netts was still watching the wall with his binoculars. None of them had reappeared. "I know this sounds weird, but I could swear one of the guys came out of that van next to the church."

This fellow had planned better than O'Brien expected. He had help lined up outside the villa.

"What do you want me to do, Henry?"

O'Brien didn't have to think. "We wait," he said with finality. "What goes in must come out. It will be much easier to nail them here where we have the element of surprise, than to go charging into the villa."

"Okay," Netts replied, and settled down for a long night.

King drew his knife and braced himself for the attack he knew was coming. But to his surprise, the dogs laid back their ears and started wagging their tails. She was making kissing noises and holding something out to them.

"What's that?" he asked.

"Doggie treats. I always keep some in my pack for my friend's dog, Sandy. The quickest way to a dog's heart is through his tummy!"

After placing a handful of treats next to the wall, they made their way toward the darkened building. Pausing under a balcony, he pulled out a small torch and drew a map of the villa from his satchel.

"Where do I find a phone?" she asked, looking over his shoulder at the layout.

"Here in the library. I'm sure he has a good phone system."

"Where are you headed?"

"He'll be asleep at this hour. I'll have to start in his bedroom. Since I don't have time to search the entire villa, I'll have to get the information out of him."

"Good luck, sport," she said, heading for the library.

"Good luck," he called after her. He couldn't believe it but he was going to miss her.

Sparks spotted the dogs as he dropped to the ground. They were munching on something and didn't threaten him. He tried to think where Melendez might be. Surely there was a service entrance.

He quietly made his way across the grounds, keeping to the shadows. Up ahead, there was a ray of light coming out of a downstairs window. Approaching it warily, he carefully stood up on his toes and looked in the window. What he saw startled him. He knew he had to work fast.

Annaliza was exhausted. Manual labor was definitely not for her! After scrubbing some three thousand feet of floors, dusting the entire place and polishing what seemed like a thousand pieces of silverware, she was ready to call it a day. Sitting down in the kitchen chair, she tilted back and placed her feet on the table with a sigh.

Just as she got comfortable, the housekeeper burst through the door. She exploded into a series of threats and, rushing over to Annaliza, slapped her across the face. Annaliza bolted up and spat in her face.

The matron was not used to retaliation from the cleaning staff. Exploding into a hysterical frenzy, she descended on Annaliza with fists and fingernails. Annaliza had no choice. As the fat matron struggled to keep her wits, Annaliza pivoted on one foot, caught the woman with her heel and sent her flying into a stack of pots and pans. The deafening noise alerted the guards.

Annaliza was just pulling the adversary to her feet for another good round when the guards descended on her. She struck out at them, hands and feet flying but there were too many. They had her on the ground and with the panting housekeeper screaming through bleeding lips, proceeded to beat her.

Sparks burst into the room, gun in hand. He had to shout to be heard above the din.

"Get off her!" he yelled in Spanish. Looking up, they quickly retreated with hands up. Slowly, she pulled herself up off the floor. Her right eye was starting to swell.

"Get some cord, tie them up and gag them," he told her in English.

Grabbing a pile of linen dish towels, she tore them into strips and bound the guards tightly after placing gags in their mouths. She took pleasure in pulling the bindings around the housekeeper's wrists until her hands turned white.

"I'll put them in the pantry," she told him. It will be a while before they're found."

He helped her, closing the door securely behind them. Their grunts could barely be heard through the thick walls and oak door.

"Come on," he grabbed her wrist and pulled her through the door. "We've gotta get out of here."

Making her way through the maze, she mistakenly opened several doors before finally discovering the library. The musty smell of old books and aged leather was heavy as she slipped through the door and sighed in relief when she saw the phone.

She reached the desk and grabbed the receiver. The droning dial tone was comforting. After a wary look over her shoulder, she connected to the international operator, and gave her the toll free number to the office. She knew the answering service would be around, at least.

"L/D Aerospace." A businesslike voice sounded across the miles.

"Is this the service?" she asked.

"Yes, it is. May I help you?"

"I need to speak to Mr. Duncan."

"Mr. Duncan is out of the country for a few days. Can someone else help you?"

"Who's on call?"

"Mrs. Crabapple."

Jen sighed with relief. Annette could fill her in on everything.

"Can you patch me through? Please, hurry." She looked around, expecting to see someone burst through the door any minute.

Three thousand miles away, the phone in Annette Crabapple's living room rang. She darted around the end of the counter, nimbly hopped over a robot lying partially disassembled on the floor, almost stepped on a Barbie Doll and avoided two youngsters lying in front of the TV. "Hello?" she said, trying not to sound out of breath.

"Annette, Annette, thank God I got you. This is Jen!"

"Jen?" Annette was amazed. "Jen, we thought you were dead! And then we found out about the hijacking! Where are you? Brent's been frantic!"

"Listen, I don't have a lot of time! Is Peeper okay? She doesn't think I'm dead, does she?"

"Oh, no. She just thinks you got tied up on the trip. She's with your mother-in-law. Don't worry about her! She's all right."

"Can you tell me where Brent's gone? They told me he's out of the country!"

"Yes, yes, he's gone to Caracas looking for you! Where are you?"

"To tell you the truth, I'm not sure myself. Somewhere in Venezuela. If you talk to him, tell him I'm all right. Tell him I'll try to find him in Caracas." She heard a noise in the hall. "I've got to go," she added in a whisper and gently hung up the phone as she hid behind the desk.

She saw the door swing open and a pair of feet shuffle across the room. A figure went to a small table on the other side of the room. As he disappeared out the door, she could make out the dark shape of a wine bottle in his hand.

Juan Carlos was jolted out of a deep sleep by a hand on his neck and a knife to his throat. A man wearing rough cotton garments stood before him. His blonde curly hair was wet with perspiration and his face was swollen with insect bites. The man's teeth gleamed in the dark as he spoke softly.

"Where is it?" the man asked.

"What?"

"You know what, the diamond, you son-of-a-bitch!"

The clipped voice was vaguely familiar. He took a guess.

"Nice of you to drop in to see an old friend, James."

The guess was right. The man clenched his fingers tighter around his throat.

"All right, I'll show you if you let me up. The man loosened his grip slightly and leaned back. Juan Carlos took advantage of this slight retreat and bursting from the bed, knocked him to the floor. He jumped on top of him, straddling his torso and went for his eyes with his fingers. King threw up his injured arm to guard his face and grunted in pain as Juan Carlos grasped it with a steel grip.

He laughed as he squeezed harder and King gritted his teeth. Pulling him roughly to his feet and holding the injured arm behind him, Juan Carlos dragged him across the room to the intercom button.

"Grog," he said. "Come up here. We have an unexpected guest."

CHAPTER 14

Jennifer's heart was pounding from the close encounter as she rushed out of the library and into the dark hallway. The monstrous villa was a maze and she was disoriented as she stumbled down the corridor, almost running into a wall as it made a sharp turn. She didn't remember it.

Hearing voices, she ducked through a doorway into a linen closet. The lights in the hallway flashed on and she heard two men talking softly as they passed her hiding place. She waited five minutes until the light went off and she was sure they were gone before slipping out of the closet and continuing her search for a way out.

Sparks grabbed Annaliza's hand and headed out the kitchen door. Running across the deserted grounds, they dodged a bubbling fountain and, reaching the wall, felt their way along until they bumped into the ladder. He pushed her ahead of him and scanned the area before following her. After they reached the top, they pulled the ladder up, threw it over the other side and were on the ground in a few moments.

"Henry." He talked into the radio while observing the scene through the night vision binoculars. "There's two of them coming over the wall. They're heading for the van."

"Move in and apprehend the suspects," O'Brien spoke decisively, ordering the six men closest to the wall.

"Here we go," Netts replied.

After reaching the van, he started the engine and wheeled around in a circle. He wanted to get out of the area before anybody came looking for them. Annaliza was slumped in the seat beside him, trembling. She was a stranger to violence and it had left her shocked and stunned. She watched Sparks as he took control. Rocks spewed from the spinning tires as he stomped the gas and headed down the gravel path.

As he started to accelerate, four men in combat fatigues jumped into the beam of the headlights, leveling their assault rifles. Two others jumped on the back bumper, ripped open the doors and were on them before he could react.

"Shit!" he shouted as the other four stormed the van, pulling open the side doors and jerking them roughly out onto the road. Throwing them to the ground, the HAT-TRIC team quickly had them pinned and cuffed. Annaliza assumed they were Juan Carlos' men and let them have it with a string of abuse in Spanish.

When they frisked Sparks they found the government issue pistol in the holster under his arm. Holding it up to the light, one of the men spoke to his partner. "Wonder where he got this piece. Must have knocked off a Fed."

Sparks was surprised at the exchange in English. "I am a Fed you stupid son-of-a-bitch!"

"Have to come up with a better story than that!" they said as they pulled them roughly to their feet and pushed them into the woods toward the chopper.

"Where are you guys taking us?" Sparks demanded.

"Straight to the pen if I have anything to say about it." Netts pushed him ahead and Sparks stumbled, almost falling. "Where is your buddy and the girl?"

"What buddy? What girl?" Sparks was confused. Obviously, they weren't associated with Juan Carlos.

As they came into a clearing, he could see the outline of a Blackhawk helicopter in the firelight. A short man with a cigar strutted up to them and squinted as if he was trying to remember a face.

Sparks tried again. "I am an investigator for United States Customs. This is my partner. Under whose authority do you detain us?"

The man removed the cigar. "That's some speech sonny. Keep it for the judge."

"I don't think that will be necessary." They turned as Brent walked into the small circle of light. "I can identify this man. He is Inspector Royce Sparks, US Customs."

"Why didn't you say so?" O'Brien asked.

"I was just getting to that but you didn't give me a chance!" He turned as O'Brien tossed a pair of keys to the man next to him to unlock the cuffs.

"I think you two have a lot of explaining to do, "O'Brien said.

"So do you," Sparks replied.

Jennifer finally found a door. She jogged across the grounds and leaned against a tree, gratefully gulping the fresh air. She was beginning to wonder if she would ever get out of that house!

She made it to the wall and felt along it to the point where she remembered leaving the ladder. It wasn't there. Fighting down a rising panic, she searched up and down . Turning around, she looked for something familiar, but it was too dark and she didn't trust her memory. As she looked back at the top of the wall, her heart sank. She could now see the grappling hook gleaming in the soft moonlight. The ladder was gone.

"Oh my God." She sank to the ground and fought the tears and fatigue.

Getting up slowly, she quietly moved along the wall, looking for another way out. Thirty minutes later, she realized she had to find some other way over the wall. Spotting a small building, she decided to hide for a while, try to get a little rest and make some plans.

She eased through the door. The room smelled faintly of gasoline and there were large red tool chests lining a wall. Another wall was covered with shovels, brooms and garden implements. A door on the far side probably led to the main building. She lay down on the dirt floor and fell asleep.

The blow echoed against the walls of the empty room and King's head snapped back as the palm of Juan Carlos' hand struck him again, leaving a large red welt on his cheek. His head lolled forward as he sat in the straight backed chair. His hands were bound behind him. Grog stood aside, quietly watching.

"I ask you again. Who are you working for?" Juan Carlos spat, his dark eyes glinting in the light of the single bulb in the room.

"I told you. I don't work for anyone. I sure as hell wouldn't split the profits."

"You're just a small time thief! There's no one who knows about the diamond except my trusted contacts in Cabo San Lucas! I must know if I've been betrayed!"

He was wasting his breath. King was out cold from pain and exhaustion.

"Grog!" Juan Carlos motioned him to his side. "We'll have to take him with us tomorrow. I must find out who the informant is! I will not be betrayed!" He stormed out of the room, slamming the door.

Grog grabbed the man and effortlessly tossed him over his shoulder.

Sparks and O'Brien compared notes as Brent and Dave listened anxiously.

"My men saw three people go over the fence tonight and one through the gate today. One of the over-the-fence crowd was you and your partner was the one who went through the gate. That leaves two unaccounted for. We believe it was King and the girl. What do you know about this?"

"I had no idea King and the girl were inside. We've been working on a smuggling ring for months and Lopez is our prime suspect. We're ready to nail him on the twenty-second."

"So, you had no information about King's operation?"

"None. I'm only interested in Lopez."

"And we're only interested in King and the girl. How are we going to work this out between us?"

Brent stepped forward. "If my wife is in the hands of that animal, I want you guys to go in after her!"

"We can't compromise the Custom's investigation! We're too close. Lopez is still not aware of our operation and I'm not anxious to blow our cover by charging in! Besides, we can't just storm the place. If he panicked, who knows what he might do to those two!"

The sun was just lighting the eastern horizon and O'Brien wondered if he would ever get another full night's sleep. This was turning into a mess. He wasn't sure how to nab his suspect, rescue the girl and get out of there without pissing off Customs. There would surely be hell to pay when he got back if he interfered with their investigation.

"Henry!" The radio crackled to life as Netts called him.

"Yeah, what is it?"

"Gates are opening up. Big black limo coming through."

"Can you tell who's in it?"

"I'll snap some pictures with the telephoto as they pass by. Randall will try to get a good look."

"Let me know what you guys see ASAP."

"Okay, Henry."

There were a few moments of tense silence. Brent held his breath. He was afraid the limo occupants might discern their next course of action.

"Henry, we've got a possible ID."

"Don't just sit there, speak man!" O'Brien said tensely into the mike.

Have to develop the pictures to be absolutely certain, but it looked like Lopez, King and some hairy looking character in the back seat."

"Any sign of the girl?"

"Couldn't really tell. Could have been another occupant, but they went by fast and the windows were tinted. Sure the one guy was King, though."

O'Brien spit his cigar. Goddamnit, now what was he going to do?

"Dave! Is that chopper safe to fly?"

"I can have it ready to go in ten minutes," Dave replied, climbing to the top of the big black bird and wielding his wrench.

"Everybody get back here," O'Brien spoke sharply into the radio. "We're leaving for Caracas!" Turning to Sparks he asked, "You sure they're planning to sail on the twenty-second?"

"Absolutely," Sparks replied.

"Wait a minute!" Brent stepped in. "How do we know for sure that my wife is with them?"

"If they have King, we have to assume they have your wife, too. King is our target and we've got to keep on top of his position while we have him. Searching the villa now would be dangerous and time consuming. If you want a ride to Caracas, you'd better come with us."

Brent didn't like the feeling of panic that came over him. He was going to have to make a decision quickly and Jennifer's life could depend on that decision. He closed his eyes, picturing her face and imagined wrapping his arms around her, never letting her go. He had not realized how much his family meant to him. He looked at the chopper and knew it was the quickest way to Caracas and he knew now that neither King nor Lopez were in the villa. They were her biggest threat. Was she still there or not? He squeezed his eyes shut and pinched the bridge of his nose with his thumb and forefinger as he tried to think. He was so damned tired and confused. Finally, he made his decision. He could think of no reason why Jen would still be in the villa. She had come with King as his hostage. He had to assume her hijacker still had her in his clutches.

Brent looked at Dave desperately. "What do you think we should do?"

Dave stopped wrenching for a moment and popped a lifesaver in his mouth. "Way I see it, all the bad guys just departed in that car. If she's not in that car the bad guys don't have her, and she's probably all right. We'll just have to trust that she can take care of herself. If she is in that car, I'd better get in gear and put this bird back together because she's going to need all the help she can get!"

"I agree," Brent said decisively. He turned to O'Brien. "We'll take the ride."

"What about you two?" O'Brien looked intently at Sparks and Melendez.

Sparks studied Annaliza. She'd had a rough day and he had to look hard for the fearless polished character he'd met just the day before. "We've had a pretty stressful twenty-four hours with no backup. If we catch a few hours of sleep in the van and then drive back to Caracas, can you maintain surveillance on that character?" Sparks didn't think he was up to a helicopter ride with a bunch of Rambo characters. If he never flew again in this lifetime, it would be too soon!

"You bet!" O'Brien was businesslike. "Look me up at the Fiesta Caracas when you get to town. I think I've got enough men to cover it until you get there."

"Thanks," Sparks said gratefully. "Come on, Annaliza, let's go get you fixed up. I have a first aid kit in the van."

They turned and walked down the incline as the HAT-TRIC team with two extras hopped into the helicopter. The rotor was already starting to spool.

In the cramped van, Sparks squinted in the dim morning light as he dabbed at the oozing abrasion on the side of her delicate chin.

"Ouch!" She jumped.

"Sorry," he said. "I'm trying to be careful."

"I know." She sighed and fought the tears that had been threatening to burst out since the shock had worn off.

"He placed a final bandage on her face and sat back for a look. "Does it hurt much?"

"Only when I laugh." She attempted a smile for his benefit. "I want to thank you. I mean, I think you saved my life."

"It's okay to let your feelings show, you know. I've been beat up with the best of them. I promise I won't tell anybody if you want to cry."

He looked at her tenderly and this show of affection was too much for her. She burst into tears and fell forward into arms that were reaching for her. "I always thought I was so strong!" She snuffled into his shirt. "I could beat everybody in my class. The last few years, nobody ever got in a lick. I'm not used to losing!" she sobbed. "Oh Royce, what am I going to do? My career is over! I've made a complete ass of myself in front of the entire FBI! What were those guys thinking? Did you see the way they looked at me?"

He gently patted her back. "Yeah," he smiled. "I saw the way they were looking at you. Even with that swollen eye, you're still a pretty foxy lady."

She stopped crying abruptly, pushed away and laid a stinging slap across his cheek.

He was startled. "What was that for?"

"That's for being a frigging male chauvinist pig like the rest of frigging mankind!" she sobbed as she dropped back into his arms. "I'm sorry. I'm just tired of being thought of as a sex object instead of a member of the team!"

He was bewildered as she clutched him and soaked the front of his shirt with her tears. "You can be a valued member of the team and still be beautiful," he said cautiously. Pulling out his handkerchief, he handed it to her.

"Thanks," she said, dabbing at her eyes and blowing her nose. "You know, you're okay." She looked at him through her good eye. "You're a regular kind of guy, somehow."

"Regular?"

"Yeah, not like some jock strutting around trying to impress the babes. I appreciate that."

He wasn't sure he liked the almost forgotten feelings that were beginning to stir. "I'm glad somebody appreciates me. I was beginning to wonder."

She said nothing, but snuggled further into the crook of his arm as her tears abated. Sighing deeply, she closed her eyes and he thought she was asleep. He sat still, not wanting to disturb her.

"Royce." Her voice startled him and he looked down at the deep brown eyes. He thought he knew what he saw and as he lowered his lips to hers, he knew he had guessed right.

Jennifer slowly opened her eyes. Her first awareness was of her aching muscles. For a moment, she couldn't remember where she was. Then the events of the last two days charged her with a rush and she groaned as she stiffly got to her feet and tried to ignore a stomach that was screaming for food. She slowly made her way across the floor of the shed and grasped the knob of the door that led into the main building. Pushing it inward, she groped along the wall to her right, searching for the light switch. As the lights flashed on, her eyes widened in disbelief as she saw what loomed in front of her. A big beautiful sunny yellow Super Cub! She looked appreciatively at the cocky little airplane perched on stumpy gear struts that looked like the legs of a knock-kneed teenager. The perky snout pointed up and she noted the long sleek cowling that housed the powerful Lycoming engine.

She gently stroked the smooth metal propeller and thanked her maker for this deliverance. It seemed to be in perfect condition, from the fabric covered wings to the oversized balloon tires. Through the cockpit door, she peered at the panel. It was well equipped with a communication radio, navigation receiver and a full compliment of flight instruments. As she opened the door, she sensed a new car smell and she ran her hand over the soft leather seats. This was somebody's baby!

She ran to the giant doors at the front of the large room and slowly pushed one open. Bright sunlight made her blink as she slipped out the door. Standing in front of the building, she looked down a gentle slope toward the wall at the far end. It was definitely wide enough but the question was, did she have enough room to take off and clear the wall? She knew this airplane was light and famous for short field performance. It could be off the ground and over a fifty foot obstacle in less than five hundred feet. But did she have five hundred feet? It was hard to judge. She started pacing, needing to be sure. Hitting that wall at eighty knots would mean instant death.

When she'd gone about a hundred feet, she heard shouting and turned to see a man in an upper window waving his arms at her angrily. When he disappeared, she knew she had to act quickly.

Running back up the hill, she heaved the door open, threw her pack into the back seat and closed the door. Racing to the tail she picked it up and swung it around until it was facing the door. Placing herself between the wing and the horizontal stabilizer, she pushed on the leading edge of the tail and hauled it out of the building. As the wings cleared, she swung it around until it was once again facing down the hill. The man had gathered reinforcements, and was running toward her.

Grabbing a rock and throwing it under the left front wheel, she reached into the cockpit and turned on the magnetos. They were a hundred yards away now and closing quickly as they shouted at her. She rushed to the prop and grabbing it in both hands, lifted a foot and pulled down smoothly as she deftly sidestepped. The engine caught, sputtered and burst to life as the prop fanned her.

She jumped into the cockpit just as they reached the plane. One man grabbed the door as she was trying to pull it shut. Knowing that she was no match for his strength, she surprised him by abruptly pushing the door outward, knocking him to the ground before pulling it closed and locking it.

Another man was pulling angrily on the other door that was, by some miracle, already locked. She stood on the brakes and shoved the throttle forward while pushing on the stick. Even though she wasn't moving, the tail was now flying from the prop wash. They were pounding frantically on the windows and as she saw a gun come up, she let go of the brakes.

Her assailants were thrown to the ground as the little plane leapt forward, bouncing over the rock and down the slope toward the wall. She watched the airspeed indicator intently as it crept slowly toward flying speed. Just when she thought she wasn't going to make it, the needle hit the right number and she yanked back on the stick. The plane went up like an elevator, the soft balloon tires missing the wall by inches.

Letting out a whoop, she climbed and turned right as she passed over the Orinoco River. She knew it would lead her to Caracas and Brent.

CHAPTER 15

Royce Sparks woke with a smile on his face. It took a few moments to become lucid after the deep sleep but as he started to move and realized who was nestled in the crook of his arm, he remembered.

Sitting up slowly, he eased away gently, laid her head on the rolled-up jacket they had used for a pillow and moved quietly to the door.

As he was climbing out of the van, he heard the buzzing of a small plane and looked up as a small yellow high-winged airplane cleared the wall by inches and turned right over the river, heading north. He could hear excited shouts on the other side and decided it was time to hit the road.

He jumped back into the van, turned the key and headed down the graveled path toward the main road. Reaching into a cooler beside him, he fished around in the sloshing water from the melted ice and pulled out a warm soda.

Annaliza was abruptly awakened by the bumping and jarring of the van and by someone whistling jauntily. She had a pounding headache and couldn't open her left eye. Touching it gingerly, she remembered the events of the past evening. Oh my God! I've slept with an inspector! That has to be the most unprofessional thing I've ever done in my life! To make matters worse, he's my partner! Her face flushed at the thought.

He heard her rustling and turned around with a gleaming smile. "Sleep well?" He was in a great mood today.

She looked at him warily. "I think we would be better off if we both just forgot about what happened between us," she said as she climbed into the seat beside him and looked out the window at the plains zinging past.

His smile left him and there was a sinking feeling in the pit of his stomach. Women! He just couldn't understand. Last night had been his best in years. He'd really felt he had connected with this woman. He was so starved for companionship and intimacy, and his feelings were blossoming. With his marriage over, standing at the brink of his new life, he was hopeful. But those hopes were quickly fading. All right, he thought, clenching his teeth. If that's the way she wants it, fine. It'll be strictly business from now on!

He stomped the accelerator and the van lurched forward over the uneven road.

Brent was sleepy from lack of rest, the motion of the helicopter and the steady beating of the rotor blades. In a way, he was grateful there were enough of the FBI guys that they didn't depend on him and Dave for watch. The chopper had climbed to fifteen thousand feet so they wouldn't be spotted. They'd had to enter a semi-hover to go slow enough to stay over the top of the limo. The driver didn't seem to be in any hurry. They took turns watching the creeping vehicle through high power binoculars.

Brent knew from eavesdropping on conversations between the Feds that they were planning on picking up Lopez and King on a cruise ship called the Pacifico Azul. He thought about their interrogation of the man at the weather desk in Cabo San Lucas. Suddenly it came to him.

"Dave!" He shook his friend awake.

Dave jumped. "Wha, what's going on?"

"Dave, it just occurred to me! Remember when we were in Cabo and that guy was puzzled because Jennifer called the airplane blue?"

"Yeah, so what?" Dave was still half asleep. He couldn't figure out what his friend was raving about.

"Pacifico Azul. Get it?"

"Get what?" Dave still wasn't functioning.

"Azul is Spanish for blue! Somehow Jennifer must have figured out she was going to end up on this ship with King!"

Dave sat up. "Of course! There's no other plausible reason for her to call the airplane blue! Why didn't we think of that before?"

Brent flopped back against the seat. "We've got some plans to make. I feel better now that I know where she's going to be! This not knowing has been driving me up a wall! The first thing we have to do when we get to Caracas is book ourselves on that ship."

"Which should be the twenty-second, right?"

"That's what they said."

"What if they don't have any accommodations left?"

"Then we'll stow away, hijack the ship, anything! No matter what happens, I plan to be on that ship!" Brent's blue eyes were flashing and Dave could tell he meant it. He couldn't get over the change in his friend. He was usually indecisive about things.

Brent's thoughts were running into and over each other. He didn't seem to be able to talk fast enough to keep up with them. "We should be in Caracas in about another hour and a half. As soon as we get there, I've got to find a phone and check on the Peep. I also need to touch base with Annette and find out if the business is still there." He looked down at his hands. "Although I'm not sure I care anymore."

"Hey, what kind of talk is that?"

"It's this business that got us into this mess, Dave. Can't you see how much I've screwed up the last couple of years?"

"You're doing the best you can. Forget the business for now and take care of your family stuff. Then you can concentrate on getting us on that ship. Let me worry about the things that don't matter so much. Everything's going to be just fine. Lifesaver?"

Brent smiled as he took the candy. They had a plan.

Jen's relief was short-lived as she looked at the fuel gauges after leveling off at twelve thousand five hundred feet northeast bound. She tapped them impatiently but they hung right on the quarter tank marks. She wondered what it was about pilots that made them tap instruments when they didn't tell them what they wanted.

She wasn't sure how big the fuel tanks in a Super Cub were, but she knew for a fact it wasn't going to be enough to cover the two hundred miles to Caracas. She had been following the giant, slow moving river for about fifteen minutes. She knew this was not the most direct route. The river emptied into the Caribbean well east of Caracas. It would probably take her an hour just to fly over the delta where it met the ocean, if she was unlucky enough to arrive at the far east end.

Then, she had an idea. Grabbing her backpack, she started pulling things out. She was looking for the aeronautical maps she'd tossed in before leaving the Lear. Near the bottom of the pack, she finally found the one that covered the area. Excited, she unfolded it, estimated her position and entered the appropriate frequency on her nav radio, turning the knob on the round indicator until the needle lined up. As she received the strong signal from the ground station, she yelled for joy and turned left on her new course.

Looking down, she watched the Guianas highlands slip under the big yellow wings and give way to the great Orinoco River Basin with its vast plains and fertile grasslands that supported great herds of cattle. She was enjoying the ride in spite of her circumstances. The feel of the engine throbbing through the stick in her hand caused a poignant euphoria to rush her as she remembered her childhood and her father's patient voice teaching her to fly. She thought about Peeper. She felt a regret at the time that had been lost in the past couple of years while they were struggling to get ahead. She wanted to leave her daughter the same legacy of love her parents had left her so long ago.

The little girl was shivering. She had stopped wondering if it was from cold, fear or lack of food. She felt a little dizzy when she stood up so she lay in her corner, wrapped in the thin smelly blanket, and thought about her father. She was beginning to wonder if he was ever going to come for her. It seemed like such a long time since she had seen him. Had it been three days? Four?

She reached and brushed a string of hair that had fallen in her eyes. Normally, she had shiny golden ringlets framing her pixie face. Now her hair was dull and lifeless. Her pink dress was torn and dirty, but she didn't care anymore. She just wanted her Dad to come and take her away from that awful man and this awful place.

The driver pulled the sleek limo under the canopy of the Caracas Hilton and jumped out to open the back door. Juan Carlos nudged King awake. They had changed his clothes and given him a shave so as not to raise suspicion. King looked at him dully

"You will follow me to my suite and say nothing to nobody! One false move, and I will have Grog break every bone in your body. Do you understand?" Juan Carlos hissed.

King glared at him through slitted eyes. He had to start planning his escape immediately. He didn't have much time.

The driver and a bell hop followed the odd trio up to the suite of rooms they had reserved. They made an interesting entourage, the tall, thin, blonde man with the swollen face and scabbed over bug bites, the tall, dark Venezuelan with the grotesquely drooping features and the short, burly, furry character who brought up the rear. The bellboy moved ahead of them to open the door, then followed them in with the six suitcases and two large trunks.

Juan Carlos glanced around warily. He didn't notice the opulence of the rooms, only the potential dangers. He was a hated and feared man and there were any number of ruthless criminals who would love to dance on his grave.

He walked swiftly across the thickly padded carpet to the gleaming windows. Heavy royal blue velvet curtains swagged the French doors that led to a private balcony.

"Grog." He moved forward immediately at the sound of his name. "Secure these rooms, close the curtains and inform the front desk that we are not to be disturbed."

A grunt was his only reply.

King stood in the middle of the living area, wondering if he could jump Juan Carlos while Grog was inspecting the other rooms.

Juan Carlos turned and fixed him with a stony glare. "Don't even think about it," he said, reading his mind.

Since he had always depended on brains and cunning to accomplish his work King was a non-violent man and had no talent for hand-to-hand combat.

Juan Carlos moved to a crystal decanter on a polished mahogany table and, turning a glass upright, poured the amber liquid into it. "I have had enough of your cat and mouse games. My patience is running thin. It is time for us to talk. Now I will ask you again. Who told you about the diamond and sent you after it?" He held the glass out to King.

King was angry and desperate. He was terrified that if Lopez got wind of who Kristen's kidnappers were, she would end up as a casualty in this clash between two powers. "Up yours you bloody son-of-a-bitch," he said, abruptly swinging his hand upward, slapping the glass from Juan Carlos' hand and soaking him.

Before he could react further, Grog plowed into him from behind, knocking him to the floor and jumping on his back with his bone crushing weight. King felt the breath rush out of his lungs and he helplessly fought for air as the powerful bodyguard jerked his arms behind him painfully, pinning him to the floor.

He could not see Juan Carlos but he could hear the cold anger in his voice. "Tie him up and throw him in the trunk. We will dispose of his worthless carcass two days out to sea!"

King felt the sweat break out on his back as he realized that they meant to kill him. He silently cursed himself for letting his emotions get away from him.

Grog bound his hands behind his back and dumped him in the large trunk. He then stuffed a dirty handkerchief in his mouth and placed a strip of silver duct tape around his head to hold it in place. As King saw the lid of the trunk lower and felt the first panic from the inky darkness, he knew he would never get out of this one alive. Forgive me, Kristen, he thought as the lid closed over him.

The chopper pilot received permission from Caracas approach to set down on the edge of town. Four of the HAT-TRIC team jumped to the ground and started toward the towering Hilton Hotel a mile away. They would be relieved from their watch once the helicopter was tucked in at the airport and the rest of the team had gotten settled at the Fiesta Caracas. Armed with radios and provisions, they disappeared into the trees as the chopper gracefully rose and turned toward the airport.

Brent and Dave had been trying to catch a few minutes sleep. They snapped awake as soon as the tires thumped firmly on the ramp and the pilot began his shutdown procedures.

Brent caught O'Brien by the shoulder as he eased out the door. "Thanks for the ride. Hope we haven't been too much trouble."

"Just stay out of the way from now on. We're doing our best to apprehend King and rescue your wife without anybody getting hurt. This damn customs investigation is just slowing us down a bit. You two just catch the next flight to the states and we'll be in touch as soon as we know something."

"Sure," Brent mumbled and cut out across the searing pavement to find the nearest phone. Dave was close on his heels.

"Nice guy." Dave didn't like the set of his friend's jaw.

"If he thinks I'm going to calmly sit around while those jerks play with themselves, he's got quite a surprise in store. The right hand doesn't even know what the left hand is doing! If we're ever going to get Jennifer back alive, we're going to have to do it ourselves, without the help of the almighty United States Government!"

Once inside the modern terminal building, they found a row of pay phones. "I'm going to call Mom and check on the Peep. Could you check in with Annette and find out what's going on there?"

"Sure," Dave said, picking up the other phone.

Brent dialed zero. He crossed his fingers and hoped he could find an operator who spoke English. Through the crackling lines, he heard a woman's voice. "Operator International?" he asked, the knowledge that he was butchering the Spanish making him cringe.

"Uno momento," she replied. There were a few more clicks before another woman came on the line.

"Operator International."

"Hablas Inglaes?" he asked hopefully.

"Si, Señor, I speak English. May I help you?"

He breathed a sigh of relief. "Yes, I have a number in the United States I would like to call collect. Can you connect me?"

"Si, Señor. Please give me the number."

After a few moments, he heard a phone ringing faintly and then his mother's voice. "Yes, yes!" she cried. "I'll accept the charges. Brent! Where are you?"

"I'm in Caracas. I'm calling to check on the Peep."

"She's fine. I'd let you talk to her, but she's at pre-school. Have you found Jennifer?"

"No, Mom, I'm afraid not. We think we have an idea where she is, but it looks like it's going to be a few more days."

"Just bring Jen home to us, Brent," his mother said. "She's the closest thing to a daughter I have."

"I know, Mom. I'm doing the best I can. We've hit a few snags down here." What an understatement. How could he describe the last couple of days?

"Okay, dear. When you see Jennifer, give her our love. Don't worry about Peeper, she's fine."

As he hung up, he looked at Dave who was waving his hands and talking excitedly. "What do you mean she didn't know where she was? How could anybody not know where they are? Look, can you just patch me through to Annette? Hold on." Brent was motioning to him.

"What is it?" he asked.

"Jen called Annette last night. This is the service. All they have is a screwed up message from Annette saying something about Jen called, didn't know where she was. Then they lost the second sheet from the notepad the message is written on. This lady is new. She doesn't even know Jen."

Brent grabbed the phone. "Hello?" He was impatient. "Hello?" he repeated.

Through the static came a faint voice. "This is the service, can I help you?"

"This is Brent Duncan. What is the message from my wife?"

"I'm sorry, sir." The voice cut out as the static started again. As it faded in she was saying, "We don't have the complete message. Mrs. Crabapple will be in this evening if you would like to speak to her."

"Just connect me to Mrs. Crabapple now! Call her on her mobile, beep her, I don't care what you need to do to get her on this line, I need to speak to her now!"

The voice faded and the static took over. "What? What?" Brent held the phone away from him and stared at it.

"Is she patching you through?" Dave asked.

"I have no idea what is going on up there!" Brent shoved the phone at him. "Near as I can tell, Annette has had some sort of family emergency. She's at the hospital getting one of the kid's stomach pumped."

"What did he eat?" Dave asked.

"I didn't catch that part." Brent sank into a chair. "This is getting worse and worse."

"What do you want me to tell them?" Dave asked as he heard the voice fade in again.

Brent stroked the stiff whiskers on his chin tiredly. "Tell them if Jen calls again to tell her we'll see her on the Pacifico Azul."

Dave had to repeat the message several times before the woman understood.

Brent got up stiffly and they approached the travel desk next to the airline counters. "Hablas Inglaes?" he asked the woman who was studying her bright red nails. She looked up and flashed a brilliant smile.

"Yes, Señor, I speak English. How may I help you?"

Those were the sweetest words he had ever heard. "I need a cabin on the Pacifico Azul, departing tomorrow for Cabo San Lucas."

The fluorescent nails clicked on the computer keys. "All I have left is a first class cabin."

"We'll take it," Brent said, flipping his credit card on the counter.

Only forty miles to go. She was surprised she'd made it this far. The fuel gauge needles had hit the E and stopped bouncing twenty minutes ago. So it came as no shock when the engine sputtered once and caught, indicating fuel starvation. She stepped on the left rudder and lowered the right wing, placing the plane into a side slip, an old trick she had learned to milk the last few drops of fuel from a tank. It bought her another five minutes. As the engine sputtered again, she reversed the slip to the opposite side, milking another three minutes out of that tank. From her altitude, she could see the city's skyscrapers on the horizon. The motor finally coughed and died, thirty-two miles from the airport. It might as well be a hundred, she thought dejectedly. There's no way I can cover thirty-two miles on foot in the next twenty-four hours in the shape I'm in.

She established a glide, and spiraled toward the ground, searching for a place to land. Although the ground looked smooth in the lush pasture land, she knew the tall grass could conceal ravines or ruts that could put the tiny plane on its nose. She was grateful for the big soft tires that could roll over some pretty rough ground without danger.

A few feet above the ground, she leveled off over the spot she'd committed to and smoothly flared the plane, waiting for the wheels to touch. She heard the grass slapping the tires, and then a soft thump as they bounced onto the moist dirt and slowly rolled to a stop. She sat for a minute listening to the quiet, not quite believing how easy it had been.

With a sigh, she reached into the seat behind her and grabbed her back pack. She wasn't looking forward to this walk. She was hungry and tired and sick of this adventure. She wondered if King had found his diamond.

After about a mile and a half, she stopped under a solitary tree for a few minutes. The heat and humidity were draining and she was dizzy from fatigue and dehydration. The canteen was empty and she knew if she didn't get something to drink soon, she was going to be in trouble.

Closing her eyes, she leaned back against the tree and closed her eyes. She didn't realize she had been dozing until she was jolted awake by warm breath on her neck. Jumping up, she startled the calf.

"Hey, fella." She held out her hand and he sniffed it warily, then turned and ran back toward his mother, kicking up his heels in the tall grass. Noting the cow's swollen udder, she had an idea.

Holding out her hand and moving forward slowly, she spoke softly. "Here, girl. Come on, and I'll scratch your ears for you."

The cow snorted and backed off a step.

Jennifer reached around and carefully unzipped her pack. The jump rope was on top and she slowly pulled it out, hiding it behind her back as she advanced step by step toward the suspicious cow.

She took one more step but it was one step too many. The cow wheeled and took off across the pasture. Jennifer saw the only meal she was likely to have moving off in a dead run. Balling her fists and taking a deep breath, she took off in hot pursuit. The cow was hindered by a full udder and small calf trying to keep up. Although she was pulling away, Jennifer was determined not to let her meal escape.

Just as she thought her lungs would burst, the cow ran up against a fence and skidded to a halt where she stood panting. Jennifer braced her hands on her knees, leaned over and gasped for breath. The cow seemed to be as winded as she was. As she straightened, she looked up and down the fence. Not forty feet away was a right angle turn where one section met another. Eureka! She thought. I've got her now.

The cow turned and faced her, the calf huddling by her side. Jennifer slowly started to approach, being careful to stay to one side so that the cow would run toward the corner. Two more steps and the cow was on her way. It only took a few moments for her to reach the corner where she turned and challenged her pursuer.

Jennifer had the jump rope out in front now, confident the cow wouldn't be able to escape. As she neared her, the animal became more agitated, snorting frequently and rolling her eyes in fear. Jennifer approached slowly.

Just as she reached the cow's head, the animal lurched forward, trying to push past to freedom, but Jennifer managed to get the loop over her head.

As she scratched the furry ears, she felt her relax. Finally, the animal was safely tied to a post. Carefully, she walked around to her side and squatted down. Her aim was rusty and it took her a couple of tries before she was able to hit her mouth with the warm milk. As the calf worked his side, she expertly emptied the other, swallowing hungrily as the milk pooled in her mouth and ran down her chin. Once her thirst was quenched and her hunger eased, she removed her canteen and filled it before letting the cow go with a pat on her back. "Thanks old girl," she said affectionately. "I needed that!"

She felt energized as she pulled out her compass and started walking toward the city. It would be another fifteen miles before the tallest buildings came into sight.

Annaliza stretched and splashed around in the cooler for something to drink. He didn't seem to be in the mood for talking, and that was fine with her. She hated to admit it, but she was attracted to the guy. Somehow, he didn't seem like the type she had always pictured herself falling for. Although she couldn't consider him handsome, he was attractive in his own way. He seemed to have a calmness about him and she had loved the way he'd taken charge in a crisis. She could really get into a guy like that.

Looking at him through the corner of her eye, she noted an errant lock of wavy brown hair that always seemed to be pulling itself loose and falling over his forehead. He frequently pushed it back into place, but it would spring loose and drop back over his eyes like it had a mind of it's own. Although his clothes were wrinkled, they hung well on his sturdy frame and she smiled to herself as she remembered the feeling of his muscled back under her hands.

He looked across at her and she turned away, embarrassed that he'd caught her examining him. As he turned back to the road, she chanced another look. The muscles in his jaw stood out as he clenched his teeth. His shirt sleeves were rolled up revealing a deep tan and bulging biceps. One wrist was draped over the steering wheel and the left elbow hung out the open window.

She pulled her bottom lip into her mouth and bit until it hurt. She didn't care how damn attractive he was. She was not going to let herself get involved with him. Her hormones had already taken over once and it was not going to happen again. They were close to busting the smuggling operation. That's what they were here for. She had to remember that.

CHAPTER 16

The rooms in the Hotel Fiesta Caracas were open and airy and the air conditioner worked well for a third world country. Henry O'Brien paced the silver carpeting. An uneaten room service meal rested on the bedside table. Although he was exhausted, he couldn't relax enough to sleep. The radio in his hand crackled to life hourly, bringing the updates he'd requested. So far there had been nothing to report. Waiting, waiting, waiting. He was damn frustrated from having his suspect holed up less than three blocks away and not being able to do anything about it. Why was everything so complicated? They should have been able to waltz in and grab the guy. Now they were having to pussy foot around this confounded customs investigation. He threw the stump of his cigar into the trash can and realized he was going through his supply at an alarming rate. He'd have to find a tobacco shop soon or he'd be going through nicotine withdrawal on top of everything else!

Dave and Brent were back in the airless grubby room of the small family hostel. The cool shower did little for their frazzled nerves. Dave lay on his lumpy bed and read an aircraft maintenance magazine while Brent tried to get some rest. Every time he closed his eyes, visions of Jennifer moved through his thoughts until he was forced to get up and pace around the room. Dave tried to ignore his agitated friend but it was difficult to concentrate on his reading with all the tension of the room.

"Want to talk?"

Brent ran a hand through his salt-and-pepper hair. "Where is she?"

Dave dropped the magazine and propped his hands behind his head, studying the network of cracks in the ceiling. "At this point, all we can do is wonder. My best guess is one of two places. Either back in that villa, or holed up in the Hilton with King and his friend."

"What if we left her back there? I just can't get over the feeling that she's on her own and needs us!"

Dave sat up in bed and swung his legs over the edge. "Well, the fact is, we don't know where she is. You've left a message at work. With the eight hundred number, it's easy enough for her to call if she's anywhere near a phone. Besides, didn't we already figure out that she expects to be on that boat tomorrow?"

"I just find it hard to believe she knew three days ago where she was going to be."

"She left us a clue. That's the only thing we have to go on. If she makes contact with the office, they'll tell her where we are. Maybe between her looking for us and our looking for her, we'll find each other."

Brent stopped pacing and looked at his friend. "If I ever find her, I'm never going to let her out of my sight again!"

"Come on, Brent. Let's go get something to eat. That'll kill a couple of hours."

The insects were back. Why didn't she think to put a can of bug spray in her pack? They didn't have insects like this in New Mexico! She was beginning to see the advantages of a dry climate.

The blisters on her feet were raw and every muscle in her body ached. She felt like someone had beaten her with a baseball bat. As she leaned against a fence post to rest, she admired a pair of horses grazing nearby. It reminded her of the ranch and made her homesick.

Plucking some grass, she held it out to the big black gelding. He stretched his nose and took a step toward her. She thought about stealing this horse. Back in New Mexico, it was considered a hanging offense to rustle stock. Hell, the penalty for horse thieving was worse than that for murder! Still, she was tempted. On horseback she could easily make Caracas by morning.

He was nuzzling her now as she scratched him under his chin. What the heck! She'd just borrow him for a few hours!

She pulled the jump rope from her pack and fashioned a crude hackemore. Grabbing a handful of long black mane, she lightly vaulted onto his back and nudged him with her heels. He willingly broke into a slow canter and she was ecstatic as she felt the rippling muscles between her legs. A low pole fence loomed in front of them and he cleared it easily. What an animal! Cowboys in Venezuela must be as proud of their ponies as their counterparts in Texas. At this rate she'd be in Caracas by nightfall.

The child was out cold. No wonder. She hadn't eaten anything for three days. He nudged the frail body with his foot but she didn't stir. Oh, well. Nobody said he had to keep her alive. Besides, she was easier to watch when she was unconscious. He scratched absently and went to find a cold brew.

The sun dipped below the horizon as they crossed the city limits into town and turned toward the Fiesta Caracas. Not two words had passed between them for the last hundred miles. Sparks was getting tired of the silent treatment.

"Look," he said. "Have I done something to make you mad? After this morning..."

"This morning didn't happen. I was upset and vulnerable. You took advantage of me."

"Hey, that's not fair. I wasn't trying to take advantage of you! I didn't hear you complaining!"

"Well, I would have if I'd been thinking straight! I'd just been through a traumatic experience and you were a handy shoulder to cry on!"

"Oh, so that's all I am, huh? A shoulder to cry on? Nothing that happened earlier meant anything to you?"

"What do you think I am?"

"I think you're a very attractive, sexy, lady."

"I rest my case."

"What do you mean?"

"I mean that you haven't acknowledged my intelligence or my expertise. All you can see is sex. Just like every other man I've ever met!"

He stomped on the brakes, bringing the van to a screeching halt. "What is your problem? Every time I compliment your looks, I'm suddenly the bad guy! Most women like it when a man says they're attractive!"

"Well, in the first place, I'm not most women. My self esteem does not rely on some horny male thinking I have a great body!"

"But you do have a great body! What's wrong with that?"

She crossed her arms and stared out the side window with her good eye. She wanted to leap into his arms and lay kisses on that craggy face. The only way she could resist was to be obstinate. "Leave me alone."

"Look," he said. "We have to work together. It's going to be a miserable couple of days if we're fighting. Yes, I admit I'm sexually attracted to you. I'm pretty vulnerable now, myself. But I'm willing to call a truce for the sake of our case. After we're done down here, I'll ask Cosgrove to assign me somewhere else so we won't have to bump into each other."

Her heart sank as he said this. With surprise, she realized that bumping into him on a daily basis sounded nice. Was she falling in love? She couldn't speak.

"Annaliza, please."

On his lips, her name sounded musical. God, how was she ever going to make it through the next few days? "Truce." Her heart was screaming, tell him! Tell him you want him as much as he wants you! Her stupid pride was getting in the way. She wanted to be professional. She felt like crying as she looked at the expression on his face as he put the van into gear and pulled onto the highway. There was so much pain there and she was responsible. "Are we almost there?" She was suddenly desperate for a hot bath.

"Almost," he replied, not taking his eyes from the road. "About five more miles."

"Do you want me to book us on the ship, or will you take care of it?"

"I'll take care of it. We'll meet in the lobby tomorrow afternoon at two, and go together."

"Henry!" The radio crackled and he jumped. He didn't realize he had dozed off.

"Wha, what is it?"

"I've been calling you for five minutes. Where were you?"

"Guess I just dropped off for a few minutes. What have you got?"

"No news. Just checking in. No movement from the room. They had some food sent up a little while ago, otherwise, no activity."

"Okay. Thanks for the update." O'Brien walked to the window and looked out at the setting sun. This was going to be a long night.

Brent and Dave let themselves into the dark room. Two glasses of wine at dinner had given them enough of a buzz that they might get some sleep. Brent stumbled into the small bathroom and brushed his teeth, careful not to swallow the water. One thing he did not need was a case of Montezuma's revenge.

He collapsed on the lumpy mattress. The days of no rest caught up with him and he dropped into a deep dreamless sleep. Dave soon joined him, snoring noisily through swollen nasal membranes. The pollen count was up.

It was dark as she approached the small stream on the edge of town. She stopped the gelding and sat quietly as he slurped the cool water. Sliding down, she removed the jump rope and gave him a slap on the rump. "Thanks for the ride fella. You'd better head for home now before somebody misses you."

She watched with longing as he disappeared into the darkness. There went her ride. She wanted to set him loose here on the edge of town where she knew he would find his way back.

She found a small rooming house just inside the city limits. The family was sitting in the living room, laughing at some program on television. The man who answered her knock looked at her strangely. No wonder. She was wearing western clothing that was dirty and wrinkled. Her face was swollen and scabbed over from bug bites. The clothing hung loosely on her slim frame and dark hair dangled limply around a gaunt face. She smelled slightly of sour milk. But she spoke cultured and fluent Spanish.

"Do you take American dollars here?" she asked.

"Yes," he stammered in surprise. Money was money.

She swung the backpack off her shoulders, found her wallet at the bottom and paid for the night.

She did not care that the accommodations were less than five star. All she could see was that shower. She stood under it for thirty minutes, feeling the water splash on her face, run down her back and soothe her aching muscles. She didn't even bother to dry off as she stumbled naked across the room, collapsed onto the narrow bed and fell asleep.

CHAPTER 17

"Henry!"

"What is it?" O'Brien said as he jumped up from the couch, almost spilling a cold cup of coffee.

"The bellboy just arrived and he's taking a truckload of baggage out of the room."

"What time is it?" O'Brien looked around for his watch. He didn't remember taking it off, but then, he didn't remember much of the night before. His fatigue had finally caught up with him just before dawn and he'd dropped off into a deep drooling sleep on the couch.

"It's ten 'til ten. Wow! I've never seen so much stuff. Looks like they're planning to be gone for a while! The way the guy was wrestling with one of those trunks it looked like it weighed a couple hundred pounds!"

O'Brien ran his fingers through his stiff hair. God, I need a bath, he thought. "Okay. I'm going to splash through the shower. Call me back in fifteen minutes with an update."

A rooster was crowing. For a moment, she was back on the ranch. Opening her eyes slowly, she focused on the room. Her head throbbed and she'd have given anything for an aspirin and a glass of red wine. Her back ached from the soft bed, but it was better than sleeping on the ground.

Crawling out of the rumpled covers, she walked stiffly across the room and looked in the mirror. She hadn't bothered to comb out her hair after the shower and it was sticking out in all directions. The swelling in her face had gone down but there were scabs all over her cheeks, forehead and neck where she'd scratched bites until they bled. Her fingernails were broken and dirty. Self-consciously, she rubbed her raw hands together and wished she had some lotion. No need to worry about that five pounds any more, she thought, looking at her gaunt figure. At this rate, she'd be trying to gain a few before it was over.

Her grumbling stomach reminded her that she hadn't had much to eat in the last couple of days. Rooting through her backpack, she found a comb and tamed the frazzled hair. Then she went to find food.

A short distance down the narrow cobbled thoroughfare she spotted a vendor selling papayas that had been peeled, placed on a stick and scored so they resembled an orange-colored pineapple. She gave him a dollar bill and he looked at it blankly. She would have to exchange some money. After handing the bill back and forth a few times, the guy finally gave up and gave her the papaya after squeezing lime juice on it and sprinkling it with chili powder. She thanked him as she bit into the sweet sticky fruit. Fragrant juice ran down her chin and dripped on the front of her soiled shirt. She didn't care. The papaya disappeared quickly and now that she felt better, she looked for a phone. Stopping a pedestrian, she asked directions. He thought a moment, scratched his head and pointed to some towering American hotels six blocks away.

The morning air smelled fresh in spite of the heavy traffic and she felt her spirits lift as she set out toward the convention area.

Going through the double glass doors of the Caracas Hilton, she was almost run over by a heavily-laden bellboy. He was carrying one large suitcase under an arm and another hung from the handle gripped in his hand on the same side. Behind him he pulled a brass cart with a large trunk on it. She dodged out of his way and nearly ran into the chest of a doorman as he blocked her entrance He wore an impressive burgundy-colored uniform and his helmet-like hat had a shimmering gold tassel that swayed gracefully as he shook his head from side to side. His arms were folded in front of his chest.

"I need to use the phone, Señor," she said.

"This is an exclusive hotel," he returned with a scowl. "Go find a phone somewhere else."

She looked down at the rough dirty garments. The ragged shorts hung to just above her knees and the skin on her legs was dry and flaky. The lightweight black boots came up to her ankles. She knew she looked pretty bad "I'm an Americano," she said, taking her pack from her back and grabbing her wallet. "See, US dollars." She held it up and was pleased to see she had his attention now. Selecting a twenty, she held it out. "See?"

He took the bill and examined it suspiciously.

"Why don't you keep it?" she asked. "Consider it payment for use of the phone."

"Be quick." He turned on his heel as the bill disappeared into his pocket. "I do not want you hanging around here any longer than necessary!"

"Si Señor!" She made for the row of phones on the far wall. She was glad they had decided to pay the price for that International 800 number. It was coming in handy.

"Annette!" she almost shouted at the sound of her friend's voice. "It's Jen!"

Annette was in the middle of working a flight and other phones were ringing furiously. "Jen! Just a second." She put the others on hold. "Okay, here I am!. Where are you?"

" In Caracas. Have you seen the Peep?"

"Yes, she's with Brent's mom. Your folks have come down and they're very upset about everything. Your dad's been camped out at the office for the last two days and your mom's been distracting Peeper so she won't worry. You okay?"

"Yeah, I've had quite an adventure. Now I'm just trying to track down Brent so we can come home together. The Lear is disabled. I need to get a couple of tires and a plane to fly some fuel into a small strip up in the highlands for repairs. It's going to be a real chore getting it out. Have you talked to him?"

"I haven't talked to him myself, but the service said he called last night. I was in the middle of a family crisis and they couldn't reach me. I guess they screwed up the message I left that you would meet him in Caracas and he left you the message that he would meet you on the Pacifico Azul. Do you know anything about that?"

"All I know is it's a big cruise ship. They go through the Panama Canal and up through the Mexican Riviera. Why would I meet him on a cruise ship?"

"No idea," Annette said. "I thought it was a little strange, myself. But they insist that's what he said."

"This isn't exactly the best time for a vacation. Will you be talking to him again?"

"I don't know. If you're in Caracas, can't you go down to the harbor and intercept them when they get on the ship?"

"Them?"

"Oh, you didn't know? Dave is there with him."

"Dave? What's Dave doing down here?"

"When you turned up missing, Dave went with him to Mexico to try to figure out what happened. They've been looking for you!"

"Well, if you talk to him, tell him I'm all right and that I'll meet them in front of the ship. When does it leave?"

"I don't know, but I can call a travel agent here and find out. Call me back in a little bit?"

"Yeah. Find out what you can. I've got to get some clothes and some money exchanged. I'll call back in an hour." She looked at her watch and noted the time. Ten thirty-five AM.

"In the meantime, maybe Brent will call again."

"Thanks, Annette." She hung up and, spotting a boutique, went to find some clothes.

II

The phone rang as she stepped out of the shower. "Annaliza?" he said carefully. "Did you sleep well?"

"Yes. Were you able to get accommodations?"

There was a slight pause. "Yes, but I have some good news and some bad news."

She wasn't in the mood for games. "Yes?"

"The good news is, all they had left was first class."

"Yes?"

"The bad news is, they only had one cabin left." The response he expected never materialized. After a few moments of silence, he asked, "Annaliza, are you still there?"

"Yes, I'm still here."

"Is, is that okay? I mean, I don't see that we have a lot of options."

She was trying to be professional. After all, it was just two customs inspectors sharing accommodations while working on a case.

"Annaliza?"

She was not a believer in love at first sight, but the rope around her heart was starting to choke. She longed to feel the muscles of his arms as they wrapped her in his warm embrace. She could still picture him bursting through that door, shouting orders, and feel the strong grip of his hand on her elbow as he steered her into the darkness. Into the darkness. Into his arms. Into her heart. She shook her head.

"Yes, Royce. That's fine."

He sighed with relief. "The ship sails at four PM. I'll be by to pick you up at two."

She swallowed. "I'll be ready."

II

The travel alarm beeping woke him up abruptly and he sat upright in the bed. Dave rolled over and pulled the pillow over his head. "That sounds like a garbage truck backing up! For God's sake, turn the damn thing off!"

Brent fumbled around on the night stand and smacked at the small object until it was silenced. He flopped back into bed and closed his eyes, not ready to start the day.

"What time is it?" Dave asked.

"Ten."

"Wow! Looks like we slept round the clock."

"Yeah, we'd better get going. I want to be on that ship early so I can look for Jennifer!"

"Wait, wait. I don't like to squash your optimism, but it may not be that easy. We figure she's still in King's custody, so you're going to have to get by him first. Besides, they've forbidden us to interfere with that investigation!"

"I don't give a rat's ass about their investigation. If I can find Jennifer, I'm going to do what I can to get her back, no matter what. We might be able to get her before the ship sails. That would certainly make things easier!"

"Well, buddy, I hope you're right. Wish I was as optimistic."

"What time is it now?"

Dave looked at his watch. "Ten thirty."

Brent jumped up and started throwing things into his bag. "Come on Dave. I don't think I can stand this place any longer. Let's get something to eat and head down to the harbor. Once we get on the boat, there'll be something we can do."

"Wait, why don't you try Annette again and see if she's heard anything."

Brent picked up the filthy receiver and after the usual language problems, was able to find an English-speaking operator. He gave her the 800 number. The line was busy. He slammed down the phone in frustration. "Who could she be talking to now?"

"Hey, take it easy. They're probably working a trip. Try again from the cruise ship terminal."

The air inside the trunk was close and stale. He felt himself being picked up and wished he could work the gag free so he could yell for help but, for now, he could only grunt. Hearing the traffic noise, he figured they had left for the harbor. Soon the strong smell of salty humid air and fish seeped into the trunk and he could hear the shouting dock workers as the trunk was swung onto a conveyor to be loaded with the rest of the baggage. He was sweating and his thirst was maddening. A terrible way to end his life, he thought.

The clothes were beautiful, but expensive. The sales clerk eyed her oddly and thought about throwing her out but as soon as the young woman handed her a credit card and started fingering the clothing, she sensed a commission.

Jennifer moved through the shop admiring the classic garments. In the children's section at the back there were pink frocks with crinolines and ribbons, black patent leather shoes and white straw hats with big bows in the back. Across the room was a fiesta dress with cutout lace and embroidered flowers on the skirt. A ruffle flounced across the shoulders. She could picture the Peep in this outfit. Standing before the little dress, she was suddenly overcome with loneliness and a craving for her family like she'd never felt. This was the first opportunity she'd had to concentrate on something besides staying alive, so she squeezed her eyes tightly shut to dam the tears and returned to the adult clothing. If she was to find Brent and get home, she had to stay focused.

After looking at everything in the shop, she settled for a simple white cotton blouse and a colorful gathered skirt that fell to her ankles. She bought several pair of underwear, a couple of bras and laid a pair of brown leather sandals on top of the pile on the counter. Then she added a pair of light blue cotton slacks and a T-shirt. "May I change here?" she asked the saleslady as she ran the credit card. The woman nodded and smiled as she handed her the package. Jen couldn't wait to get into some clean clothes. No wonder they didn't want her in this place!

She pulled the shirt off and dropped it into a small trash can in the dressing room. The shorts followed. Then she changed into the beautiful skirt and blouse, pulling the colorful belt snugly around her shrunken waist. After removing the boots, she dropped them in her back pack and slipped on the cool sandals. Relief, at last.

She whisked out of the boutique, humming under her breath. She stopped at a nearby shop and looked in the window longingly. Small amber bottles of perfume glinted in the bright lights. What the hell, she thought.

Inside, she grabbed a bottle of her favorite scent, a lipstick, a fingernail file and a large bottle of moisturizing lotion and piled them on the counter with her credit card. On her way to the bathroom for a needed makeover, she felt better already.

Twenty minutes later, she was back at a phone. Annette picked up the receiver on the second ring. "L/D Aerospace."

"Hi, Annette. Jen again."

"Jen! I spoke to the travel agent a few minutes ago. The Pacifico Azul is sailing today at four. They're not supposed to give out passenger information but the agent's a friend of mine and I was able to find out that Brent is registered in a first class cabin. She wouldn't tell me any more than that."

"Wow!" It was almost noon. "I'd better get down there if I'm going to intercept them! Thanks a million, Annette. I'll call if anything else comes up."

She hurried to the front desk, exchanged some money for the local currency and asked the man at the desk for the best way to get to the Pacifico Azul. He called a cab and she stepped past the towering doorman to the front steps.

"Señora." He bowed and held out his hand. She smiled as she remembered the other reception. The cab screeched to a halt and she jumped in, instructed the driver and leaned back to relax during the forty minute drive.

Henry O'Brien faced a tough decision. He was going to have to split up his team. He hated to do that but they might need the chopper. After selecting six men to accompany him on the ship, he sent the other two on to Acapulco in the Blackhawk. They would rendezvous there when the ship arrived four days later. Maybe King would be in custody by then. Meanwhile, at least some of his team would be getting a little R and R on the beaches of Southern Mexico.

The selected team members piled into a taxi and headed for the harbor. The limo had departed a half hour ago and the helicopter was already hovering overhead, insuring that the waterfront was the destination. As the taxi pulled up in front of the ship's loading ramp, O'Brien gave the guys in the chopper final instructions over the radio and released them to Acapulco. His stomach gave a lurch as he saw the black dot become smaller on the horizon. He hoped he hadn't acted too soon.

Brent and Dave were at the terminal within an hour. It took a while to find a pay phone, work through the operator and put through the call to the office. A busy signal. Brent slammed down the receiver and looked at his watch. Eleven forty. For all he knew, Jennifer was already on the ship. That was the plan. Why were they wasting time trying to call the office? He had a gut feeling she was close by.

Although they were early, there was already a line. When they finally stepped up the gang plank, he relaxed. The purser gave them a map of the ship with directions to their cabin. Champagne was being served in the ballroom. Musicians were playing and there was a holiday atmosphere. Brent felt his spirits lift. He felt the closest he'd been to Jen since this all started. Now if they only knew what room King was in.

Juan Carlos had bribed the right people and was allowed to board the ship through a service entrance on the side. Crowds always made him nervous. You never could tell when a knife-wielding assassin would slip up on you, cut your liver out and be gone before anyone noticed. He couldn't be too careful.

His cabin was a suite of two bedrooms with a palatial living room set between. A wet bar on one end was well stocked with liquor. Two small port holes revealed a scrap of water and a bit of sky, little else. The luggage had arrived earlier. Suitcases were unpacked, clothing hung in the closets. The two trunks were stacked in Grog's quarters and Juan Carlos gave little thought to his captive as he sipped the refreshing room service lemonade. To him, King was already dead, another casualty of his personal war. He would have to figure out another way to find the informer.

O'Brien had been busy. The first order of business was surveillance for the druggie's room. That had been easy enough. The tiny lenses on their cameras were easy to hide. Next, he was able to use his authority to obtain a position in the kitchen for one of his men. In this way, they had a good excuse to be in the room and speak to the occupants. The agent had just delivered iced lemonade to the room. He had not seen King. This had O'Brien a little nervous. King had not been seen since he went by in the limo outside the villa. They had maintained constant surveillance since then and he was sure if King had left the company of Lopez, they would have known it. Still, it would have made him feel better if his agent had actually seen him in the room.

He unwrapped a fresh cigar. One advantage of being in South America was good Cuban cigars. In the States, he had to rely on the black market. Guilt niggled him, but not for long. A man needed a good cigar.

CHAPTER 18

Jen had been pacing in front of the cruise ship terminal for over an hour. As she looked at her watch for the twentieth time, she silently cursed her punctual husband. Why did he always have to be early? If he had been. She approached the purser once, hoping he would let her board the ship to look. But he merely looked down his beaky nose and informed the Señora that no one boarded without a ticket. The rascal wouldn't even take a bribe!

It was fifteen minutes to four. The all-aboard preparation to depart whistle had already sounded and passengers were lining the rails, waving to loved ones and tossing confetti. A band played a rousing Venezuelan folk dance and everyone was in a party mood. Her eyes frantically scanned the faces lining the rail. No Brent. No Dave. What was she going to do?

As she turned to look through the crowd, she saw a truck parked along the dock. Two men were hurriedly unloading boxes of provisions into the side entrance. She ran down to the dock and cautiously peered around the truck. The sounds of a busy kitchen could be heard as dishes clanked, water sloshed and someone shouted orders.

On an impulse, she picked up one of the boxes and started through the door. She almost ran into one of the workers rushing out for another load. Their eyes locked for a moment but for reasons she couldn't fathom, he grunted and hurried on to the truck for another carton. She entered the busy kitchen, dumped the box on the nearest counter and looked around. It was like an ant pile in a rain storm. Workers were running back and forth in every direction, sweating in the heat from the ovens and cursing as they bumped into each other. It didn't take long to make her decision. No one could recognize a stranger in this melee. She threw her back pack under a counter and grabbed a white apron.

As she moved to a sink, picked up a carrot and started peeling it, the final whistle blew and the service door clanked shut. Nobody seemed to notice. They had a lot of work to do to prepare the lavish dinner they'd be serving tonight.

She frantically tried to come up with a plan. It looked like she was committed, like it or not. She hoped Annette was right. If Brent was on this ship, she was going to find him!

A short, red faced man with fat cheeks and a bushy mustache started shouting incomprehensibly to her. It took a moment, but she realized he was speaking

Portuguese. Wide eyed, she looked down at the carrot and continued peeling. This seemed to make him more angry. Grabbing the carrot from her hand, he waved it around in the air and pushed at her. Confused, she looked around to see if anybody was watching. It was obviously a common event, as all the workers within earshot were ignoring him.

He pushed her toward a doorway and she figured out he wanted her to get something.

Stepping through the arched metal door, she peered around a dark, cool store room. Strangely the shouting man retreated, giving her a moment to let her eyes adjust. There were sacks of flour and sugar among gallon jugs of molasses and maple syrup. Towers of neatly stacked canned goods in cartons stood beside bags of every kind of rice and pasta imaginable She decided this would be a perfect hiding place until she could escape the red faced man in the chef's hat and go looking for Brent.

She pulled some sacks of flour and sugar around, and made a reasonable blockade and a fairly soft bed. Maybe she wouldn't be missed.

Annaliza looked around the small cabin. Somehow when he'd said first class, she had expected something bigger. At least there were two separate compartments, a sitting room and a bedroom with a double bed. He was unpacking his clothes.

"I'll flip you for the bed," she said.

He didn't turn around. "That's okay. I'll take the couch. I don't mind. Besides, one of us will be spending a lot of time in O'Brien's cabin monitoring the bugs. With any luck, we won't have to spend too much time together."

He was certainly being understanding. He had been courteous when he picked her up and on the long drive to the harbor. Almost too courteous. She wished he would grab her and crush her to him, forcing her to forget about convention and allow them to explore their feelings for one another.

"Do you want me to take the first shift?" He turned and leveled a cool gaze in her direction.

Flustered, she replied, "No, I mean, why don't you get some rest. I'll go first." She grabbed her clutch and pushed through the door, hoping to escape before he saw her tears.

Juan Carlos leaned back in the recliner and closed his eyes. The ship was moving slowly and they wouldn't extend the stabilizers until cruising speed. That was hours away. Until then, the rolling was going to be uncomfortable. The lemonade helped settle his stomach but it was still going to be a rough couple of hours.

"Grog." As usual, he was at his side instantly and he patiently awaited the expected command. "Have you made contact with D'Orino?"

"Uhh."

"When does he want to transfer the merchandise and funds?"

"Tomorrow night."

"Where will we meet?"

"Engine room."

"Is our privacy assured?"

"Your privacy is assured."

"Does he have the money?"

"Argh."

"Bring me the wine, Grog."

He disappeared into his quarters and returned with a silver zero case. Opening it, Juan Carlos carefully lifted out the bottle. Shaking it slightly, he heard the stone clink softly against the side. He smiled crookedly. It was so easy. The movement of his lips caused a dribble of saliva to escape and he reached up with his handkerchief to dab it away. "So, my pretty," he addressed the wine. "We will soon part. What a shame. It has been a very satisfactory relationship." He cackled softly in the closest thing he ever came to a laugh.

Carefully placing the bottle on the table next to the recliner, he got up to go to the bedroom. "I'm going to lie down for a few minutes, Grog." Thumping the trunk on his way, he threw over his shoulder. "Make sure our extra baggage has been disposed of before tomorrow night."

"Argh."

Since the surveillance cameras were outside the door, Annaliza could not see the exchange. But she heard it. Clicking off the recorder, she rewound the tape and listened. It sounded like he was talking to someone besides the goon in the room. A woman? Lopez had been under almost constant surveillance the past two days. And he had not been accompanied by a woman. She was puzzled.

Grabbing a phone, she dialed her cabin. Sparks sounded sleepy as he answered.

"Royce, "she said excitedly. "Listen, I just heard a conversation between Lopez and his ape that might mean something. Come down here right away."

Sparks sat up in the bed and ran his fingers through his hair. "Have you figured out how they're moving the diamonds?"

"No, but there's going to be some sort of transfer between Lopez and a guy named D'Orino tomorrow night in the engine room."

"D'Orino's the one they identified as the fence in Cabo! I wonder why he's on this ship? I wouldn't expect him to meet Lopez until Baja!"

"There's something else that's got me puzzled. Get on down and listen to this tape."

"Be right there."

Dave leaned back in his chair, patted his stomach and belched. "That's what I like the best about a cruise, the food."

"Dave, you're disgusting. This is supposed to be a formal dinner. Brent looked around at the well-dressed couples in the dining room. They'd managed to get a private table, almost unheard of on a cruise. Usually, you were expected to share a table with four, eight, even ten other couples. "I do admit, though, that was good. First decent meal we've had in days."

Dave scanned the room as he had done a hundred times already this evening. "Seen anybody we know?"

"No one. Not King, not Lopez, not even any of the Feds. Wonder what they're up to?"

"I don't know, but I'd give my eye teeth to find out."

"Do you still have your FM receiver?"

"Sure do." Dave pulled it out of his pocket and passed it to his friend.

"Think we could bug the Fed's phone?"

"I doubt it. I had the impression there was going to be somebody in the room around the clock. Since we haven't seen any of them around here, I imagine they're holed up in their cabin doing their spy thing."

"Feel like taking a walk? I'd like to cover every inch of this ship. Maybe we'll stumble onto something."

"Yeah, I could stand a walk. I feel like I've just swallowed a basketball."

Jen bolted awake and quickly brushed the flour off her clothes. The dust made her sneeze as she made her way to the kitchen and quietly peered in.

The frantic rush of a few hours before had slowed but there was still activity. With six meals and an unending supply of snacks to prepare, the kitchen was rarely idle.

Slipping inside, she swung her backpack over her shoulder, keeping the apron on until she reached the steps that led to the upper decks. Then she slipped it over her head, rolled it into a ball and tossed it into a corner.

Couples in evening wear strolled the decks, faces close, sharing kisses and secrets. She had to swallow a lump in her throat as she thought about how much she missed her husband. But back to reality. She would spend the night moving around the ship, mentally mapping everything. The first destination was First Class but it might take her all night to figure out where it was. She thought about simply asking someone for directions but it might look strange if someone didn't know how to find their own cabin at this late date. Thank goodness she had new clothes!

As she reached the Promenade deck she stepped out into the balmy Caribbean air, drew deep breaths and reveled at being alive. Walking to the rail, she admired the golden ray of light dancing on the gentle swells under a full moon. Although it was late, a few couples were strolling the decks but none of them noticed her solitary figure.

Grog looked at his watch. Two AM. This had to be the quietest time of the night. Anybody still up would either be in the Casinos or too drunk to notice.

He opened the door and scanned the hall. All clear. Heaving the heavy trunk onto his back and holding it with one hand over his head, he made his way down the narrow hallway toward the Promenade deck.

O'Brien sat up as he saw the door open. He watched as the Neanderthal character with a large object on his back looked up and down the hall, then headed for the Promenade deck.

"Al, come here." He motioned to Netts.

The older man looked over his shoulder. " I'll be damned. I wonder what that character is up to now? What's in that trunk?"

"Don't know. You'd better grab Peterson and hustle up there to take a look."

"I'm on my way."

Jennifer heard the door behind her open and turned around just in time to see a burly character wrestling with a trunk, trying to get it through the door. She was partially behind a life raft and he didn't notice her as he pulled the thing across the deck and propped it on the rails. Curious, she moved forward, careful to stay in the shadows.

He had his back to her and was struggling with the heavy trunk, trying to heave it over the rail.

"What are you doing?" she heard herself ask. The last thing she expected to see on a cruise ship was somebody trying to throw a trunk over the rail in the middle of the night.

He whirled around, momentarily losing his balance. The voice from the shadows had startled him. He still had a grip on the trunk and he balanced it on the rail as he stared in her direction.

Was the moonlight playing tricks? Maybe it was fatigue or the culmination of days of uncertainty. Whatever the reason it looked like a grotesque, hairy beast. She let out a scream and became rooted to the deck, feet refusing to move.

Grog was taken by surprise. Physical combat he could handle but a screaming woman was beyond the abilities of his limited intellect. He had to move quickly. He turned and ducked through the door, his foot steps echoing off the steel walls.

The trunk teetered on the rail. But she was still unable to move, frozen in place by shock and surprise.

It seemed she stood there for an hour although it was seconds. As she watched the trunk, it appeared to move in slow motion, such was the state of her mind. She knew it was going over the edge, taking its mysterious cargo it into the blue depths of the Caribbean. Then it happened.

The ship had been swaying since leaving port. During the night, the swells had increased in depth, the aftermath of a minor tropical storm in the eastern Caribbean. Just as the trunk leaned toward the ocean, the ship lurched suddenly toward the starboard side. Her stabilizers were still retracted as the straining engines thumped on, trying to achieve an optimum cruising speed. She was susceptible to the increasing swell. The sudden movement was just enough to tilt the trunk in the opposite direction and it crashed to the deck. Jen was thrown to the steel surface, skinning her elbows and knees.

As the ship righted itself, it took her a moment to stand. Holding her stomach to fend off the wave of nausea, she grabbed for something to give her balance and looked at where the trunk had fallen. She was astonished to see a pair of boots sticking out the end that had smashed on impact.

"Oh my God!" she said, hand over mouth. Running over she cleared away the debris and looked inside. Starring back at her from sunken sockets were a pair of gray eyes. Under the eyes was a strip of gray duct tape. James Dover King!

As he moved weakly, she peeled the tape off his mouth.

"Ouch!" he yelled. "Jennifer! Untie me! Quick!"

Pulling her Swiss Army knife from her pack, she unfolded the large blade and sawed at the bonds around his wrists. As he yanked his hands free, he reached down to untie the ankle bindings.

She helped him to his feet but there was no time for questions. They heard running feet and saw two dark figures bearing down on them.

"Come on." She quickly put an arm around his waist to give him support. "We've gotta get outta here!"

Netts and Peterson were amazed at the sight. The girl was helping King through a door. As they moved quickly into the dim hallway, they were faced with three choices. The main hallway they had entered was bisected by another taking off at right angles in two different directions They looked at each other. Three directions, two guys. It was impossible to tell which direction they'd gone as the echoes bounced around their ears, confusing their sense of direction.

Netts took command. "You take the left, I'll go straight," he said, slapping his friend lightly on the shoulder and taking off down the hall.

Jennifer heard the pursuing footsteps and knew she had to come up with a plan. The hallway was lined with cabin doors. Jen tried one and found it locked. She tried the next and the next, her heart sinking as she heard the footsteps closing in on them.

Finally, the fifth door yielded and she fell into the cabin, yanking him in behind her and shutting the door firmly. As the door clicked, the cabin lights flashed on. A startled couple sat up in their bed, staring with unbelieving eyes.

Both parties were speechless as the slim, dark-haired woman in the long skirt and the gaunt, hollow-eyed apparition beside her slumped back against the door.

Jen finally broke the stunned silence. "Could we get a drink of water?" she asked cautiously, moving toward the bathroom. The couple remained frozen as Jen grabbed a pitcher of water and handed it to the man who gulped the contents and begged for more in a hoarse whisper.

"That's enough," she said after the second. "You'll make yourself sick!"

Thanking the couple, they backed out the door. She'd heard footsteps pass shortly after they had entered the cabin and felt they were safe for now.

Three doors down, they found an elevator and she punched the down button.

"Where are we going?" he whispered.

"The ship's levels are labeled by letter, A is the top deck and it goes down from there. We need to go to U deck."

"What's on U deck.?"

"A good hiding place."

The doors slid open quietly. They stepped in and it smoothly started its descent.

But after several seconds, it bumped to a stop and the doors swooshed open to reveal a large woman bent over in drunken laughter. Jen held the open button and gazed at the figure. Her hair was flaming red teased and sprayed until it capped her head in a varnished helmet. She was wearing a bright orange muumuu, not the right color to go with the hair. One of the flat soled shoes had a yawning hole in the side from which protruded a large bunion. Tears of mirth slid down her cheeks, leaving a trail of black mascara. Purple eye shadow extended to black penciled brows.

"Is this U?" Jen asked, uncertain.

The woman's face puckered up and she managed to choke, "Yeah, this is me," before collapsing into another state of hysterics.

Jen released the button and the elevator continued its descent.

"Why don't you just push the button marked "U"?" he said dryly.

"Haven't lost your smart mouth, I see."

He smiled, grateful to be standing in this elevator bantering instead of sinking to the bottom of the ocean.

They reached U deck without incident and she led him through the labyrinth to the kitchen. A single pastry chef was on the far side, her back to them, preparing the morning's buffet.

Jen placed a finger to her lips and motioned for him to follow her. They eased across the deserted kitchen and slipped into the store room. She led him to the flour and sugar fortress where they both collapsed.

"I could just kiss you, Jenny," he said gratefully.

CHAPTER 19

Antonio D'Orino was used to getting his way. He never expected the deal he'd made with Lopez to get this far. Where was King? After all the trouble he'd gone through to get him to steal the rock so he wouldn't have to pay for it, King had disappeared and he was strapped with a whining kid.

Just before boarding the ship he'd talked with the bad choice he'd left to guard her on the boat. The connection was scratchy and he'd had to have his office in Cabo patch him through on a radio telephone to the ship in the harbor.

"Yeah, boss," he heard through the static.

"Have you heard from King?"

"No, boss, I ain't heard nothing. You want me to start cutting off the kid's fingers?"

"Naw, that won't do us any good! I have to meet with Lopez tomorrow night for the transfer. King has until then to get his hands on the rock. If you haven't heard from me by midnight tomorrow, waste the kid."

"How you want me to do the job, boss?"

"I don't care!" he growled. "Handle it. It's just a kid, for God's sake!"

The static increased and he didn't hear the reply. Slamming down the phone with disgust, he cursed all the incompetents in the world.

Now he lay in his dark cabin, sleepless. The ship was still rolling, and he felt his stomach grumble.

His thin lips were pursed tightly as he thought of the exchange. One billion! What rock was worth one billion bucks? The last several years had taught him money was no object for the right stone. Besides, this one had a legend. A legend of power and mystery. He smiled to himself. Sometimes power was worth more than money! After all, wasn't that what most people bought with money?

His smuggling ring had advanced his position in the "family". A lot of men owed him favors. And a lot more would owe him before it was over.

Want a politician? Snap your fingers. Get rid of one? Snap your fingers. Kill a man? Snap your fingers. Kill a little girl?

He sat up and swung his legs over the side of the bed, pausing to get his balance before heading for the liquor cabinet. Grabbing a bottle by the neck, he poured a straight whiskey and raised it in a silent toast to himself. You're going to be mine tomorrow, he thought. The whiskey was tossed in a single gulp. One way or another.

"Hey, kid!" He nudged her with his foot.

It took her a moment to fight out of the black void. She struggled for consciousness and slowly opened her eyes. Everything was spinning.

"I thought you was still with us!" he cackled. "But not for long! Your Daddy don't deliver the goods, you is shark food! Here fishy fishy," he sang in a high voice as he turned to leave. "Supper time!"

"Here!" Annaliza said as she rewound the tape. "Listen to this."

Sparks had arrived a few minutes before. Together with O'Brien, they leaned expectantly toward the tape recorder.

As Annaliza played back the exchange between Lopez and Grog, Sparks looked puzzled. "That doesn't make sense," he said as she turned off the recorder.

"Didn't it sound like he was talking to a woman?" Annaliza asked, studying his face.

"What doesn't make sense is his request for wine. According to his dossier, he's a conspicuous non-drinker."

They were quiet for a moment, O'Brien's cigar bobbing in front of his face as he pondered the mystery. "So you all are trying to figure how they're transporting the diamonds from South Africa to the US?"

"If we solve that puzzle," Sparks replied, "we can nail them at the border. So far we have who and what, but not how."

"They make wine in South Africa?"

Sparks and Annaliza looked at each other. "Of course!" he said. "It's simple! The diamonds are in the wine! With a dark red wine and green bottle, you'd never see them!"

"How can we be sure?" Annaliza asked.

"We're going to crash their little party tomorrow night."

"If they know we're on to them, they'll never let themselves be caught at the border! That's the only place we have jurisdiction to make arrests!"

"I know. That's why we'll watch the exchange from a safe place. I think it's safe to let the HAT-TRIC team track down King and make the arrest. You with us, Henry?" Sparks turned to O'Brien.

"Wouldn't miss it for anything."

Suddenly, Netts and Peterson burst into the room. "Henry! We've found King and the girl!"

"You're kidding. Where?"

"You're not going to believe this. King was in that trunk the goon wrestled out of Lopez' room a little while ago. Seems he was going to go for a little swim!"

O'Brien's eyes opened in surprise and he stopped chomping momentarily. "They tried to kill him?"

"We didn't see the whole thing, but it seems the girl stepped in and broke up the party. She helped him get away."

"The girl? Where in tarnation did the girl come from?" The cigar was disappearing rapidly.

"Don't know, Henry. But she was definitely helping him. He wasn't tracking too good!"

"Where'd they go?"

"We lost them. They disappeared down a dark hallway. Could be anywhere on the ship."

O'Brien turned to Sparks. "Looks like our boy is not too popular with Lopez. Think he'll be at the party tomorrow?"

"I'll bet you a box of good Cuban cigars he will!"

O'Brien laughed. "That's one bet I'm not going to make!"

"So, I take it you didn't get the diamond?"

She was sitting on a flour sack, leaning toward him, dark eyes flashing in the dim light.

"No diamond. Lopez overpowered me and took me prisoner. They tried to beat information out of me but I wouldn't talk."

"That's why Lopez decided to make fish food out of you?"

"Yeah." He picked up a raw potato and rubbed it against his pants before taking a bite.

"You have a plan?"

"I thought I was dead so I haven't been thinking much about the future."

"What about Kristen?"

He stopped chewing. "I heard most of their conversations while I was in that trunk so I'm privy to their plans. The diamond transfer is going to take place tomorrow night. I've got to get my hands on it before then!"

"Do you know where it is?"

"Yes. In a bottle of South African red wine."

"And where is this bottle?"

"When I saw it, it was sitting on a table."

"Isn't he worried about it being stolen?"

"Lopez is clever. He knows humans generally overlook the obvious."

"It sounds like you and Lopez have met before."

"We have. In another lifetime." He paused. "Did you find your phone?"

"Yes," she said, getting up and arching her back, hands on hips, to work the kinks out. "But I seem to have lost my husband."

"What are you doing on this ship?"

"For some reason my husband and his best friend are on this ship. He left a message for me to meet him here, but didn't say where. The only information I have is that they're in a First Class cabin. I was looking for them when I stumbled on you and your friend."

"Why in the middle of the night? Couldn't you just have them page him?"

"I'm afraid I'm a stowaway."

"What? The virtuous Jennifer Duncan doing something dishonest?"

"I was desperate."

"Ahh," he replied, getting up stiffly and stabbing another potato with his knife. "Seems we have something in common. But I know where the First Class cabins are. Interested in trading services?"

"Does this mean you're no longer demanding my services at knife point?"

He grinned and wiped the knife on his pants leg before handing it to her, handle first. "If you'll help me get the diamond, I'll help you find your husband."

"I'm not into stealing. I'll find my husband by myself."

He put his hands on her shoulders. "Jenny, please. I'm asking you as the mother of a little girl. Please. I need your help to get Lopez out of his cabin."

She looked into the sunken gray eyes and thought of the child. "Okay. What do you want me to do?"

Annaliza was asleep in front of the monitor. It was now the early hours of the morning and there wasn't much going on. Royce walked across the dim room and looked down at her. The swelling around her eye had gone down. Asleep, she looked peaceful. When awake, she always had that hunted look about her, as if she had to constantly keep up a guard, not let anyone too close. He wondered if she had been hurt, as he had.

He went into one of the bedrooms to find a blanket. O'Brien was sprawled across the bed, fully clothed. Sparks eased around the bed and opened the chest of drawers. They were empty. He finally found some blankets in the closet on the top shelf and carried one back into the sitting room. Gently, he picked her up and moved her to the couch. He spread the blanket over her and leaned down and kissed her on the cheek. "Good night Annaliza."

CHAPTER 20

The morning dawned with a brilliant show over the western Caribbean. The sun cast streaks of gold across the indigo water and the air tasted tangy and felt soft against the skin.

Tourists were already at the rail, straining to see the distant shore of Panama, anxious for a ring side seat at the crossing of the Panama Canal. They whispered to each other, intimidated in the early morning light. Colorful cotton garments flapped in the gentle breeze.

Brent and Dave had risen early after a fitful night's sleep and on the deck, they scanned the crowd for a familiar face. Brent was edgy.

"What are we going to do, Dave? I thought it would be easy to find her once we got on the ship."

"It's a big ship. You're just going to have to be patient. We've still got eight more days before we reach Cabo."

"Yeah, but only three more before Acapulco. Any port is an opportunity for them to take Jen off the ship. We've got to find them before then."

"Since there is no way they're going to release information about passenger cabins, the only way I see to find them is to keep walking and hope for the best. I don't see how they can stay in their cabin the whole time. They've got to eat."

"How about room service?"

"That's a point."

"Do you think we're right about her being here?"

"I guess there's a possibility she's not, but it still seems our best bet, based on what we know so far."

"The fact that the Feds are on this boat makes me think we may be close. Damn! I wish they'd share information with us! When we were tagging along with them, we were privy to a lot more facts. Seems like we've been floundering around ever since we left them." Brent turned to look at his friend who was staring blankly into the distance. Brent followed his gaze. A bronze bodied blonde with the briefest of bikinis was eyeing him. "Dave! Pay attention, for God's sake!" he said as he poked him in the ribs.

"What? What were you saying?"

"I said, pay attention. After we find Jen, you can have all the women you want. Until then, I need you!"

"Sorry, I'm just a little distracted this morning."

"I can see that. Come on, let's get going. We've got a lot of ship to cover."

Sparks was on his fourth cup of coffee. He'd just sat down in front of the screen when he saw movement and a woman stopped in front of Lopez' cabin. He sat up and leaned forward. It was Jennifer Duncan.

She looked up and down the hall, then knocked loudly on the door. Moments later and the Cro-Magnon equivalent was at the doorway and she was speaking to him in rapid Spanish. Sparks had to listen closely.

"Señor Lopez?"

"No, he is not to be disturbed."

"I come with a message from the Captain. There is a phone call."

"Can it be transferred to the cabin?"

"No, cabin phones are only for calls within the ship. This call is on the ship-to-shore radio. Tell Señor Lopez he must come quickly. The Captain cannot tie up the communication lines any longer than necessary."

Soon Lopez appeared at the door, buttoning his shirt and cursing. The hairy man accompanied him as he hurried down the hall.

Suddenly, King appeared with the girl. He expertly picked the lock and they were inside in seconds.

"Annaliza, wake up!" he called.

"What is it?"

"King and the girl just broke into Lopez' cabin. Go get Henry!"

She disappeared, and came back a few moments later with him in tow. His hair was sticking up and he was squinting in the bright light. "You have King?"

"Quiet." Sparks put a finger to his mouth as he listened to King and the girl.

King didn't have any trouble with the lock, but then breaking and entering was his business.

Jen couldn't believe how easy it was. There was the wine, setting on the table.

"Is that it?"

"That's it!"

"How can you be sure?" He picked it up and rocked it gently. "Hear that?"

"Can we go?"

"The sooner the better."

The three Feds watched as the pair reappeared in the door and then rushed down the hall with the bottle of wine.

"Well, I'll be damned. That son-of-a-bitch got the diamond after all!"

"We've got a bigger problem." Spark's face was wrinkled in a frown. "If Lopez doesn't have the diamond in his possession, the transfer won't take place tonight. All parties will be spooked and we'll have a hell of a time proving anything!" Suddenly, his face relaxed. "Annaliza, do they have South African wine on this ship?"

"I don't know, I can check. What label?"

He turned and rewound the tape and forwarded it to the frame that showed the bottle of wine in King's hand. Then he used the lap top computer to enlarge the picture.

Annaliza squinted at the monitor. "Got it!" she said and picked up the phone.

Sparks rushed for the door "I've got to get something out of my cabin. Be right back!"

Lopez wondered who could be calling him. He hoped it wasn't bad news from D'Orino. This deal was too important. Damn that Italian! He could visualize the bastard backing out at the last minute!

Grog moved in front of him as they approached the bridge. The officer looked questioningly as they approached. "I'm here for the phone call," Lopez said impatiently. "They sent for me."

The man looked at him blankly.

"Señor Lopez. My name is Señor Lopez. A girl came to get me for a phone call?"

The officer replied rapidly and Lopez realized he was speaking Portuguese. "For God's sake, find someone who can speak Spanish!" he shouted at the man.

The officer continued speaking as he pushed them away from the door. Grog was like a dog who felt his master threatened. He grabbed him, spinning him around until he had his right arm pinned to his back. Two ship's officers appeared and a fight broke out. Fists flew and Portuguese and Spanish curses split the air. Suddenly the Captain arrived and angrily shouted his men into order.

"What is this?" he shot at the Chief Petty Officer who was wiping blood from the corner of his mouth.

"These men were trying to force entry."

"What do they want?"

"We don't know, they speak only Spanish."

"Then find someone who speaks Spanish so we can find out what they want! You seem to forget these people are our guests! I want them treated with respect. Now offer them refreshments, make them comfortable and find an interpreter immediately!"

II

By the time Sparks returned Annaliza had ordered the bottle of South African wine from room service.

"Thank God they had the brand," Sparks remarked.

"What's this all about?" she asked.

"You'll see. Just be patient."

There was a knock on the door and there was the wine. The waiter held it up with a flourish and whipped a corkscrew out of his pocket.

"No, no!" Sparks jumped forward and grabbed the wine. "We can't open it!" He pressed a couple of bills into the man's hand and ushered him out the door. "Come on, Annaliza, we don't have much time!"

Sparks grabbed her hand and headed out the door.

Outside Lopez' cabin, he stopped and looked at her. "Shall we knock first to make sure they're not back?"

She tapped on the door. No answer.

"How are you at picking locks?" he asked.

"Criminology 101," she said, reaching for a hairpin.

Once inside, they looked around to get their bearings. From the conversations they'd overheard he figured the wine had been on the table.

He set the bottle down and reached into his pocket and pulled out a small brown paper parcel.

"What's that?" she asked, leaning closer. As the paper fell away, she drew in her breath and stared at the magnificent stone. "That looks like the Heart of Aphrodite! I read about it last month. Wasn't it stolen from a museum in Turkey?"

"Yes, it was. Cosgrove read that same article and sent this to me on a hunch that this was the stone causing all the fracas down here between King and Lopez."

"But, how did he get it?"

"This one is a fake."

She took it in her hands and held it to the light. "But we don't know for sure that this is Lopez' merchandise."

"We're just working on hunches here. A hunch that this is the stone. A hunch that they're transporting the diamond in the wine."

"I'd say the second one is accurate. Why would King break in here just to steal a bottle of wine?"

"Just one problem. How do we get this stone into that bottle?"

She looked helplessly at the large diamond in her hand. And how did they get the real diamond in their bottle in the first place?"

"Must have been placed in the bottle as it was blown. That's got to take some talent!"

"I have an idea, give me the bottle."

He handed her the wine. "Hurry, they'll be back any minute!"

She raised the bottle by the neck and cracked it against the side of the table, releasing the rich red fluid that spread like a pool of blood on the beige carpet. Then she dropped the pieces of the bottle on the floor next to the table.

"Annaliza! What are you doing?"

"Watch this." She placed the diamond in the middle of the pieces as if the bottle had fallen from the table, broken and released its precious cargo.

"You're brilliant! Come on, let's get out of here!" He laced his fingers with hers. "Thank you."

She squeezed his hand as they slipped through the door.

It didn't take long to find a Spanish interpreter for the strange pair waiting in the Captain's lounge. They were all scratching their heads. No one had sent for Señor Lopez. In fact, there had been no calls on the ship-to-shore radio. Perhaps the Señor was mistaken?

Juan Carlos stood up abruptly, knocking his chair over as he stalked toward the door. The startled ship's officers looked at each other, shrugged their shoulders and circled their ear with the end of an index finger. "Loco."

Juan Carlos Lopez was panting as he reached the cabin. His hand shook as he pulled the key out of his pocket and he dropped it once before finally forcing it into the lock and shoving the door open.

Sparks and Melendez watched with interest. "Looks like he's worried," she observed.

"Let's hope the little charade convinces him!"

They listened as the door slammed behind the two.

"Grog, the bottle! Where is the bottle?"

"Broken." He was standing beside the table, looking down. The diamond sparkled in the light.

Lopez snatched the stone and held it up to the lamp. "Check the cabin. We must have almost caught them stealing it! I'm glad the exchange is tonight. I am tired of these games!" He closed his fist on the diamond and disappeared into his bedroom.

Two decks down, Royce Sparks and Annaliza Melendez sighed with relief.

CHAPTER 21

Pacifico Azul had been cutting its speed for hours, the massive hulk reluctant to give up the headway it had worked so hard to gain over the past fourteen hours. But now she came to rest inside the deep water anchorage assigned to ships awaiting canal passage. The ship was magnificent, an aging matron dressed for the party. Gleaming white paint was a fitting contrast to colorful flags and streamers. Twin stacks painted the national colors of Brazil, green, gold and blue tilted back at a jaunty angle. In respect for the host country a red, white and blue Panamanian flag flew from the masthead.

Passengers crowded to the rail as a white launch approached the ship, bringing the required canal pilot whose responsibility was to see the ship safely through the locks. The city of Colon sparkled against the deep green of the forested hills rising from the sea.

As the crew welcomed the canal pilot aboard, a commentary on the history of the Panama Canal was being broadcast over the PA system rotating the monologue in Portuguese, Spanish and finally, English.

Annaliza and Sparks were shoved about by the crowd of tourists as they attempted to push their way to the rail for a better view. O'Brien had dismissed them an hour ago with a wave of his hand. Under his gruffness was the sentimentality of a doting grandfather and he was not blind to the budding interest between the two. He offered to cover the surveillance while they took a few hours off to enjoy the crossing. "I get claustrophobic in crowds," he growled. "You two go without me. I don't expect anything major to happen here for the next several hours, anyway."

As they reached the rail, someone was pushed into Annaliza, almost knocking her down. "Excuse me!" the offender said as he reached to steady her.

"Brent Duncan!" she said with surprise. "What are you doing here?" Equally surprised, he replied, "Looking for my wife!"

Annaliza glanced at Royce. Now they had a dilemma. Should they pass on classified information to ease his mind? Royce took the initiative. "We've seen your wife, Brent. She's okay."

"Does King still have her?"

Royce looked at Annaliza. "Yes, but I don't think she's his captive any longer. We saw her helping him escape."

Brent looked startled. "Are you guys accusing Jennifer of aiding a criminal?"

"No, no!" Royce said. "We just have no idea what's going on right now."

"I've been patient for an awful long time! I'm getting sick of sitting around on the sidelines while you guys play games with my wife's life!" Brent's fists were clenched and he was moving toward Sparks when Dave grabbed him.

"Inspector Sparks, when will you tell us Mrs. Duncan's whereabouts?"

"We should know more after tonight. If you give me your cabin number, I'll come by tomorrow and tell you what I can."

"Tell you what," Dave released Brent and took a pen and notepad out of his pocket. "Tell us your cabin number and we'll be by first thing in the morning to talk to you."

Sparks paused for a moment. "E-37. Come by about eight."

"We'll be there." Dave turned and pushed his friend back into the crowd.

"Dave, what are you doing?"

"I have a feeling something big is coming off tonight. When they take off, we'll follow them."

The ship began to move. "The Isthmus of Panama," the loudspeaker boomed, "is the tiny sliver of land which joins North and South America. The carefully manicured ten mile wide canal zone is separated from the rest of the country by an imposing series of barbed wire fences."

As they approached the first lock, the crumbling colonial housing that made up the city of Colon could be seen easily.

The ship was harnessed to two tiny locomotives. Although she was moving into the lock under her own power, once inside the locomotives would tighten the cables to hold her in position. Steel doors were slowly opening, pushing thousands of gallons of sea water before them as the ship passed into the massive tank a thousand feet long and one hundred and ten feet wide. A small sailboat entered the lock behind the ship and bobbed around in the wake as the doors slowly closed, the sound of grinding metal, throbbing turbines and crunching gears echoing through the still morning.

The process continued until the ship reached the top level, fresh water Gatun Lake, eighty-five feet above sea level. As the last lock filled with fresh water, the ship rolled gently in the currents. Once the waters were still, the final gate opened and the cables dropped away as the ship slowly motored into the glassy lake, free from her bonds until the descent on the far side.

The speaker was still active. "The dirt excavated from the canal prism would be enough to build a wall the size of the Great Wall of China from San Francisco to New York."

To the right loomed the massive wall of Gatun Dam, built from the excavation of Culebra Cut ahead, blocking off the Chagres River and creating Gatun Lake.

Bare branches of trees sacrificed to the lake rose above the still surface of the water. Small islands protruded here and there, plant life clinging desperately to small patches of dirt.

"The French were the first to attempt to build a canal across the Isthmus of Panama," the loudspeaker droned. "The French contractors imported people from Central and South America, blacks from the Caribbean Islands, Italians, Greeks and Chinese. Working conditions were extreme. They worked in swamps. Swarms of mosquitoes and other flying insects as well as unsanitary living conditions contributed to epidemics of malaria, yellow fever, tuberculosis, typhus and cholera. Before the French gave up and pulled out, twenty-five thousand lost their lives to the project. After ten years they were defeated by the colossal project. That's when the Americans took over."

The tourists became quiet as they eased into the eerie lake, thinking of the sacrifices made for this waterway. Sacrifices of men, machinery, money, plant and animal life, a way of life.

The pilot maneuvered the massive ship carefully, staying in the deep of the narrow channel They soon approached Culebra Cut between Gatun Lake and the first lock on the far side, Pedro Miguel.

"The channel through these cliffs was the most difficult of the construction," the loudspeaker continued, "because they had to dig through the Continental Divide, three hundred and ten feet high and nine miles wide. This was the project that finally defeated the French. They did not have enough workers or resources to press on. When the Americans took over, they hired eighty-six thousand people of which seven thousand died. The main causes of death for the workers at this site were premature dynamite firings.

The ship descended into Mira Flora Lake and the Mira Flora locks. The locks were emptying now and this meant less rocking and more comfortable movement.

Fifteen hours after they had entered the Canal, they slowly slid past the Balboa Yacht Club and met with the launch that would pick up the canal pilot for his return trip. The crew waved him off and the ship was under way, Acapulco their next destination.

Asleep in the store room, Jennifer was unaware that she had just passed through the Panama Canal. She stretched and squinted at her watch. She hadn't seen daylight in almost two days and was anxious to get out of this hole and into fresh air.

He was still sleeping on a pile of flour sacks, recovering slowly from his ordeal. She thought about the Peeper. How must he feel, knowing his daughter was in danger? Knowing she was in the hands of animals with no respect for human dignity? No sympathy for the suffering of a child?

She was beginning to sympathize with his predicament.

The wine bottle lay safely in the crook of his arm, the ace in his hand, the ticket that would release the little girl.

They knew D'Orino was on the ship but they didn't like the idea of meeting up with him and Lopez. Tonight was his only opportunity to make contact with D'Orino and negotiate for Kristen's release.

She shook his shoulder gently. "Hey, Kimosabe. Wake up. It's time to go do your thing."

He opened his eyes slowly and blinked. The difficulties of the past several days were written across his face and she thought how much he'd aged since she'd met him.

"Jenny, what time is it?"

"Nine PM. What time did you say they were going to meet?"

"Ten."

"Then we'd better get down to the engine room."

Annaliza had relieved O'Brien a few hours before they completed the canal crossing. Sparks was already back in the cabin catching up on his sleep after a night of stakeout. O'Brien was in his room and the other four members of the HAT-TRIC Team were hanging around the cabin reading magazines, playing solitaire and sleeping. It was quiet.

Her part of the investigation was drawing to an end. Now that they knew how the diamonds were being brought into the United States, all that was left was the transfer between Lopez and D'Orino. That would be the final nail in the lid to their case. A lengthy report would be prepared and forwarded to the Customs teams in Los Angeles, Cabo San Lucas and Caracas. Then her life could get back to normal.

She wondered what she wanted. Until a few days ago, it had been easy. She'd been aiming for success in her career for as long as she could remember. And this case was going to be a feather in her cap. Why did Royce Sparks have to come into her life? Why did he have to be ten years older? Why was she so attracted to him?

There was something about his maturity that was definitely a turn on. He was much more sensitive than other men she'd known, yet he seemed to know when to take charge. She closed her eyes and imagined his lips on hers, reliving the moments she'd spent with him, locking them away to pull out and savor in quiet times when she could think.

Should she request a transfer? What if it was pure love? Was it true that everyone only had one person out there who was just right for them? What if he was that person?

The touch on her shoulder made her jump. "Sorry to bother you, Annaliza, but we need to get ready to go. You want to wake up Sparks and get back here for the brief?"

"Yes," she said, rising from her chair and smoothing her slacks. She was not used to being flustered. "Let me change and wake up Royce and we'll be back here in twenty minutes."

As the door closed softly behind her, five pairs of male eyes watched her retreat appreciatively. "What does she see in that old man?" Peterson asked.

"Watch what you say about us old men!" Netts punched him lightly on his way to the bathroom to shave. "We've got a lot over you youngsters that you haven't even figured out yet!"

O'Brien watched the exchange. He'd sure be glad to get out of this tin can and plant his feet firmly on US soil.

Down the hall and around the corner, Dave and Brent heard Annaliza step into her cabin, calling out to Sparks. Five minutes later, they came out together and moved back down the hallway in the direction from which she'd come. They could hear them talking softly, unaware of the two men dogging their activities.

O'Brien opened the door, waving them in.

"Bingo!" Brent said, peering around the corner. "You were right, Dave. Something is definitely coming off tonight."

They settled down for the wait. Dave munched lifesavers. Brent thought about Jennifer.

After about fifteen minutes, the door opened suddenly and the two Customs agents, accompanied by O'Brien and his men, moved down the hall toward the stairway. Brent and Dave jumped to their feet and followed at a safe distance.

As they passed through the doors to the stairwell, Brent heard Sparks ask O'Brien, "Where did you say the engine room is located?"

"W deck at the stern end of the ship."

The door clanked shut behind them and Brent could hear their footsteps echoing as they clambered down the stairs. "Did you hear that?"

"Yeah. Why do you suppose they're going to the engine room?"

"I guess we'll find out!"

Lopez was almost through dressing. Carefully, he combed the long mustache, covering his drooping mouth and the perpetual frown. Grog stood at the doorway, waiting.

"Did you have any problems disposing of King?"

"No," he lied and hoped the trunk had gone over the rail.

"I'm anxious to question D'Orino about King's mission. Bet that little worm is going to squirm when he figures out I'm on to him. No one else could have sent King for the diamond."

"Argh."

"Are you ready, Grog?" He had turned from the mirror and adjusted the silver bollo around his neck. "Let us go."

D'Orino was nervous. Although he had come prepared, he hadn't counted on actually having to go through with the deal. He waited until the last moment. No word from Cabo. King had not shown up with the diamond. He hadn't expected to hear anything from them because Lopez had not been in contact to let him know the plan had changed. There was always the freak chance.

He hated the thought of a face-to-face encounter with Lopez. The man gave him the creeps. That droopy face and sinister mustache. He could take the guy's appearance if it wasn't for that creature hanging around in the shadows. He shuddered as he thought about those two. Better get this over. Even if I have to pay for the rock, my profit is still going to be phenomenal. He snapped his fingers as he approached the door and his two bodyguards fell in behind him.

Nick Latelli leaned back in the old chair and took a bite out of the thick ham sandwich. Not a sound from the rotten kid. No word from Tony. He looked at his watch. Just two more hours and he could pitch her over the rail and be done with it. Just enough time for a little snack and a nap. He was going to have to ask Tony for a bonus. He finished off the sandwich, licked the grease off his fingers. Closing his eyes, he dreamed about what he was going to do with that bonus.

CHAPTER 22

They could hear the throbbing engines long before they reached the engine room. They would not be disturbed here because the ship's engineers and mechanics monitored all the systems in the comfort and quiet of an insulated room a deck above. No one would come down here unless there was a mechanical problem.

Cat walks crisscrossed the cavernous chamber and pipes of every diameter surrounded them like giant spaghetti. In the center of the long enclosure, down low, they could see the turning shafts of the twin screws driving the ship on to Acapulco. The noise was deafening.

Lopez did not like being out in the open. Too many places for assailants to hide and Grog's presence gave him little solace. He hoped D'Orino wouldn't be late. The stone was starting to burn a hole in his pocket and he wanted to be rid of it. There had been nothing but trouble since it came into his possession two months ago.

D'Orino arrived, flanked by two body guards. Juan Carlos eyed him narrowly, not trusting the Italian.

D'Orino had a confidant smile on his face as he approached, holding out his hand. "Juan Carlos, my friend! You are looking good."

D'Orino's Spanish had a heavy American accent and Juan Carlos had to strain to hear him above the roar of the machinery.

"You have betrayed me, Antonio."

D'Orino's brows shot up in mock surprise. "To what do you refer, Juan Carlos?"

"I think you know what I mean! You sent that two-bit thief King to steal the diamond! Very clever of you to avoid paying what you owe."

"Simply smart business. I take it he failed?"

"He has stolen his last diamond unless he can return from the bottom of the ocean."

D'Orino made a clucking sound with his tongue. "And I always admired him for his cleverness. I guess he was not smart enough for you, was he?"

"I thought I could trust you, Antonio. This will be the last arrangement between us. I'm going to stick with cocaine from now on."

"Did you bring the stone?"

"And you the money?"

D'Orino pulled a cellular phone from a leather sling hanging from his belt. "Let me have the stone." He held out his hand.

Lopez reached into his coat pocket and produced the diamond, holding it up to the light. "Not until the transfer is complete."

"Is your man in Buenaventura awaiting your call?"

"Yes. He flew to Colombia before I left."

D'Orino punched a series of numbers on his phone, gave some directions and hung up. He then handed the phone and a piece of paper to Lopez. "Here is the number for the banker in Grand Cayman. He is available twenty-four hours a day. The money has been transferred into the account on the paper. I will give you a password. Once you use it, I will no longer have access to the account. A new password, known only to you will be the only access. I will be locked out."

Lopez quickly dialed the number in Buenaventura and provided the information along with instructions to call the bank immediately, confirm the transfer of the funds and provide the new password.

He hung up and waited for the return call. The phone rang. "Yes?" Juan Carlos gripped the instrument with white knuckled hands. His face relaxed as the transfer of fifty billion Bolivar was confirmed. Dropping the phone to his side, he turned to D'Orino. "The password."

D'Orino smiled his crooked smile. "The diamond."

Lopez handed the stone to him and he snatched it greedily, fitting a jeweler's glass to his eye and examining the gem closely. The glass dropped from his eye and clattered to the floor. D'Orino's face was purple with rage. "This is a fake!" he screamed, throwing the stone at Lopez' feet, where it shattered against the metal mesh.

Juan Carlos was stunned and stood gaping at the sparkling fragments. D'Orino lunged for him, hands outstretched for his throat.

Grog jumped between the two, catching the brunt of D'Orino's charge. He grunted as the man slammed into him, bouncing off to be caught by his two bodyguards who had pulled their guns. Juan Carlos' eyes were bulging and his breath was coming in short puffs. "For God's sake, have them put away their guns."

D'Orino nodded at the two men and they reluctantly replaced their weapons. "I can't believe you'd try to pull such a scam, Juan Carlos!" he said angrily through gritted teeth. "Did you think I am stupid? Where is the real diamond?"

"It's right here." Both men spun around at the voice from the shadows. King held up the diamond for all to see as he slowly stepped into the light. "Thought you were rid of me, huh? Your friend there didn't finish his job. Just a little bit short of the mark." He nodded to Grog. "Now, Antonio, I believe we have some negotiating to do."

"What do you want?"

"I want you to tell me where I can find my daughter. I want her released safely into my hands."

"You will give me the diamond?"

"That is the deal."

"She's on a ship in the harbor at Cabo San Lucas."

"The name of the ship?"

"Hand me the diamond first."

"You'll get the diamond when I have my daughter. The name of the ship?"

"Anna Maria."

"See ya." As he quickly backed away, D'Orino nudged his bodyguards. They immediately grabbed his arms. As King struggled against them, the diamond rattled to the floor. As D'Orino moved to pick it up, he was stopped by a voice from the shadows. "Let him go."

D'Orino froze. Jennifer moved into the light and leveled the gleaming barrel of the vintage Colt on him. "Now stand up, slowly," she said, keeping a safe distance. D'Orino nodded to the bodyguards and King was free.

"Jenny, the diamond!" he barked.

With her free hand, she grabbed the stone.

But without warning, Grog slammed into her from behind, knocking her to the floor and the gun went off. The discharge was thunderous in the enclosed space, the report echoing from metal walls as the bullet ricocheted off pipes, walls, ceiling, whining its way with deadly inaccuracy.

"Jesus Christ!" D'Orino yelled as he and the others hit the deck. But the bullet had lodged harmlessly and all that could be heard was the thumping of the massive engines.

Jennifer was still clutching the diamond but the gun was beyond her reach. Grog pulled her toward him and lifted her into his arms, one furry hand bending her wrist until she cried out in pain.

Brent and Dave had seen the action from a catwalk above Lopez. Brent dropped the twenty feet and landed on Grog, catching him off guard. Spinning him around, Brent landed a right punch in the center of the man's bulbous nose, smashing it. "That's my wife you're pawing, you stupid son-of-a bitch!" he yelled as he backed off, waiting for the heavier man's move.

"Brent!" Jennifer cried, starting toward him. Grog suddenly regained his wits and plowed into him, growling with rage. Jennifer jumped on his back, clawing. Her weight was no more than a gnat to him, but it created a distraction. She still had the diamond in her right hand and the punches were beginning to make an impression.

Lopez grabbed D'Orino, thumbs poised at his wind pipe in a death grip. "The password, you bastard! The password!"

The two bodyguards rushed forward but D'Orino put up his hand. "Stop! He will kill me!"

"The password!" Lopez tightened his grip.

"Heart...of...Stone." Lopez released him and he dropped to the floor, clutching his throat.

The Feds had watched the confrontation from behind a bank of machinery. Things were not going as planned. After seeing Grog easily grab Brent in one arm and Jennifer in the other, Sparks and Melendez both came to the conclusion that the investigation wasn't worth two lives.

Dave dropped into the fight in a last ditch attempt to save his friends. The body guards immediately pounced on him and he was as helpless as Jennifer and Brent. King was wrestling with Lopez for the gun and D'Orino, recovered, was shouting orders.

"You guys get King and help the civilians. Lopez and D'Orino are ours," Sparks yelled to O'Brien as Melendez plowed into the struggle.

Grog didn't know what hit him. Karate chops to his shoulders almost cracked his collarbones and he released his captives. Spinning around, he was surprised to see a slim dark woman, eyes flashing, crouched in a classic martial arts stance. He lunged at her but she deflected his bulk easily, jumping lightly to the side and landing a double kick to his midsection and jaw.

After kicking the gun out of reach of the two wrestling men, Sparks grabbed Lopez, pulled him to his feet and punched him in the jaw, driving him to the floor. Lopez lay dazed, Sparks grabbed his hand with pain and gasped as he examined his bruised knuckles. O'Brien yanked King to his feet, cuffed him and shoved him into the waiting hands of Alan Netts who pushed him against the wall to check for weapons.

The other three men from HAT-TRIC were occupied with the body guards who were still bent on beating the hell out of Dave.

Melendez had immobilized Grog, who was whimpering in a corner with a broken elbow and bruised windpipe. Now she turned to D'Orino, who was still blindly screaming orders even though he realized they were losing. He put up a good fight, but he was no match for the blur of feet and hands that came at him, beating him back until he was trapped against a transverse pipe, holding up his arms to protect his face. "Get her off me!" he screamed.

Sparks put a hand on her shoulder and she wheeled around, hair flying, eyes bright from the adrenaline rush. She looked at him wildly. "Annaliza," he said quietly. "It's over." He handed her a pair of handcuffs and she looked at them, dazed, as D'Orino crouched on the floor.

Sparks had Lopez cuffed and shoved against a pipe, frisking him. After D'Orino was immobilized, Annaliza stalked over to where Lopez was standing. She looked at him with disgust for a moment. Then, with a swift movement she stomped down on the arch of his foot. "AAAAAGGGGG!" he yelled and doubled over in pain. Without hesitation, she kneed him in the groin and leveled an undercut to the jaw with both fists clenched.

Sparks watched with amazement. "That was for Charlie," she said through clenched teeth.

The bodyguards had been apprehended by the HAT-TRIC Team and Jennifer, Brent and Dave looked around at the damages.

O'Brien spoke first. "God damnit, it's about time! Come on, King. The party's over!"

O'Brien pushed him through the door, But King pleaded. "They have my child. Please let me get her back, then I'll go with you peacefully!" He struggled as O'Brien pushed him down the hall. "Jenny, help me!" he called over his shoulder.

Jennifer was in Brent's arms, her face buried in his shoulder as he held her tightly and stroked her gently, whispering. Her heart was pounding and she was dizzy from the harrowing experience. She heard King's pleas over the sound of the engines and every fiber in her body screamed NO! Don't get involved! You don't owe this man anything. He kidnapped you, took you away from you family and endangered your life. But she remembered the past several days. What would she have done in his place? What if it was Peeper?

"Brent." She pushed away from his chest and looked into his eyes. I know you're not going to be happy about this but I hope you love me enough to understand what I have to do."

"Just don't leave me. I've had a lot of time to think the last few days. Some things are going to change."

"I know. I've been thinking, too. But there's one more thing I have to do." She turned and ran toward the retreating HAT-TRIC Team.

"Wait!" Jennifer called. You heard D'Orino! His little girl is a captive on a ship in Cabo San Lucas. We've got to get her out of there. "

O'Brien paused, trying to comprehend this new angle.

"Please," Jennifer said. "They'll kill her."

"Son-of-a-bitch!" O'Brien shouted as he threw his cigar on the floor and stamped his foot. "Isn't anything easy?"

The rest of the team surrounded him and they were joined by Sparks and Melendez. Everyone was quiet as they waited for a response. All had treasured children in their lives. Sons, daughters, grandkids, nieces, nephews. He looked around at the circle of faces, and he knew he had no choice

"Okay," he said finally. A cheer went up , "Now settle down!" he growled. "You," he pointed to King, "remain in our custody. We'll help get your kid back but then you're going directly to jail. Do you understand?"

"Thank you, sir. We do not have much time before they harm my daughter!"

"Then let's go, folks."

CHAPTER 23

Nick Latelli yawned, stretched and looked at his watch. Shit, he thought. I slept through the night. He pulled his legs from the top of the desk, leaned the chair forward with a creak as the wooden limbs thumped to the floor. Rising unsteadily, he yawned again and peered around the door at the child. She was still huddled in the corner on the blanket. It was going to be easy to toss her over the rail. Hell, she probably wouldn't even wake up! The way his head was pounding, he needed a cup of coffee before he could get moving.

Filling the battered tin coffeepot with water, he lit the stove and used the match to light a cigarette while he waited for it to boil. It was early in the morning and there wasn't much going on as he stalked out to the deck and gazed across the harbor, smoking leisurely. Just a few sports fishing boats heading out for a day of marlin or mahi mahi fishing.

He finished the cigarette and made his way back inside to find the water steaming. Grabbing a cup, he dumped instant coffee into it and picked up the pot. His hand was unsteady from the hangover. The throbbing headache made him regret the beer and whiskey he'd guzzled the evening before. As he looked at the cup, it divided into two, then four identical images. He blinked his eyes, trying to get into focus as he tipped the pot to pour the water.

"AAAAHHHHHH," he screamed as his shoe filled with boiling water. Hopping around on one foot, he tried to get the shoe untied but the laces were in a knot. Falling to the floor, he grabbed the toe with both hands and tried to pull the shoe off. He winced with pain as the shoe finally pulled free of his seared flesh. Growling with pain and anger, he got up from the floor and limped to the door. He was going to have to go down to the clinic in town to get fixed up. The sleeping child in the other room was, for the moment, the last thing in his mind.

They had spent half the night in O'Brien's cabin, formulating a rescue plan. It was smoothly outlined who was going to go to Cabo San Lucas, who would stay on the ship, who would get off at the fuel stop in Acapulco.

Brent was tired of the adventure. Besides, he had a pair of airplanes sitting in a rain forest in South America to pick up. It was time to get off the ship, tie up the loose ends and go home. But Jennifer was worried about Kristen. She knew King was going to be taken into custody and it could be years before he got out of prison. In the meantime, there was no one to take care of the little girl, no family, no close friends. She finally convinced Brent to go along. After the child was safe, they could return to Venezuela and take care of the airplanes.

Sparks and Melendez decided they would go on to Cabo while two of the HAT-TRIC Team would remain on the ship to turn the criminals over to the appropriate authorities, once in port.

Near dawn, O'Brien went to the Captain's quarters and, through an interpreter, explained his need to contact the rest of his team in Acapulco. The Captain arranged a phone patch and the Blackhawk helicopter was soon on its way. If the sea remained calm there would be enough room on the forward deck to land it. They expected the team by late morning. In the meantime, everyone caught up on some sleep after the criminals had been placed in secure quarters until Mexican and South American authorities could deal with them.

Dave glanced at the lovebirds in Brent's cabin and then took his battered face, sprained wrist and a blanket and went to catch a few winks on deck.

Jennifer and Brent gazed uneasily at each other. After days of uncertainty and yearning, why did they suddenly feel awkward?

"Hi," Jen said as she smiled at her husband of twelve years.

"Hi yourself." His gray eyes were piercing. "You've lost weight."

"You too." She took a step forward and placed her hand on his chest.

One arm pulled her closer. With his index finger, he gently touched her face. "Looks like you had a pretty rough time."

She mentally mapped the familiar face. "The worst part was being away from you, and the Peep."

He bent down and kissed her gently on her lips, then kissed each of her closed eyes as he massaged the small of her back. "I love you," he whispered.

"Oh, Brent." Her breath caught in a sob. "I never thought I'd see you again! I was so scared!" She stuttered and gripped him tighter as tears flowed freely.

"I know." He swallowed his own tears. "I was scared, too. Everything is going to be all right, now. I promise."

Picking her up, he carried her to the bed and lay her gently on the soft comforter. "What do you say we spend what's left of the night getting reacquainted?" She smiled as he kissed the tears off her face and moved to her waiting mouth.

Sparks and Melendez returned to their cabin, congratulated each other on blowing their case, patted each other on the back for saving a few lives and fell into bed. Exhaustion exceeded desire. They were asleep in minutes.

King sat in his locked room and prayed for the helicopter. He hoped they weren't too late to reach Kristen.

Kristen awoke suddenly and sat up, fighting waves of dizziness. She was thirsty and rose on unsteady legs to find something to drink. She peeked into the room where the man stayed but no one was there. Only a broken coffee cup in a puddle of water on the floor. The gas burner was on but no sign of the man. It looked like he might have left quickly, intending to return any moment, so she hurried to the refrigerator. Inside were two cases of beer, a chunk of moldy cheese, a lump of something wrapped in foil, a half bottle of milk and a partial loaf of bread. She grabbed the milk and drank thirstily from the bottle. She felt stronger now.

Cautiously, remembering the last time on deck, she passed through the door. Was it possible he'd left? Everything was quiet, only faint strains of music from the distant shore and a few boats puttering around the bay but other than that, she was alone. Maybe she could hide. She began to explore her prison, convinced in her young mind that she could be safely hidden away by the time he came back.

Nick hobbled up the cobblestone street stopping frequently to ask directions, when he could find someone who spoke English. Finally, at the top of the hill, he came upon the small clinic. He was now sweating freely in the hot humid air and the burn on his foot was throbbing.

The clinic was a small white plastered building, sitting in a grove of date palms. A bougainvillea bush flowered by the front door, its pink blossoms the only splash of color against the pale building and brown earth.

As he approached, a young man limped out the door assisted by a woman of about twenty-five. He had a large bandage wrapped about his head and his right leg was in a cast to the hip, his right arm in a sling. He was awkwardly trying to maneuver with a crutch, the one good arm and leg, and the assistance of the young woman. The rest of his skin was covered in cuts, bruises and abrasions.

It was cool inside the building and it took a few moments for his eyes to adjust to the dimness. As things came into focus, he scanned a small waiting area crowded with sweating bodies—howling babies on the laps of matronly women, old men sneezing and coughing, young men who showed early signs of starvation or malnutrition, pregnant women, broken legs, seeping wounds, a study in human suffering.

He hobbled to a door where an older woman in a soiled white nurse's uniform sat. Giving her his name and complaint, he noted her disinterest. She tiredly wrote the information on a pad of paper and told him in broken English to have a seat.

There were no seats so he wedged himself between an old man having a coughing fit and a young woman with a blank stare. As he turned and leaned his back against the wall, the old man finally hacked up a glob of sputum onto the floor where it lay in a lump, yellow and streaked with blood. Nick, the jailer of children, fought the bile rising in his throat.

O'Brien was on the deck in the hot late morning sun, squinting at the blue sky to the northwest. He'd been in radio contact for almost an hour now and should have visual contact any minute. Beside him, Jennifer gazed in the same direction, a hand shading her eyes. "There," she said, pointing. Years of flying had sharpened her eyes to the tiny dots of traffic in the sky.

O'Brien soon picked it up. "Round everybody up. I want to leave as soon as possible."

Jennifer was already on her way.

The pilot looked despairingly at the small white ship. When he'd joined this team, nobody told him he would have to become a carrier pilot. Fortunately, the sea was fairly calm and the wind light.

As they hovered a hundred feet above the deck, he could make out a diminutive O'Brien waving his arms. Slowly he lowered the big chopper closer to the deck, mentally gauging the diameter of the rotor against obstructions, as well as the vertical motion caused by the swell. The closer he got, the easier it seemed.

The fore deck, as promised, had been cleared of people, lounge chairs and other items that might pose a problem. The helicopter slowed it's descent as it neared the deck. O'Brien was standing next to the Captain, who didn't look pleased with a US Government helicopter using his ship for a landing pad.

The chopper eased down with a thump, the descent perfectly timed so the wheels reached the deck just as the ship was hitting the bottom of a swell. The passengers were well organized, traveling light and were soon aboard.

The pilot looked over his shoulder to make sure everyone was safely buckled in before liftoff and O'Brien leaned forward. "Dan, this is James King. He's the one we've been chasing but we've agreed to help him find his daughter. She's being held hostage, as I told you on the phone. How long before we get to Cabo San Lucas?"

"This thing is slow," he apologized. "And we're also going to need fuel before we leave the Mexican mainland and strike out over the water. I'd say we'll be lucky if we make it before dark."

"Let's get moving, then!" O'Brien sank into the co-pilot's seat and peered out the window as the chopper lifted smoothly from the deck and took off northwest. The Pacifico Azul was soon a white dot in the background.

On the upper portion of the cabin, Kristen found a round vent sticking out of the roof, facing forward like a periscope. The round hole was close enough to the top of the deck so she could crawl in. It was a tight fit but she found that she could maneuver herself into a comfortable position. After taking a final long look around, hesitant to leave the warm sunshine on the deck, she eased into her hiding place to wait. She knew her father loved her and would come.

It was early evening before the nurse called his name. He followed her into the depths of the clinic and tried to ignore the moans and cries coming from behind the doors along the hallway.

She motioned him into a room, then turned and shut the door behind her without a word. The only furnishings were a rusty exam table covered with a soiled sheet, a sagging wooden book case with an assortment of medical manuals and reference books and an orange chair covered in cracked vinyl. He sat in the chair and waited.

An hour and fifteen minutes later, the young physician whisked through the door in a flurry of white lab coat and tennis shoes. He had a clip board in his hand and held it in front of him as he peered over his glasses at the patient and fired three questions at him in rapid Spanish.

"No hablas Español," Nick said, the only Spanish phrase he knew as he shrugged his shoulders.

"Americano?"

"Yes."

"Problemo?"

Nick held up his foot, indicating the angry red flesh.

"EEEE," the doctor whistled as he poked at the flesh gingerly. "Uno momento." He held up a finger and left the room.

Nick was soon propped on the table as the young physician wielded a pair of hemostats and cleaned the wounded flesh as Nick tried not to scream. The doctor then smeared it with a white cream and wrapped the foot tightly in a white bandage. "No agua." He pointed to the foot, trying to speak simply. "Comprende?"

"Yes, Si, gracias," he replied, anxious to get out of the torture chamber.

The nurse wrote out a bill and he counted out the appropriate pesos, pushed through the undiminished crowd and limped back down the hill toward the ship.

The farther they traveled north, the stronger the head wind. King ground his teeth as he looked out over the dark Pacific, straining to see the lights of Cabo San Lucas. They'd had to make two fuel stops, one in Acapulco, the other in Ixtapa. The passengers were quiet as they entered the final leg of their trip.

After what seemed like hours, they made out a faint glow on the horizon which soon yielded the lights of the distant village forming a curve around the harbor. The pilot slowed to a semi-hover as they passed five hundred feet above the water, all eyes searching for a ship named Anna Maria.

After several tries, the pilot turned to O'Brien. "I think this is futile. It's just too dark to read the name on the stern of a ship."

"Can you find a clear area on the beach somewhere to drop us off?"

"I'll have to turn on the spot light."

"That's okay. Everybody knows we're here by now anyway. I'm already going to have a lot of explaining to do to the Mexican authorities."

They found a large, mostly empty parking lot and the pilot expertly maneuvered the chopper down between a few parked cars.

"You can't leave it here," O'Brien shouted as they piled out. "Go ten miles up the coast and set down on the beach. I'll contact you on the radio when we're ready to leave."

From out of nowhere a large crowd had gathered. The masses of tourists and Mexicans parted as O'Brien pushed his way through, growling at King who was stumbling ahead of him in handcuffs. The curious fell in behind them as they headed for the pier.

Timothy Andrews had moved to Cabo San Lucas five years before, had bought a sport fishing boat and was making a good living in an enviable way, escorting fisherman into the Sea of Cortez and the deeper Pacific waters. He'd had a good day. Of the four men who hired his boat, three had come back with trophies and the evening had been spent taking pictures and gutting fish. Now he was alone stuck with boat cleaning and re-provisioning.

He was spraying the blood and fish scales off his boat when he felt a tap on the shoulder. He turned his red head with the dark brown freckles around and had to look down to meet the eyes of the man peering over the top of a bobbing cigar. Stringing out behind the man stood a group of locals and tourists, looking on with interest.

"May I help you?" he asked.

A silver shield in a leather case appeared and he growled around the cigar, "Henry O'Brien, FBI. Need your boat."

"Where do you need to go?"

"Know a ship by the name of Anna Maria?"

"Yes, I know her. Pass her every day on my way out. She's been anchored in the harbor for a couple of weeks."

"Seems she's got something we need. Can you give us a lift?"

"Who's us?"

O'Brien had to think a moment. "Five of us ought to be enough to lift the kid. How many men on guard?" he asked King.

"I don't know. How many men does it take?"

"Can't be too many. Besides, they're not expecting us. Who's going?"

"I'm definitely going!" King stepped forward.

"Me, too!" Alan Netts had five little granddaughters.

"Count me in, too." Peterson stepped forward.

"I've come this far," Jennifer said. "I guess I'd better help finish it."

"If she goes, I'm going!" Brent moved beside his wife.

"Hold on, hold on now!" O'Brien was holding up his hands. "We don't need the whole group! King, you can come along but no funny business! We'll take the cuffs off on the boat. As soon as we get our feet back on dry land, you're back in custody." He looked up and spread his hands. "Why do I get myself into these things? "Netts and Peterson, you guys back me up. That's it. No more. Everybody else stays here."

"Wait a minute, Agent O'Brien." Jen put a hand on his arm. "She's just a child. She's going to be frightened. Don't you think it would be good to have a woman along?"

"Okay," he said gruffly. "But that's it!" He put out a hand as Brent started to protest. "I said, that's it!" He turned to Jen. "There's liable to be some shooting. I want you to stay in the boat. As soon as we have the kid, we'll be back."

CHAPTER 24

It was dark by the time Nick reached the ship He stumbled on board and bumped around in the blackness until he found the door. As he flipped on the lights, his eyes fell on the empty blanket. Oh no, he thought. I forgot all about the kid.

In the galley, he looked under the table, in corners, on the far side of the refrigerator. He tried to suppress the panic that threatened to overcome him. If he screwed up on this, he'd be floating face down in the harbor.

Taking a breath, he tried to think. It was a half mile to shore. There was no way she could swim that far. She was either still on the boat, or drowned and floating in the water

He grabbed a flashlight and went out on deck. Weakened by the pain in his foot, he limped around, looking, calling out to her with empty hope.

The fishing boat moved smoothly over the glassy water, its twin diesel engines rhythmic at the low RPM. Timothy Andrews knew every rock, weed and sand bar in the bay, but tonight he was hampered by a cloud-covered moon and an uneasy feeling. He squinted ahead past O'Brien who was poised on the bow like a hood ornament.

"It's darker than the inside of a bruised crow out here!" O'Brien growled under his breath. "I hope this kid knows where he's going."

Suddenly the dark ship loomed before them, less than forty feet away. He knew Timothy had seen it in time and reduced power. The boat slowed and everyone on board held their breath as their craft moved alongside the ship. Slowly, they inched along, looking for a place to board. The ship was dark except for a single light coming from a forward porthole.

Timothy killed the engines so as not to over-advertise their presence. He joined the men on the port side to help pull their boat along the iron hull. She was in poor repair. They could feel blisters passing under their palms and their hands were covered with rust from her weeping wounds.

As they eased around the stern, O'Brien's hand closed around a pipe. "Bingo," he whispered. "A ladder."

He motioned for the men to follow him as he quietly made his way up and over the top onto the deserted deck, revolver in his hand, ready for action. Timothy stayed with Jennifer. The men fanned out, Netts and Peterson going left, O'Brien and King right. Suddenly, a flashlight beam sliced the night and then disappeared. "Down!" O'Brien whispered.

How many places were there to hide on a ship this size? He tried to remember how big she was but couldn't. The pain in his foot was a distraction and if he didn't take something for it soon, he was going to be in real trouble. But there was nothing to take. Walking around had not been good. He could feel the dampness in the bandage. He needed to rest and get the foot up. Damn her! It was all her fault.

He'd look around the aft end of the ship and if she didn't turn up there, he'd just have to assume she'd jumped overboard. He'd tell the boss he did her in. Nobody would know the difference.

As he swept his light and turned to go back inside, a hand clamped over his mouth and he felt a gun against the base of his skull. "Make a move and you're dead," a voice hissed.

His bulging eyes strained to see his attacker, but he couldn't move.

"How many are there?" the voice whispered, as the hand came away from his mouth.

"How many what?"

"How many are there on the boat?"

"My partner is going to be back any minute," he lied.

His hands were quickly tied tightly behind him, a gag shoved in his mouth and he was forced to the deck. "If you move, I'll kill you," the voice came back. Then the two figures moved off into the darkness.

Netts and Peterson stood at the starboard side entrance, one on either side of the thin sliver of light coming from the cracked door. Peterson leaned over and peered through the crack. Inside was a crude galley, an ancient stove and a small refrigerator, an old formica dinette table with a single chair and a broken coffee mug on the floor. No sign of life.

They held their gun barrels pointed up, beside their right ears and cautiously pushed the door open. The only sound was the creaking of the door and the humming of the old refrigerator.

Moving into the room, their eyes carefully scanned every inch. Netts saw the door first, and eased along the wall until he could look into the tiny enclosure. The room was empty except for a frayed blanket.

"All clear?" O'Brien and King had appeared at the doorway.

Peterson and Netts lowered their guns. "Nobody in here. Looks deserted. How about you?"

"We've got one tied up out on the deck. Claims he's got a partner coming back soon. Find any sign of the kid?"

"Just an old blanket in the other room."

"Come on." O'Brien waved his cigar. "Let's see what we can get out of this character."

Jennifer was worried. It had been fifteen minutes. She had expected to hear shouts, gunshots, anything but silence. Timothy was sitting patiently, waiting to speed them away.

"What do you think?" she whispered.

"You're asking me? I don't have a clue!"

She resisted the urge to board and find out what was going on. But she'd made that promise to Brent not to get involved.

Figures approached through the darkness. As they got closer, Nick could see that there were four of them. He figured he was dead.

"Where's the kid?" one man asked, squatting down and yanking the gag out of his mouth.

"What kid?"

Nick was caught off guard as a fist slammed into his face, knocking him flat. "You dirty son-of-a-bitch, where's my daughter?"

The other two grabbed the owner of the knuckles and pulled him off. Nick saw stars as the short one grabbed him by the shirt and yanked him upright.

"Memory improving?" he growled.

Nick was too stunned to speak. The fist was struggling against the other two. "Let me at him!" he shouted. "If he hurt her, I'm going to kill him!"

"If you don't start talking, I'll be tempted to let him go. Then I can't be responsible. "You're not real popular with him right now," the short man threatened.

"I don't know!" Nick blurted. "I went to town. When I come back, the kid was gone. I don't know where she is!"

"You lying bastard!" King shouted. "What have you done with her?"

"Daddy?" King stopped struggling. "Daddy?" King looked around frantically.

"Kristen? Kristen, baby, is that you?"

O'Brien picked up the fallen flashlight.

"Kristen? Kristen, speak so we can find you!"

The beam of light fell on the vent. A small pale face was framed by the round enclosure, limp blonde curls falling forward over her eyes.

King reached in and pulled the emaciated child to him.

She blinked her eyes slowly and put her arms around him. "Daddy, is it really you? He told me you wouldn't come for me unless I was good!" she sobbed. "I tried and tried and tried to be good."

"Oh, Kristen, can you forgive me?" He held her away from him so he could wipe the tears from her face and looked into her eyes. "I love you, Kristen, please say you forgive me for taking so long!"

"I love you, too, Daddy. Please never leave me again."

King looked around the circle of men. "Kristen, there's someone I want you to meet." He stood and lifted the child into his arms.

O'Brien was the first down, followed by Nick between Netts and Peterson, and last, King with Kristen in his arms. The boat rocked slightly under the weight of the men and Timothy moved forward to start the engines.

"Jenny. This is Kristen."

The child's face was buried in his neck, her arms locked behind his head. She turned slowly and looked warily at the woman.

"Kristen." King looked down into her face. "This is Jennifer. She's." He paused as their eyes met. "She's my friend."

Jennifer wiped the tears away, embarrassed by her show of emotion. "Hi, Kristen. I've heard a lot about you." She placed her hand gently on the child's back.

Timothy gunned the engines, no need for silence now, and they shot toward the sparkling shore lights. O'Brien pulled his radio and called the helicopter.

As they neared the dock, Jennifer could see Brent and Dave silhouetted against the bright lights. The crowd was still hanging there, hoping for excitement.

Timothy docked the boat and O'Brien shoved a card in his hands. "Call this number and they'll tell you where to send the bill." As they disappeared over the hill, he wondered if it had really happened. He looked at the card in his hand. It read, Chief Agent Henry O'Brien, Federal Bureau of Investigation, Hijacking and Terrorist Tactical Response International Cooperative Division, Houston, Texas, USA. There were phone and FAX numbers at the bottom. He whistled through his teeth as he shoved the card into his back pocket and went back to spraying the fish scales off his boat.

The helicopter touched down lightly and the pilot waited for everyone to board. O'Brien was embarrassed. "Sorry, King," he said, looking at the ground. But it's time to go."

King hugged his daughter to him, his heart breaking.

"Kristen," he said gently. "I'm afraid I have to go away again for a while but Jennifer is going to take care of you."

"No," she said softly. Then louder. "No."

The tourists were pressing close now, straining to see. O'Brien turned on them. "Back off!" he shouted angrily and waved his cigar threateningly. "Get out of here! Show's over!"

The crowd dissipated as quickly as they had come. Royce Sparks placed a hand on King's shoulder. "Good luck. I'm sure we'll be talking to you later." He and Melendez turned and left.

The little girl clutched her father desperately. The helicopter was running and the pilot was waiting.

"I'm sorry," O'Brien said. "We have to go."

King couldn't hold back the tears as he held his daughter in one final embrace and buried his face in her hair. "I'm sorry. I'm so sorry, Kristen." He grabbed her hands to pull them from around his neck.

"No!" She was holding on frantically. "No, Daddy! The child pounded her fists at Jennifer and screamed as they placed cuffs on King and led him to the waiting chopper.

The child finally collapsed against Jennifer as the helicopter lifted off the pavement, tilted and moved north. "No," she mumbled weakly. "No."

Brent had moved beside them. "Come on, Jen. Let's get some rest."

CHAPTER 25

If they didn't waste any time, the case might be salvaged. Sparks and Annaliza tried to close out the screams of the little girl as they hurried down the waterfront to the hotel. Wally answered on the first knock.

"You said D'Orino was on the cruise ship?" Wally asked, trying to assimilate the information.

"Yes, but he's in custody now. I guess we've blown the case."

"Now, wait a minute! Do any of his people know he's been caught?"

"Probably not. He's still on the ship. I doubt he's had his one phone call yet."

Wally stood up and rubbed his chin thoughtfully. "Did you find out how they're transporting the diamonds?"

"Yes," Sparks smiled. "South African red wine."

Wally spun around. "No! That's so simple! Why didn't we think of it?"

"Sometimes the simplest means are the hardest to crack."

"When is the next shipment?"

"We don't know."

Wally moved to the phone. "I'm going to call Customs in LA. With a little luck they might be able to make a bust before word gets back that we've broken the case."

"What about Lopez? That's been bothering me. I don't see that we've got anything on him because he's not the one bringing the stones over the border. When we arrested him on the ship, we were treading on thin ice," he smiled. "Excuse the pun. Anyway, we were able to hold him for possession of stolen property, namely the Heart of Aphrodite. But he'll be off on that charge before you know it."

"Don't be so sure." Wally had the phone to one ear, waiting for the international connection to go through. "Law enforcement in Mexico and South America is not as soft on criminals as we are. Besides, we can pass on all the information we've gathered from our investigation. Since he was involved in a smuggling operation on their soil, they can nab him and put him away for a long time if they want. I expect the South African authorities will be anxious to dry up a South American drug source."

"By the way," he continued. "Where is the Heart of Aphrodite, anyway?"

Sparks reached into his pocket. "I hate to carry this thing around with me, but I don't know what else to do for the time being. Jennifer gave it to me while we were on ship. She didn't want to be responsible for it."

"I'll check with the hotel and see if they have a safe." He paused. "Oh, hello," he spoke into the mouthpiece. "This is US Customs, El Paso. We have some very interesting information for you guys."

Annaliza wasn't able to sleep. Every time she closed her eyes, she was haunted by the scene of the little girl clinging to her father and sobbing. She got up and paced around the room and, flipping on the TV, found nothing but late night re-runs. The hotel didn't have cable. She shut it off and continued her pacing. She'd been thinking a lot about family this trip. Remembering the early times with her brothers made her smile. She missed the closeness of a family. Her father's lifestyle in the Marines meant never settling anywhere very long and it had been hard to form close friendships. Her Dad was doing a tour of duty in Singapore now and her brothers were scattered all over the United States. She had never felt so lonely.

Royce Sparks lay in his dark hotel room, hands behind his head, staring at the ceiling. He had given up on sleep hours ago and was resigned to another miserable night of tossing on the bed, trying to blot out images of other times.

Suddenly, there was a muted knock on his door.

"Royce," she called softly as she tapped again. "It's me, Annaliza. Let me in."

He jumped up and pulled on a pair of pants before opening the door. She eased past him and turned, looking at him intently. "I couldn't sleep. Did I wake you?"

"No," he admitted. "I couldn't sleep, either."

After the balmy air in the passageway, the air conditioning chilled her and she shuddered. "I've been thinking about kids."

"Oh?" He reached for a light.

"No," she said as she put out her hand. "It's peaceful here in the dark." She moved to a chair by the window and looked out at the lights. "I miss my family tonight. Do you ever miss yours?" She turned to look at him.

"What family? My old man left for work one day when I was four and never came home. After that, it was just my mom and me. She worked herself to death. I was an orphan by the time I was fourteen."

"How awful. I came from a large, loving family. What about your wife?"

"We can't even be civil to one another anymore." He ran his hand through his hair and sat down on the bed.

"Any kids?"

"I wanted children, but she didn't want to be bothered. Now I guess I'm glad we didn't because that would just make the divorce more painful than it is already."

She was quiet for a moment, then looked back at the lights reflected on the harbor. "I've been thinking about that little girl. How much pain she's in." She turned to him, dark eyes shining. "What does it all mean, Royce? Am I just being philosophical or am I missing the reason we're put here? All these years I've been striving toward a successful career, but somehow tonight that seems insignificant. I suddenly feel like I'm standing on the platform watching my train disappear down the tracks. It makes me afraid. I've always known exactly where I was going and how I was going to get there. Now I just feel adrift."

She could feel his eyes through the darkness. "I think I know what it means." He got up from the bed slowly and walked toward her across the room. "I think it means that we spend too much time worrying about things that aren't important. I think we should hold on to the people we love. Spend time with them while we can. Not look back thirty years from now with regrets."

She rose to her feet. He spread his arms wide and she hesitated only a moment before walking into his embrace.

Kristen had been huddled in a chair on the balcony, looking out over the water for hours. Her arms were wrapped around her drawn-up knees and she was staring straight ahead. Jen would rather have the tears than this. She carried a tray with a sandwich and glass of milk and set it on a table next to the child.

"Hungry?" she asked.

The little girl shook her head. "Why doesn't my daddy love me any more?" she asked as a tear slid down her pale cheek.

Jennifer drew a breath. "He loves you very much, honey. The things that have happened over the last several days are not his fault. I'll tell you the whole story soon. Then you'll understand what he went through to get you away from that horrible man."

The child turned her head and looked into Jen's face. She liked the woman who had rocked her and stroked her head after coming to the hotel. Once she was able to stop crying, the woman had not asked questions or lectured. She reminded Kristen of her mother. But this thought fostered more tears. "What is going to happen to me?"

"You are going to come to New Mexico and live with me and my family for a while until your daddy can come and get you. Do you know where New Mexico is?"

"Aren't we in Mexico already?"

Jen smiled. "Yes honey, we're in Mexico but New Mexico is a state in the USA. You'll like it there. I have a little girl and she's going to be very excited to have you stay with us."

Kristen's eyes widened. "You do? Does she speak English?"

Jen laughed. "Yes, most of the time. I talked to her a little while ago. You see, she hasn't seen her daddy for a long time, either. She's very anxious for us to come home. I think you two will be the best of friends."

"I haven't ever had a friend, truly. We were always moving and daddy was afraid for me to go to public school, so I had a nanny and a tutor. But that wasn't the same! They were terribly old! I always wanted to play with other children. What is your little girl's name?"

Jennifer was glad to see the child perk up, and she enjoyed the British accent. "Her name is Lisa, but everyone calls her Peeper. I can't wait to have you meet her."

Kristen climbed into Jen's lap and snuggled into her arms. "When will that be?"

"In a few days. I'm afraid there are still a few things we have to do before we go home. Do you like airplanes?"

"Yes, very much."

"Then you'll enjoy our home. Everybody is always talking about airplanes. Here," she said, reaching for the sandwich. "You eat this and I'll share a poem with you."

"A poem?" she asked as she bit into the sandwich.

"Yes. My great, great aunt wrote it when she was a girl. They spent months traveling across the country in a covered wagon. After they homesteaded their place in New Mexico, they had to endure the hardships of a winter in the high country. Finally, spring came and her father built a log cabin for his family. They were very grateful for any convenience in those days, no matter how small. One summer night she sat on the stoop of the cabin and composed this poem.

"As I stand in the door of my cabin
And look down the valley tonight,
The scene that meets my vision
Makes my heart beat fast with delight."

Kristen took a small bite of the sandwich and snuggled into the crook of Jennifer's arm. Jen smiled as small dimpled arms circled her in a tentative hug.

"The moon, sailing high in the heavens,
Casts down her wonderful light
And makes of the earth a jewel case,
Lined with silver, shining and bright."

The musical cadence of the poem soothed the child and with a shuddering sigh, her head sagged against Jen's side.

"The dew drops are diamonds all scattered
As if dropped by some fair lady's hand;
The pearls with their soft subdued luster
Are the white pebbles there in the sand.

The fireflies flicking and dancing
Are sparks from a red ruby's glare
And the illusive soft light around me
Are the blue green sapphires there.

The grim mountains surrounding the treasures
Are tall sentinels standing there
To guard the matchless treasure
Made of moonlight and air."

Jennifer paused, looked down at the closed eyes of the exhausted child and continued in a whisper.

"I wake with a start from my dreaming
To see the moon sink in the west
As she throws out her arms of jeweled splendor
To give me a good night caress.

I kneel in this pathway of beauty
And thank God for his watchful care
For the valley of peace and plenty,
And the loved ones with me there."

Kristen was asleep and Jen realized how tired she was herself. She placed the partially-eaten sandwich back on the plate, rose stiffly and carried the child to her bed before undressing and climbing into her own.

It was so quiet she could hear her watch ticking She spooned against Brent's back, her hands fanned across his ribs and her face buried in his soft hair. She could tell he was still awake.

"Brent?"

"Hmm?"

"I've been thinking about a lot of things."

He rolled to face her, folding her into his arms and lightly stroking her shoulder. "That could be dangerous."

She smiled. " Seriously, I was thinking about the reward for the diamond. Do you think it's possible?"

"I don't see why not. Royce Sparks has named you as the person who recovered it."

"I had a little help."

"I know, but technically the Feds can't claim any part of the reward. They were on official US Government business. That makes them ineligible."

"What about James?"

"James is pretty wealthy in his own right. Seems all those years of robbing rich old ladies has put him in pretty good shape."

"Doesn't seem like the money has brought him much happiness. He almost lost his little girl." She shuddered at the thought.

He kissed her on the nose. "So, Mrs. Duncan, what are you going to buy with all that money?"

"Time."

"Time?"

"I'm going to pay off some debts so we don't have to work so hard. I want to see my daughter grow up. I don't want to explain to her any more why I can't go to her Christmas program, or the mother's tea at school. I've already missed the loss of her first tooth, the first time she rode a two-wheeler and her first day of school. I don't want to miss any more firsts. They're too important to both of us."

"What about the business?"

"Think Dave could handle things by himself for a while?"

"Why, are you planning to move?"

She cupped his face in her hands and looked into his eyes. "I want to go back to the ranch. I want to pass on to my child the same legacy of love my folks passed on to me. I had a wonderful childhood."

He laughed. "That's an understatement!" Then they were quiet for a moment. "What about my career?"

"I've been thinking about that, too. Your real gift as an engineer is in design. I've felt for years that you weren't really reaching your full potential because of your job."

"You're right. I've always wanted to do some free-lance design and consulting."

"Well, here's your chance! We can set you up an office with a PC and a drafting table. If you need to go to Albuquerque or Santa Fe, it's just a little over an hour in dad's 180. Once the Lear's paid off, we should have a pretty decent income from our share of the business. Besides," She stroked his chest. "We could get reacquainted. What do you think?"

He rolled her on her back and pinned her down playfully. "Now, what was that you said about getting reacquainted?"

CHAPTER 26

The small group gathered on the hot soft asphalt ramp at Albuquerque International Airport. Nobody was talking. Roy Nolan stood with his old felt hat pulled low over his lined face as he squinted down the taxi-way. Mary Nolan wrung her hands. It had been a difficult few days for all of them, wondering what had happened to Jennifer. Wondering if they would ever see her alive again. In front of them was their flaxen-haired granddaughter, oblivious to the ordeal the older members of the family had been through. She bounced up and down with impatience.

"When are they going to be here, Grampie?" she asked, turning to hug his legs.

"Supposed to be here by now," he said gruffly, trying to make out the shape of an airplane.

Martha Duncan stood to the side. "Are you sure they were supposed to be back today?"

"I checked with flight service an hour ago. According to them, their flight plan puts them in here," he paused to look at his watch, "five minutes ago."

Peeper jumped up and down. "There they are, there they are!" She pointed to the east.

Through the heat waves shimmering above the pavement, a Learjet materialized. Now they could hear the whining jet engines as it taxied around the circular strip leading to the General Aviation ramp and moved toward them.

The line boy from the fixed base operator marshaled the plane into a parking place and the door swung open while the engines were still whining down. Brent Duncan appeared in the doorway, blinking in the bright light. As he started down the steps, Peeper broke loose from the group and ran toward her father. "Daddy!" She jumped into his arms and he hugged and kissed her.

"Hello, Munchkin! I'm sure glad to see you!"

Jen appeared in the doorway. "Peeper!" she yelled and held out her arms.

The child struggled out of her father's embrace and shot up the stairs to her mother.

Jen had tears in her eyes as she hugged and kissed her daughter. "Mom, Dad." She held out her arms and they embraced, Peeper in the middle.

"Hi, guys." Dave started down the steps. Sitting on his arm was a little girl with glossy blonde curls wearing a pink embroidered fiesta dress.

Peeper looked at the stranger in her idol's arms. Dave tried to set the little girl down on the pavement but she clung to him with one arm, the other hand tightly clutching a roll of lifesavers.

"Come here, Peeper," he said. "I have someone I want you to meet."

Peeper took a step closer.

"This is Kristen," Dave continued. "She really needs a big sister. Do you think you could be her big sister for a while?"

Peeper's face slowly brightened and she hugged Dave who caught her with his other arm. "I always wanted a sister!" She reached out to a startled Kristen, drew the girl to her and kissed her on her forehead.

Jen was surprised to find her mother had been at work in her kitchen and had a big meal waiting. She was hungry for real food. Brent sat in the den with his father-in-law, telling about the last few days.

After taking a long pull from a can of soda, he continued. "So, once we got Kristen, we headed back down to Caracas to pick up the airplanes. You wouldn't believe how Jen handled that landing strip, Roy. It would be a challenge for your 180, let alone a Learjet!"

Roy was proud of his daughter. "Did a pretty good job getting her in there, did she?"

"Yeah, but the anti-skid failed, so the two left mains were toast. Besides that, she was running on fumes."

"Where did you get fuel? Wasn't this place in the middle of nowhere?"

"Couldn't get much more remote. Used to be a drug-runner's field. We were able to hire a Twin Otter in Caracas to haul five fifty-five gallon drums of Jet-A in there so we could get her out. It took us all day to change the two tires and fuel up. Then, that was enough to get us over to Caracas where we were able to completely fill up."

"What about the 421?"

"That was much easier. It has a prop seal leak, but that's more of a nuisance than anything. Made a major mess of the right nacelle. We were able to ferry it to Caracas. Dave is going to get a new part and go back down to install it before he flies it home."

"So, tell me about this big diamond that was causing all the fracas."

"Oh, yeah. We handed it over to Customs and they notified the authorities in Turkey that it had been recovered. Turns out there's a big reward attached to it and Jen is going to get it!" Brent smiled. "About a million bucks!"

"A million? Wow! You guys could retire on that!"

"Better yet, we can pay off the Lear!"

Jen came to the door and called the men to dinner. As they sat down, Peeper raised her hand. "Mommy, can I say grace?"

Jennifer smiled. Her daughter was growing up.

CHAPTER 27
FOURTEEN MONTHS LATER

Jennifer Duncan sat on the ranch house porch swing next to her mother. They were quiet as they enjoyed the late afternoon northern New Mexican sun. In the distance, they could see a cloud of dust kicked up by a vehicle coming up the dirt road.

"That must be him." Jennifer pointed to the approaching dust cloud.

Her mother nodded. "First company we've had in a month."

They were quiet again as a late model sedan pulled into the driveway and stopped in a swirl of dust. They remained on the swing, content to let the visitor come to them.

The car door opened slowly and a tall man with blonde curly hair and piercing gray eyes unfolded himself and stood stiffly.

"That him?" her mother asked.

"Yes," she said, standing.

The man walked toward her and paused at the bottom of the steps. "You're looking good, Jenny. Life on the ranch agrees with you."

"Yes, James," she said with a smile. "You're looking a little pale, yourself."

"Haven't seen much of the sun the past fourteen months." He looked around.

"They're down in the pasture." She pointed toward a fenced meadow where hoof-beats and the shouts of small children could be heard. "Your daughter has turned into quite a rider. Come on up and have a seat." She sat down close to her mother to make room for him on the swing. "This is my mom, Mary Nolan."

"Nice to meet you, mam." He held out his hand as he mounted the steps.

"They'll be up in a few minutes." Jen could tell he was anxious. "They haven't eaten in a whole hour. Riding horses makes them hungry. They'll be looking for a snack before long. Just relax for a few minutes."

"How is she?"

"She's done very well. The ranch has been wonderful for them both. They've become the best of friends and they're growing like weeds. Peeper is going to be sorry to see her go. Would you like some iced tea?"

"No, thanks." He was admiring the view. "This is some place."

"I never knew how much I missed it until I came home."

"How's the business?"

"Since we paid off the Lear, we were able to put it in Dave's able hands. He's in hog heaven, running around like a chicken with it's head cut off. And I've got to say I haven't been this happy in a long time. It is so good to be home with my family."

"Have you heard from Inspector Sparks?"

"We went to the wedding last month." Jen smiled.

"No kidding?"

"Yep, Royce and Annaliza tied the knot as soon as his divorce was final."

"Do you see them?"

"He's trying to get me to fly for Customs. I think I'm ready for a break, personally."

"What about Agent O'Brien?"

"Well, you know how bad he felt about bringing you in. He really is a pretty decent guy. I think he was the one who got your sentence shortened. After all, it was extenuating circumstances."

King nodded. "When did you get back from Turkey? Did you have a good trip?"

"It was some experience. I got to visit the museum the diamond calls home. It's built on the site of Aphrodisias, home of the goddess Aphrodite. There is so much to see. I could have spent another six months and not experienced everything."

"I guess they were relieved to get it back."

"I felt guilty taking the reward, but the diamond is a priceless antiquity and they insisted. They also gave me this." She reached for the gold medallion hanging from a heavy chain around her neck. "When they told me the legend of the Heart of Aphrodite and showed me where it had been found, I was fascinated and asked all kinds of questions. Seems this medallion was found close by. Nobody knows if there's any connection to the stone. Even though its very valuable, they gave it to me. I couldn't believe it. The only strange thing is the dream."

"The dream?" he asked. The sound of a crying infant could be heard through the open door. Jen started to get up, but her mother said, "I'll get her, Jen."

King raised an eyebrow. "A new addition to the family?"

Jen smiled. "Yes, a sister Peeper has been wanting for so long."

"You were about to tell me about the dream?"

"Oh, yes. When I was pregnant, I started having this dream. There is a beautiful girl in the dream. She has dark slanting eyes, full lips. She is holding the diamond in her hand and trying to speak."

"What does she say?"

"I can't tell, but there is another person in the dream. A handsome young man with shiny dark curls and dark eyes. He is wearing my medallion, holding his hand out to the girl and calling her name.

"What name?"

"Lydia." Her mother returned and placed the baby in Jen's outstretched arms. "James King," she said to him with a smile. "Meet Lydia."

"You named her after the girl in the dream?"

"Yes. Just felt I should."

"How's the rest of your family?" he asked, holding out his hand to the little girl.

Jen grinned. "Let me show you something." She got up and led the way to the barn next to the driveway. Holding the baby in one arm, she used the other to shove the door open. Inside was a shining yellow Super Cub. "A souvenir from my trip to Venezuela," she said.

"Did this belong to Juan Carlos?"

"Sure did. After I told Royce Sparks about my escape from the villa, he mentioned the plane to Customs in Venezuela. After Juan Carlos' arrest, it came up at auction. He made sure my bid got into the right hands and before I knew it, I was the owner of a Super Cub! My dad's wanted one for a long time so I gave it to him. His only gripe is that it's in perfect condition so there's nothing to work on!"

They heard the sound of approaching hoof beats on the hard ground and turned as the two little girls thundered up. "Daddy!" Kristen was off her mount and running into his arms almost before the horse had skidded to a stop. Her cheeks were flushed and long curls bounced around her shoulders as she leapt into his arms.

"Hello Princess." He squeezed his eyes shut to stop the stinging. "I've missed you so much."

"You're not taking her away, are you?" Peeper asked.

"We're going to come back often for visits."

Suddenly, another car pulled into the drive. "That's strange," Jen observed. "We rarely get visitors out here."

A young couple got out of the car, followed by a toddler who clung to his mother's hand. The woman walked toward them and held out her hand, "Hi, we're your new neighbors. We bought the Larson's place down the road."

Jen held out her hand. "Nice to meet you. What brings you to this part of the world?"

"The woman looked at her husband. "It's strange," she said. "We grew up in California and thought we would always call it home. But one day we woke up with this desire to move to New Mexico."

The little boy pulled away from his mother and ran up to Jen where he stood staring at the baby. "That's odd," the woman said. "I've never seen him take any interest in babies at all."

The little boy looked intently into the infant's eyes. Her tiny hand griped his finger.

"What's his name?" Jen asked.

"Jason," the woman replied.

ACKNOWLEDGMENTS

I'd like to thank my editor, Jim Smith, for his patience and perseverance in this project. The many hours he spent on the book made it a better product and he unselfishly dedicated extra time to help me improve as a writer.

My husband, Grant, deserves a lot of credit for the culmination of this venture. Without his extensive knowledge of computers and a lot of patience, I'd never have had the courage to tackle a PC, let alone use one to write a novel. He was also tireless in his assistance during the editing process.

Several of my fellow pilots helped me out with information on specific aircraft. Captain Mike Ash was of tremendous assistance in calculations of complex Learjet performance and his systems knowledge was invaluable. I also gratefully drew on his extensive background in the culture and geography of Mexico. Captain Jerry Marshall deserves a big thanks for his contribution of expertise on Blackhawk helicopters. To many more un-named men and women with whom I've shared a flight deck over the years, thanks for those colorful stories which have given me inspiration.

I wouldn't have made it very far without the excellent staff and reference material at the Albuquerque Public Library. I'd also like to commend the National Natural History Museums in Washington, DC and New York City for their impressive displays and presentations on flora, fauna and Indian culture of South American rain forests.

In memory of my Great Aunt, Irma Hinds, a thank you for a poem she wrote as a young girl in nineteen nineteen, after traveling across the country in a covered wagon to our family's homestead in the Sunshine Valley of Northern New Mexico. This poem, which appears in Chapter 25, originally appeared in the *Animal News* in nineteen twenty-one. I know she'd be pleased.

A big thanks to Grant and my daughter, Lisa, who made a lot of sacrifices to help me realize a dream and to my mother and father for teaching me by example the importance of family.

And finally last, but certainly not least, I salute my neighbor and friend, Neva King, who harassed me without mercy until this project was finished and never once let me believe it wasn't possible. Anyone fortunate enough to have a friend like you will find they can achieve anything.

—Anne Denton
Tijeras, NM
1994